HIDDEN VILLAINS: CRIMINALS

Edited by
ROBYN HUSS

Inkd
Publishing

Inkd Publishing LLC

HIDDEN VILLAINS: CRIMINALS

CONTENTS

INTRODUCTION

Dear Readers,

Welcome to the fourth anthology in the *Hidden Villains* series. Some of these authors have names you will recognize, and others are publishing their first short story. I have enjoyed reading, editing, and compiling all of them for you.

I know you will find these stories an eclectic collection, as usual, and each will be an enjoyable read. Wherever these hidden criminals lurk, whether in this world or in another, I hope they remain fiction!

Robyn Huss, Editor

Robyn Huss is a freelance editor who specializes in heavy developmental and copy editing; she is a thorough grammarian and has a good eye for inconsistencies. She is able to focus on character development, dialogue, paragraphing, sequencing of events and details, theme, and symbolism, in addition to providing a thorough review of grammar, usage, style, and word choice.

Robyn has spent a lifetime analyzing fiction and writing. Her bachelor's degree is in English with teaching certification; she taught literature and writing for more than thirty years to writers in grades six through college, and she has been editing professionally since 2013.

To learn more about Robyn and see samples of her work, visit www.HussEditing.com

THE RESURRECTION OF MISS LILA DYER

JANCI PATTERSON

I lay reclined on the chaise in the sitting room, the second volume of *The Romance of Lady Burton* open on my skirts, when I heard the groaning coming from the back of the house. I ignored it at first, imagining it originated in one of the houses next door. The air was so thick and stuffy in Port Said that we didn't dare shut up the windows for fear we'd roast alive. The voluminous sleeves of my dress pressed against my sticky skin such that I longed to peel it off, though with all the windows open, there was no real privacy to speak of.

The groaning came again, this time accompanied by a loud thump that shook the floorboards. Whatever made that sound was inside the house. I sat up straight in my chair and smoothed my skirts. Father was already out for the afternoon with his business partner, Garai Amin, and he'd yet to find me a proper companion since we'd arrived in Egypt. The closest I had was Lady Caldwell, who lived in the house across the street, watching from her veranda and reporting to Father if I so much as set one foot outside in the sun.

Perhaps one of the local boys had broken in to get a peep at whatever relic father had brought home this time. He touted his discoveries as "rare," but the ease with which he'd acquired them led me to believe this was something of a misnomer. I focused my eyes on the pages of my book, mouthing the words to maintain my concentration. I'd just reached the part where Lady Burton, accompanied by her husband, explorer Sir Richard Francis Burton, arrived in Port Said. A quick skim ahead revealed that she departed the very next day; I admired her ability to pass it by, as I seemed to be stuck here until Father concluded his business with the antiquities, however long that might be.

I did take pleasure in her descriptions of the city, which had remained largely unchanged in the two decades between Lady Burton's visit and my own. The slave trade had been abolished since then, but she focused her descriptions on the rows of wooden houses lined up like toys; the broad, dirty streets; the feral dogs; the music halls and dancing saloons. Not that I'd had the opportunity to visit any of those—Father wouldn't stand for me wandering the city, though he apparently had no compunctions about leaving me in this empty house alone. In England, I would always have been accompanied, but things were different now. The only person Father had hired since he arrived was his assistant Garai, and he was hardly a suitable chaperone.

The groaning came again—a low, guttural moan, deep with pain. If one of the locals had come in through the window, it sounded as though he'd hurt himself on whatever Father had stashed back there. I sincerely hoped it wasn't an animal of some kind. Father had surely learned his lesson after the incident with the ratting dogs.

Then again, if he were capable of learning a lesson, we would still be in London where we belonged, not hiding in Port Said.

A crash came then, with the sound of shattering glass. I stood from my chair, book falling to the floor. On our estate in London, I would have escaped to the gardens and let the servants take care of the disturbance, but here all we had was a small house on a dusty street. There was barely enough space for the show furniture Father had bought—let alone room enough to escape from whatever was making the noise.

I stood taller after picking up my book from the floor and holding it tightly in my hands. Even still, my hands shook.

The groaning grew louder. At least the growl of a ratting dog would have been familiar—this moan was distinctly human. Since there were no servants here, and I had no way to know when Father would be back, I was going to have to investigate myself. It was what Lady Burton would have done, surely. She had no fear of traveling without her husband, passing port after port, even exploring strange cities while on her way to meet him on faraway continents. She likely would have thought nothing of investigating a strange moan at the back of her house. She was in her forties at the time of her travels, and I had barely passed the age of seventeen, but if I longed for her freedom, perhaps I'd need to summon a bit of her bravery as well.

I took a deep breath to steel myself and then walked purposefully through the hallway to the back of the house. The door to father's study was closed but unlocked. I hesitated with my hand on the doorknob, listening.

Silence. Perhaps the noise had wafted in through the open windows after all.

Nothing to be afraid of then. I turned the handle and pushed the door into the dark room. The damask curtains—one of Father's showpieces—kept out the mid-afternoon sun, but not the stifling heat. The room was filled with boxes and cases—things Father had shipped with us on the boat from England or acquired since. Our insurance, he called it.

I didn't ask exactly what he'd stolen. I didn't want to know.

The large table at the center of the room was Father's pride and joy—the wood was real oak, imported of course. Atop it lay a disheveled bed sheet, rumpled and wadded as if it had been used to cover something precious from view and then dramatically thrown aside in a grand reveal. At the far end of the table lay a stone tablet, though I couldn't see its detail. Around the table sat a number of chairs piled with books and sheets of paper. More books were scattered across the floor, as if someone had shoved them off the table—probably the source of the crashing noise. Perhaps one of the local boys had entered by the window, wounded himself, and then fled again.

The darkness might have obscured my vision, but it did nothing to mask the smell. The room reeked of bodies—Father must have neglected to open the window during his hours of meetings—but under that I detected something older. Mustier. Rotten. As I stepped in, glass crunched under my feet. The remains of a lamp lay a few feet from the door, oil spread slick over the floor.

How had the lamp fallen? I peered around, half expecting to find some mongrel dog hiding under the table, but I couldn't make out anything moving in the shadows.

This was foolish. I shuffled past the glass and around the table to the windows, reaching up with both hands to shove the curtains aside and let in more light.

The groaning came again, this time from behind me.

I wheeled around, and in the shadow of the corner, behind one of the large crates, stood an Egyptian man, illuminated by the light that now poured in from the window. He was bald, shirtless, and unshaven.

He was also utterly naked.

I screamed and leapt back against the window. The man stared at me wide-eyed, his mouth open, revealing yellowed teeth. He let out an indecipherable yell, higher pitched than the previous groans. Something about his complexion didn't look quite right. Jaundiced perhaps. Had Father taken to experimenting with those awful curing elixirs? He'd always said those were quite the swindle, though I'd tried to ignore the longing in his voice.

I tried to rip my eyes away from the man's exposed body, fighting between the urge to run for the door and the desire to stay as far away from him as possible. I considered the tablet on the table—with the curtains open, I could make out scrawls of foreign writing across the stone face, and an arrow-shaped carving at the top, pointing sideways at the wall toward the neighbor's house. I wasn't certain I could heft it, let alone use it to defend myself.

As I hesitated, the man lunged for the bedsheet on the table between us and then hunched down behind a traveling trunk with the cloth wrapped around him. He stared at me in shock, as if he was as surprised as I was to find himself naked. He seemed to have no desire to come any closer.

I edged toward the door, bent down, and snatched up the remains of the shade from the oil lamp, careful not to cut my fingers on the jagged glass. I straightened up, holding the sliver of glass before myself like a weapon.

This man was clearly not a thief—a thief would have kept his clothes on. I cursed Father for leaving me alone in the house. Had he no sense of propriety remaining? Though, offering me warning would have led to questions, and questions were not something Father was fond of, especially about matters of business. It didn't take a scholar to figure out why.

The man tightened the sheet around his mid-section,

looking at me wide-eyed. "Who are you?" he said, his voice shaking. His voice was lightly accented, but his English clear. "Where am I?"

"Who am *I*?" I asked. "Who are *you*?"

The man's eyes widened again, and he flinched. "I..." He paused, his eyes twitching back and forth. He let out another inarticulate groan and slammed the heel of his hand against his temple.

"Whoever you are, my father will be home soon," I said. "He'll be furious if anything happens to me."

He hadn't taken much care for my safety in the last few weeks, but this man didn't have to know that. Better he think that Father treasured me. That might put some fear into him.

I needn't have worried. The man lifted the corner of the sheet, tying it around his chest like a toga. Then he flattened himself against the wall, edging toward the door, wincing as his feet met the shards of broken glass.

"Let me go," he said.

I raised my hands in surrender. If Father meant to keep the man here, he might be furious at his escape, but he certainly couldn't blame me for it. The man took one more confused glance around the room and then ran for the doorway, sheet flying out behind him. His feet pounded away, then I heard the front door open and shut.

I breathed a sigh of relief. I almost hoped that Lady Caldwell was out on her veranda at that moment to see the sheeted man run by. She would faint from the impropriety, to be sure. I wished for the gumption to take such an action, to run away from these suffocating walls and never return.

Instead, I checked the rest of the study thoroughly to be sure no more surprises lurked in the corners, though I stopped short of opening the crates. Unless Father had more naked men stuffed in his travel trunks, I was well and truly alone, for the moment at least.

After locking the front door, I settled back into my chair in the parlor and opened my book again, but it was no use. The incident had me too rattled; there was no chance I could concentrate on Lady Burton's journey to India now.

When Father returned, I'd be ready for him. I was going to give him a piece of my mind.

* * *

WHEN FATHER RETURNED AN HOUR LATER, I was still waiting for him in the front parlor. He whistled as he came through the door, dropped his bowler onto the hat stand, and stripped off his morning coat.

I sat in my chair facing the door, drumming my fingers on the armrest.

"Ah, Lila," Father said, turning his sales-pitch smile on me. "How was your afternoon?"

"Divine," I said, "unless you count being frightened nearly to death by the nude gentleman in your meeting room."

Father's smile melted away. He swept past me down the hallway and paused, staring at the open study door. He stalked into the room and out of my sight, though I could hear glass crunching under his shoes. A moment later he returned, his face pale. He stared at me for a moment, then ran a hand through his hair, disturbing the crisp horseshoe part that encircled his head. He sank onto the loveseat opposite me.

"Lila," he said wearily, "who took the body?"

I narrowed my eyes. The body? Dear Lord, I hoped he hadn't involved himself in a murder. "What body?" I asked.

Father sneered at me. "Don't be pert. The body on the table, of course."

I sat forward in my chair, giving him a hard stare. "It got up and walked out. Or sprinted, more accurately. I think its owner was shocked at finding himself naked in a dark room with a strange girl, and I shared the sentiment."

Father sprang up out of his chair and stepped closer to me. "It walked out," he repeated. *"Alive?"*

"Alive, yes." I glared at him. "Unless the dead can run like madmen." Good heavens. Not only was Father involved in a murder, but he'd managed to bungle it. How long before the naked man brought the police to our door?

A look crossed Father's face then. Was it fear? Anger? The expression faded away before I could decide. He stared at the ceiling.

"What was that man *doing* in the study?" I asked. "Why would you leave me alone with him?"

Father shook his head. "I didn't know."

No, he'd thought he left me alone with a *dead body,* which I didn't find to be significantly preferable.

I waited for him to explain, but he only paced down the hall to have another look at the study. This didn't bode well for us. We'd left London to escape the men who wanted to break Father's legs for one reason or another. We'd only been here a few weeks, and he'd gone and ruined Port Said for us, too. Where would we run to next? America?

"You can't keep doing this," I said. "If you want to put yourself in danger, that's your right, but you're dragging me through it with you, and it isn't fair."

"I know," Father said. "When I make this next sale, I promise things will be different. I'll have enough to set us up anywhere in the world. You pick the destination, Lila. Anywhere you want."

I stared at him. He promised me the literal world—the one thing he knew that I wanted—to travel, to be free. But I'd never be free as long as I was with him, and I had no money or contacts to travel the world alone. I'd heard this story before. One more deal. One more sale. "The next one is always the one that solves all of our problems," I said. "But instead, it only creates more."

Father wouldn't meet my eyes. "Be a good girl and go sit in your bedroom for a while," he said. "Garai will be here in a moment."

He knew I was right, but he'd never admit it. It would do no good to stay; Father wouldn't tolerate me speaking to his business partner besides simple pleasantries, but I had the sense that he saw Father as an opportunity, that he was also seeking a way to improve his fortunes and escape from this miserable place. He worked as a guide to foreigners who came to Port Said and was new to schemes like my father's, though he seemed to be adapting to them quickly enough. I wanted to warn him that the only opportunities he'd find here were the kind that were likely to ruin him. Though if he was helping my father collect bodies that weren't quite dead, he probably should have figured this out on his own, no matter how desperate his circumstances.

I collected Lady Burton from the sitting room and stalked to my bedroom, slamming the door behind me. Once, my father would have lectured me about my lack of refined manners, but now he had no standing to instruct me on such things. I flopped on my bed, fanning my face.

My room bore the brunt of the morning sunlight, and by mid-afternoon grew oppressively hot. I pulled my hair free of its knot, allowing it to frizz about my face.

Through the open shutters, I heard a knock on our front door, and Garai's voice greeting Father. If they were having one of their business meetings, I could be stuck in here for hours, wondering what foolishness Father was cooking up in the other room. This was going to be London all over again, only this time I could see it coming. I should have seen it even then. First Mother's jewelry disappeared. Then the artwork straight from the walls—even the seascape Mother had loved. Then the curtains. Soon it was all gone, and a few weeks later, so were we.

This time I knew what kind of man Father was. I needed to listen, so I could prepare for what would come next. I couldn't listen from the hall; if Father opened the door to the study, he'd discover me instantly. Instead, I hitched up my skirts and sat on the window ledge, swinging my legs over and lowering myself onto the stone path in the alley. The space between our house and the next was narrow, no more than a yard and a half. I walked slowly along the back of the house toward the study window. In London, I never would have thought of sneaking about like this. Back then, I hadn't known there was a need.

Garai's voice grew louder as I approached. As I'd hoped, Father had left the shutters open to allow in the breeze.

"You should have waited until I finished the translation," Garai said. "You shouldn't have gone ahead without me."

"I think you're missing the point, friend," Father said. "It *works*."

"How do we know it works?" Garai said. "There's no body to prove it."

"If we acquired one body, we can acquire another."

Garai's tone grew sharper. "I took risks to get you the first one! You claim he walked out of here alive, but I haven't seen him. You might have disposed of the body yourself."

"If you don't believe me, ask my daughter. She saw him."

I stiffened. If Garai came looking for me, I might not be able to get back through my window in time. I wanted to believe that Father wouldn't send a strange man into my bed chamber to interrogate me, but by now, nothing could surprise me.

Thankfully Garai didn't seem eager to chase after me. "If

what you say is true, you've already exposed us. How could you let him escape? He knows where to find us. He could turn us in."

"You let me worry about that," Father said. That's what he always said when he didn't have an answer. Garai was at much greater risk than Father. This was one reason we'd come to Egypt from London; Father had learned of the Capitulations, laws that forbid the local law enforcement from imposing on British citizens. If they were caught committing a crime, Garai might be arrested, but Father would only face consequences if the British Consular Court took an interest, and they overlooked all but the most public of cases.

"There won't be another body," Garai said. "If that one is really walking around somewhere, we need to find it and bring it back. That's your proof."

"All right," Father said. "We'll go out together, and we'll look."

Wailing rose toward the front of the house. Inside the study, footsteps approached the window, and I flattened myself against the wall so I wouldn't be seen. Father's hand gripped the shutters, and he slammed them closed, shutting out the noise. I heard the latch scrape shut inside, and the voices resumed, muffled now. I could have pressed my ear to the shutters to listen, but I'd have risked casting a shadow through the shutter slats.

The wailing continued near the street, breaking into wracking sobs. I edged around the corner of the house, passing by the window of my bedroom to investigate the sound.

A wagon waited on the street. I stepped onto our porch, watching as two men hauled a body wrapped in black cloth out of the house next door. An Arab woman followed after them, crying into the cloth that covered her hair and part of her face.

I shivered. Two bodies in one day, though from the look of it, this one wouldn't be running away naked down the street.

The woman didn't look toward me as they loaded the body into the wagon and drove him away. She stood by the road, crying.

I hadn't watched when they took mother away. Father wouldn't let me see her after she grew sick, wouldn't risk that the illness that wracked her body might transfer to me. He didn't tell me they'd come to take her until she was already gone. I wanted to say something to the woman, some words that might be of comfort, but I already knew there was no comfort, not in times like these. Instead, I retreated back into the house by way of the front door.

Options for eavesdropping now closed, I retrieved my book from my room and settled in the parlor again. I couldn't imagine what Father might be involved in that he'd need to show a body to an interested party. I was amazed that the frightened man hadn't returned with law enforcement yet, though of course they wouldn't be able to do anything to Father.

I needn't have worried about eavesdropping. Garai came storming out of the study not ten minutes later. He took a swipe at his nose as he stalked to the door. He was always doing that, as if he had some perennial problem with his sinuses that caused him constant discomfort.

"Good day," I said. He didn't even turn to look at me—just pushed out the door and let it close behind him.

Father emerged after him and sank onto the loveseat opposite me. He looked too wrung out to scold me for not following his instruction that I remain in my room.

"This has been quite the day," he said.

"I would imagine so," I said. "It's not every day you're part of a foiled kidnapping."

"We didn't kidnap anyone," Father said sharply. "What would give you that idea?"

"Only the man who didn't know where he was or why," I said. "If not foiled kidnapping, a bungled murder then. Even better."

"This city has sharpened your tongue," Father said. "You never would have spoken to me this way in London."

It wasn't Port Said that sharpened my tongue, but he was right. I would never have spoken to him like this when I'd believed him to be respectable.

"I'm sorry," I said. "It must be the shock from my encounter with the body."

"That may be," Father said. "Perhaps you should retire to bed until you recover."

"So you don't deny you're involved in a murder," I said.

"Of course I'm not," Father snapped.

"How do you explain the body, then?"

Father leaned back in his chair. "That is my business. You let me worry about it."

But Father never worried enough about his plans. If he did, we might still be back on our London estate. The law might not be able to catch him here, but it wasn't the law we were running from in London. I imagined men with a grievance could break a man's legs here as easily as they could there, and without consequence if they came from the right nation.

Father closed his eyes, and we sat in silence. I opened my book, but I didn't read. Not even Lady Burton's descriptions of Jeddah could engage me.

A knock came at the door. Father jumped, the way he had those last few days in London anytime a visitor came to call.

But instead of hiding, he stood up and answered the door. That was a good sign, anyway.

A local officer stood outside. Father nodded to him politely, but the man didn't look pleased. He offered a few words in Arabic—an Islamic greeting, I thought, though I hadn't yet had the opportunity to memorize the local customs.

"I'm looking for Mr. William Dyer," the officer said in English.

"Well, you've found him," Father said. "How can I help you?"

I stood to get a better look outside the door. I half expected to see the naked man from the study, but the officer appeared to be alone.

"I'm searching for information regarding the disappearance of a valuable artifact from the home of Mr. Arthur Conway. Do you know him?"

"Yes," Father said. "I'm sorry to hear he's been robbed."

"May I come in?" the officer asked.

"I'd rather you didn't," Father said, nodding toward me. "My daughter is at home, and she has...delicate sensibilities."

At least he hadn't given me some horrible contagious disease. The officer wouldn't be permitted to force his way in, and he didn't try.

"Yes, well, Arthur named you as a potential buyer of the object in question—a tablet he acquired some weeks back. Do you remember it?"

"Of course," Father said. "His price was too high. I told him last week that I wasn't interested."

"The very next day the tablet disappeared," the officer said. "You won't mind if I come in to look around your home?"

"I most certainly would mind," Father said. "I have a

respectable reputation. If Arthur is going to accuse me of stealing from him, he can come here and do it himself."

I cringed. The law might not be able to touch Father in Egypt, but this Arthur fellow could, if he put a mind to it.

The officer stared Father down, but he didn't press the issue. "Thank you, sir," he said. "I'll be back if I have further questions."

"You might want to direct those questions elsewhere," Father said. "I've told you all that I know."

The officer nodded, no doubt aware there was nothing he could do, even if he knew Father had committed the crime.

Father closed the door after him. He paused, resting his forehead against it. I watched out the window as the officer headed down the street. He said he might be back, but I didn't imagine he would be. What would be the point?

"So the tablet in your study is stolen, then," I said.

Father gave me a sharp look. "Go back to your book, Lila," he said. "Leave my affairs to me."

He retired to the study, and I settled back into my chair. If we had more guests in the evening, I wasn't going to miss them.

* * *

As it turned out, I did miss the trouble, which instead arrived next door, and not until the middle of the night. I heard about it only the next morning from Lady Caldwell, who called down to me from her veranda the moment I opened our front door.

"I hope you're safe, dear," she said, fanning herself furiously with her wooden folding fan. "Did you hear of the break in next door? Terrible thing. A man tried to enter their house in the middle of the night! And after a death in the family, too. It's a terrible thing."

I glanced next door, to the house where the dead man had been taken away. It did seem a terrible thing, someone trying to victimize the family when they'd just lost a loved one. "Is everyone all right?" I asked.

"All except the intruder!" Lady Caldwell said. "He died when the police arrived to subdue him. Hard to say he didn't deserve it. I'm glad you missed it, dearie. A young girl like you shouldn't be exposed to such violence."

I thanked her for sharing the gossip all the same and ducked back inside the house, locking the door behind me. It was a strange collection of events. Father had left the house early that morning, and being left alone for hours on end did nothing to quiet my nerves.

It was late afternoon before Father and Garai returned, backing a wagon up to our front door and unloading a coffin-sized crate into our front parlor. I watched from the hallway to my room. The neighbors might talk, but unless they'd seen the naked man the day before, they would probably assume the box contained more furniture rather than a corpse. I, on the other hand, couldn't imagine that it contained anything else.

"What is that?" I asked as Garai and Father carried the box through the doorway into the study.

"Nothing you need to worry about," Garai told me, though I had a feeling it was quite the opposite.

As Father closed the door behind them, he gave me a weary look. "Why don't you go out for a while, dear," he said. "Go down and look at the canal."

The first few days we were here, Father wouldn't even let me answer the door alone. But as his desperation increased, his memory for propriety suffered.

Still, I retrieved my hat and gloves. If he thought I had gone out, he wouldn't come looking for me. I shut the front door extra hard on my way out, so he would believe I had gone. Then I slipped behind the house and arranged myself in the shadow behind our building where I wouldn't cast a silhouette on the wall opposite. The shutters to the study were open again, allowing in the morning breeze. I'd left them open early that morning in preparation.

They both grunted as they hefted the crate onto the large table with a thud. I wondered now if the table had been built specifically to examine bodies.

"Well, we found it," Garai said, "but the body is as dead as ever."

"The point is," Father said, "that it *wasn't*. It was alive and well last night when it tried to break in next door. That's proof enough that it works."

"Who do you expect to believe it?" Garai asked. "And why would the man escape from here only to break in next door?"

"It must have gotten confused," Father said, "which is just as well. I wouldn't have liked it breaking in here."

I closed my eyes. So they were all connected—the naked man from yesterday, the break-in, and this body, now returned and freshly dead. I didn't know if that made me feel better or worse.

"What do you mean to do now?" Garai asked.

"We'll try it again," Father said.

"I don't know what will be different," Garai said. "The original pronunciation is lost. Without that, it may never work properly."

"But it *did* work," Father insisted. "Say the words again. Slowly this time."

Garai began to speak in Arabic, though he could have been reading today's newspaper for all I understood of the language.

Someone else shouted in Arabic, his voice drowning out Garai's. I looked up to see a man leaning out of a window in the house behind ours, waving his arm at me.

As word spread about the break in, I imagined the neighborhood would be on high alert. I tried to smile and wave at him, hoping he would realize I was harmless, but I was too late. Father's head emerged from the window, and he turned, laying eyes on me. His gaze hardened into a formidable stare, and he reached through the window and grabbed me by the arm. "Get in here this instant," he said through clenched teeth. "What have you heard?"

"Nothing!" I said. Though I had no excuse for skulking behind our building.

Inside, Garai stopped speaking. Father pulled me toward the window, looking as if he might grab me by the arms and haul me right through, when behind him, Garai let out a loud grunt. Father turned, and I watched through the open window as Garai rubbed his nose once in that way of his, and then stumbled back against the wall, his eyes unfocusing. The papers that had been in his hands fluttered to the floor, and he slumped, his knees giving out from beneath him as he fell to the ground.

Father loosened his grip on me in shock. I could have wrenched away and run, but I didn't know where I would go, so instead I lifted myself onto the windowsill and swung my legs into the room. Father dropped my arm and moved over to Garai.

I pulled the shutters closed. I didn't want the man in the window to witness this scene. The room grew dark, the only light filtering in through the dusty shutter slats.

Father shook Garai, but his body flopped lifelessly. He lifted Garai's arm and pressed a finger to his wrist.

"He's dead," Father said.

Another one? "Can you resuscitate him?"

Father shook his head. "It's better this way. He knew too much and was starting to get twitchy. I'll have to find another local man to find me bodies."

I backed up against the shutters. Father was going to continue with whatever mad scheme this was, even with two dead men on his hands. This was worse than London. Father had left a lot of angry people there, but not a trail of bodies. "Surely you don't think we should stay."

Father waved a dismissive hand at me, then picked up the papers Garai had dropped. "We'll go just as soon as I find a buyer for the artifact."

The thick stone tablet lay on the table, though it had been turned so it now pointed at Garai's fallen body. "How did Garai die?" I asked, pressing harder against the shutters, blocking more of the light. Father lit a lamp and looked over the papers. "Did the artifact kill him? Or the incantation?"

Father shook his head. "I don't know. But finding another with access to bodies who speaks English and reads Arabic will be difficult." He gave Garai's body an annoyed look, as if his sudden demise was an inconvenience at best.

"If the artifact killed him," I said, "why would anyone want to buy it? A...death rock?"

Father didn't respond, as if my question was of no consequence. I couldn't imagine what I might do to stop him from proceeding with his mad plans. And wherever his schemes took him, he'd drag me right along.

At that moment, the body in the crate on the table began to groan again.

I jumped back. One of the unlatched shutters fell open a few inches, casting a ray of light onto the body's swollen face. I watched as the swelling faded and the body's muscles grew gradually more taught. My knees buckled, and I fell beneath the window, scrambling into the corner as the body opened its eyes.

Father stood in the middle of the room, still holding the papers. "Fascinating," he said. "I told him it worked."

I could barely squeak words between gasped breaths. "You—expected this?"

Heavens, had he stumbled upon some kind of *resurrection*?

Father watched raptly as the bald man recoiled inside the crate, grabbing at the sheet that covered his lower half and pulling it up to its chest. He seemed to be struggling with his own tongue. Color restored slowly to his face.

"What was wrong with him?" I asked. This was unmistakably the same man I'd discovered yesterday in this very room. If Lady Caldwell was to be believed, he'd been killed the night before as he resisted arrest. "Was he mistaken for dead? *Twice*?"

"No," Father said. "He was certainly dead both times. So it works more than once. That'll make a fine selling point."

A *selling point*? "You plan to sell this…what *is* it? Some kind of circle of death?"

"Yes, there is that problem," Father said. "How do we get it to bring the bodies back without killing the witnesses? This won't be much of a source for labor if the cost is one for one."

I tried to make sense of that statement. Father's artifact brought days-old bodies back from the dead, but it killed bystanders in the process.

The man who died yesterday, the one I'd seen taken from the house next door. Had he died because of this artifact? Was it some kind of terrible *cost*?

The tablet, I realized, had been pointing next door when that family had suffered a loss. The carved arrow at the top was pointing to Garai now, who still lay slumped on the floor, lifeless and unmoving.

"What do you mean, use it for labor?" I asked. "You want to—to resurrect the dead and put them to work?"

"Not me," Father said. "That's the beauty of it. There's a shortage now, a need, since the end of the slave trade. Make the sale quiet enough, and there are rich people all over the world who would pay for an extra set of hands. It may be illegal to sell a person, but it's not yet illegal to sell the means to bring them to life. And once they're back from the dead, well. Dead men don't have rights. Not yet, anyway." He shook his head. "There has to be some way to keep it from killing. Garai made an error in the translation, that's all. We'll try again."

"This is mad," I said. "Who ever heard of such a plan?"

"That's why I tried to keep you out of it," Father said, looking pointedly at me. "But no, you had to keep pressing your nose where it didn't belong. Now you're in this, so you're damn well going to make yourself *useful*."

I opened my mouth, but no sound came out.

The man in the crate moaned again, and then he reached up, swiping a hand across his nose in exactly the way I'd seen Garai do, time and time again.

I looked down at Garai's still body.

Oh, God. Yesterday, the naked man had run from here, only to return *next door* in the night...perhaps returning to his own home? Did Father's artifact resurrect the dead, or did it transfer a soul from one body to another?

"Garai?" I asked.

"He's dead, Lila," my father said. "He won't hear you."

The naked man rocked back and forth, gnawing on the knuckle of his ring finger. He didn't respond.

I wanted to look away. I shouldn't be here. Father and I should both be back in London. I should be out calling. Father should be off on business.

Not here.

Not here.

"What are you going to do now?" I asked Father.

Father reached into his pocket and pulled out a pistol. My hands trembled as he looked at it, considering, as if he thought he might shoot the body in the head and be done with it.

"Don't!" I said. "He's your proof that it works, isn't he?"

"I wonder if it wouldn't be better to start over," Father said, running a finger down the barrel. "We'll leave, go to Cairo, find a fresh translator and demonstrate again, in front of a buyer this time."

I steadied myself against the wall, still not ready to stand on my own. Father couldn't possibly expect me to go along with this madness. But no, it hadn't even crossed his mind that I might turn against him. That I might go to the police. But what if I did? They couldn't touch him. The laws gave Father the perfect haven for his schemes. He wasn't going to stop, now or ever. He would go on endangering lives, including my own.

"All right," I said, trying to think. "Is there room enough to load the bodies into the wagon?"

"If I move some things," Father said, and he stumbled out of the office, still carrying his pistol at his side.

Leaving me alone with the naked man. Again.

The sun had begun to go down—I could see the reflections of the red light on the wall behind our house, gleaming through the shutters. I stepped past Garai's body, approaching the crate. The man inside swiped at his nose again.

"Garai?" I asked. "Is that you?"

Garai blinked at me. "Where am I?" he asked in English. "What did—what did I do?"

"Do you remember your name?" I asked.

He nodded, stumbling over his words. "Garai Amin," he said. "You—you're Lila."

His voice was different, but the cadence of his speech matched Garai's. It seemed almost unbelievable that his soul could have been in one body and was now in another, and yet the proof was right in front of me.

I wanted to shake Garai for his foolishness, but I had a limited time before Father returned, and Garai was my only possible ally. "You used the artifact to transfer yourself into a dead man's body," I said. "Did you know that's what it would do?"

Garai shook his head. "I don't know," he said. "I don't know."

I moved to the tablet and picked up Garai's notes. Garai's scribbles looped and twisted across the page—written in Arabic. I cursed myself for not learning any of the language, though I hadn't known I might have need of it until these last few weeks.

Could I use these words to put Garai back in his body? Point the artifact where he sat in the crate and complete the transfer?

There, near the bottom of the page, I found the English transcription of the words Garai had spoken. The inscription of the artifact, translated from an old Egyptian language into Arabic, and then into English. I could ask Garai for help, but he seemed to know very little of how this worked. If he had understood he would never have spoken the words, particularly not with the carved arrow pointing at himself.

My king, the words read. *Rise from my words and begin life anew. Take from my meaning and lead us once more.*

I didn't know who might have been raised with the artifact before it was buried long ago, but it must have been someone for whom the speaker was willing to die. Perhaps of the ancient Egyptian kings, revered as deity, being reclaimed from heaven to rule again.

In the crate, Garai covered himself further with the sheet, staring at his own hands where they gripped the fabric. He was still disoriented, so I didn't think he'd be much help, even if he understood the full implications of what he'd done.

If Father returned, he might shoot Garai. He'd drag me along in the company of two bodies, and to whatever he did next, I'd be an accomplice.

I couldn't let him do that. I couldn't. I turned the stone on the table, working its orientation so the part that had been pointing toward Garai before now pointed to the door.

Father's footsteps pounded down the hall. His schemes were leading us both into the depths of hell, and I had only moments to act.

I picked up the notes again, muttering the words under my breath.

Father appeared in the doorway. "Lila," he said. "What are you doing?"

"Lead us once more," I said, finishing the incantation.

Father looked at the notes in my hand, and then at the tablet, at the arrow pointed directly at him. I had done something terrible. I'd either attempted to use a deadly artifact against my father, right in front of him where he could easily discern my intent, or...

Father pulled the revolver out of his pocket, this time pointing it squarely at me. "Lila," he said. "What have you—"

The words died on his lips as he groaned and stumbled forward, the gun slipping from his grasp and clattering to the floor before his body fell alongside it.

I'd killed my own father.

Behind me, Garai's old body groaned. I looked down at my father, lifeless on the floor. If the artifact had transferred his soul, it was nothing but an empty shell.

I'd done that. I'd killed him, though his soul was very much alive and now in Garai's old body behind me.

What would I do now? Leave them this way? When my father got over the initial disorientation, he would only continue with his terrible schemes. He never learned, no matter the consequences.

I stepped over to the crate, looking into the eyes of the naked man who now contained Garai's soul. I couldn't imagine Garai wanted to remain in this man's corpse. He looked terrified, which told me he was beginning to understand the gravity of what they'd done, what we'd *all* done.

If I returned my father's soul to his own body, I knew better than to believe he would change his ways. I'd plead with him to change, but he had refused.

With my father dead, what would become of me?

A damning plan began to form in my own mind. It was terrible even to think, but I didn't know how long my father's disorientation would last, and I wanted to make good use of it. I turned the artifact again, this time pointing it at the naked man's body, currently possessed by Garai. I spoke the incantation again.

Garai rocked up on his knees in the crate, reaching out as if to stop me, but he was too late. He slumped immediately over, his head lolling over the crate's side, and my father's body shuddered and then scrambled a bit on the floor, as if the person inside had suffered a shock.

I didn't have time to wait for the disorientation to wear off. I knelt before my father's body, pulling Garai upright. "I need your help," I told him. "You have my father's face. Egyptian law can't touch you now. Help me leave the country, and you can keep it."

My father's eyes widened in shock as Garai took in my words. Garai looked down at his new hands, which trembled in fear. I took a step back. It was uncanny, to see a person transform so entirely, wearing another's skin.

"This is an abomination," Garai said in my father's voice, and this time, when he looked up at me, there was anger in his eyes.

We agreed on that, but I didn't know how to fix the situation without him. "You can help me get out, and then you can have his life."

Garai looked at me in horror, and I heard my father shuffling around behind me in the body Garai had left.

"I don't want it," Garai said to me. "Do *you*?"

My head swam with the possibilities. Garai could work the artifact and give me my father's body. I'd have all his power to book a ship anywhere I wanted to go, and no one would look askance at me as I traveled alone. I would have all his freedom, all the safety that came with being an Englishman, however despicable his past deeds.

But my stomach turned at the thought of living the rest of my life in the body of a man, let alone one I hated. "No," I said. "No, I don't want it."

Garai's hands tightened around mine. My father's hands. The ones neither of us could stomach claiming, even with the benefits attached.

"Put me back," Garai said.

I nodded. When I turned to the artifact, my father was already standing. He looked over at Garai wearing his body, horror in his eyes. And then his gaze shifted to his pistol, still lying on the floor.

Garai sprang for the gun while I threw myself at the table, dragging the artifact to point at my father in Garai's body. I didn't need to read the incantation this time, having said it twice before. I shouted the words as Garai leveled the pistol at his own body, his hands shaking so hard that the barrel wavered this way and that.

"My king," I cried. "Rise from my words and begin life anew. Take from my meaning and lead us once more."

Father took one stumbling step toward me, and then he fell to the ground. The body of the naked man in the crate lifted its head again, groaning. My father was going through the disorientation of the transfer again, which bought us precious moments. I turned the artifact to point at my father's body. Garai nodded to me once as I said the words, and then my father's body fell to the floor again, and Garai's body moaned as he returned to his own skin. My father's body lay inert. The naked man groaned in the chest as my father began to recover from his latest transfer.

It wasn't over. Not yet. Not until I made sure my father couldn't do anything like this again. I picked up my father's pistol from where it had fallen to the floor. His body was lifeless. Empty. Nothing.

I repeated these words over to myself as I fired a single bullet into my dead father's head, to eliminate confusion about his cause of death. Then I returned to the tablet and shoved it off the table and onto the floor. The stone tablet made a satisfying sound as it hit the floor, fracturing into a hundred crumbled pieces.

"You should go," I said to Garai. "Save yourself."

As I ran to get the local authorities, that's exactly what I intended to do.

* * *

MY FATHER WAS ARRESTED a few hours later, though it was a local man's name that graced the arrest warrant. Omar Darwish—the man whose body Garai and Father had originally stolen—was charged with the murder of Mr. William Dyer, a British National, and therefore would have the full force of the law brought against him.

When the disorientation wore off, Omar told the court his name was William Dyer, though no one but me believed him.

The story I told wasn't as clean as I would have liked it to be. My father was a thief, of course, and he'd been working with Darwish, who was presumed to have faked his death in the first place to avoid his responsibilities and begin his underground dealings with my father. They'd stolen the artifact, and then Darwish turned on my father, preferring to keep the money for himself.

The question of how I—a girl of slight frame—had hit Darwish hard enough over the head with the artifact to make him forget who he was, let alone bound him to the table leg without his preventing me, remained unanswered. But the officers seemed happy to have a local man to blame—one that they could charge under the law. If they suspected that events had not played out exactly as I described, they did not let on.

I set immediately about selling the rest of the contents of our Port Said residence—on the legal market, of course, rather than Father's underground one. Garai offered to buy me passage on whatever ship I chose. The money from the sale of Father's assets would last for a while, giving me time to find legal means to support myself. I had done terrible things, things no decent person should ever contemplate, but I vowed that I would leave the poison behind with my father, that whatever I did from now I would do honestly, free from my father's influence and his legacy. I meant to keep traveling as long as my legs would carry me—my life was mine, and mine alone, and there was an entire world beyond that had been out of reach only a few days before.

One which Lady Burton surely would not have hesitated to explore.

Janci Patterson writes young adult science fiction and fantasy, romantic comedy, and epic fantasy. She has co-authored many books, including the sixth book in the Alcatraz vs the Evil Librarian series and the Skyward Flight collection with Brandon

Sanderson. Janci and Brandon will be continuing the Skyward universe with a new co-authored trilogy, debuting in 2025. As a hybrid author, Janci has published forty books both independently and traditionally. She lives in Orem, Utah with her husband, two children, and her energetic border collie. In her spare time, she plays games of all kinds, customizes barbie dolls, and watches too much reality TV.

CIRCLES

MICHAEL BOULERICE

Fresh snow crunched under Stavro's loafers as he trudged back to the boarding house from the old grocery store down the street. The sun dipped behind the buildings of North Street, warm peach-pinks quickly ceding to the navies and ceruleans of an impending night sky. His pomaded hair, inky black from a box of men's comb-in colorant, stiffened with frost in the northern New Hampshire air.

Stavro's only Christmas tradition was to put as much distance as he could between himself and the moldering mansion he both lived in and managed. Last year was midnight mass and mai tais in Oahu. The year before that was a Caribbean cruise and several days on the Dutch side of St. Maarten, and before that was Ibiza, where he was almost beaten for groping a cocktail waitress at one of the few dance clubs open in December.

This time, he was traveling to Albania to stay with his last remaining family, a pair of spinster cousins who hadn't seen Stavro in so long they'd forgotten how much they disliked him.

He kept one hand warm in the thinly lined pocket of his leather jacket. The other, quickly losing feeling in the chill, held a plastic shopping bag with a pre-made Italian sub and a quart of chocolate milk: lunch to eat in the car tomorrow on his way to the international departures gate. His flight wouldn't start boarding until eight at night, but he wanted to beat the Christmas Eve traffic. Nothing about his holiday itinerary could ever be left to chance. The stakes were too high.

He was thinking about how smart he was for having decided to pack early when the orange snowplow hopped the curb. Stavro, struck with terror, watched as the driver violently swung the steering wheel to the left. He managed to put his truck back on the road, but not before the edge of the blade clipped Stavro's right side, sending his fragile body spinning into a frozen snowbank.

Even as the truck driver draped his Carhartt jacket over Stavro as he convulsed on the frozen sidewalk, the aging swindler could think of nothing but getting on that plane and escaping that backwater hamlet before it was too late. Before the circles came for him.

The strobes of an inbound ambulance illuminated the scene of the accident in an offensive red and white staccato. Stavro stared at the plastic bag that once held tomorrow's lunch, torn and empty after the impact, drifting in listless circles in the middle of the street.

SEVEN YEARS EARLIER

"It's not the end of the world, but it's not looking great, either," Thomas said.

The stifling August humidity drew beads of sweat that trickled down Stavro's nose and dripped on the painted floor as he eavesdropped on the conversation between Thomas and his elderly father, Guillaume.

"A lot of these bills are second and third notice. It's a problem we're gonna need to address at some point, Pop. Your manager isn't managing anything."

As someone who understood the connection between information and power, that was not the first time Stavro stood in the locked hallway separating the boarding house from the lower living quarters, listening to the conversations taking place in the kitchen. The walls and door were just thin enough to pick up voices at normal speaking volumes, but that was a two-way street, and one had to stand completely still to keep the hallway floorboards from creaking, which could be heard from the kitchen.

"He's had plenty of time to visit the bank and withdraw cash out of the boarding house account. That's *on top* of his paycheck. He's not paying bills with that money. It clearly isn't for renovations or repairs, because it looks like absolute shit up there."

Guillaume said something in his garbled Quebecois that Stavro couldn't make out.

"I have no problem with you paying him more. That's your prerogative, but right now he's not asking before he takes it. That's stealing, Pop. I'm gonna have a talk with him."

Stavro quietly closed the front door of the boarding house, slowly twisting his key to relock it as quietly as possible. He stormed into the blast furnace of Main Street, his gold-plated Italian cornetto swinging violently with every step.

Thomas, that ungrateful fuck. Causing problems where there weren't any. Sure, Stavro skimmed money, but he deserved it. As far as he was concerned, he deserved everything he earned, as well as everything he took.

IRONICALLY, it was the cycle of indiscriminate taking and spending that landed him in that depressing boarding house a decade earlier. Nearly penniless, he'd been on the run from a couple mobbed up Irish hardcases after scamming one of their gum-smacking idiot wives out of a few hundred bucks in Buffalo.

But Thomas seemed set on throwing a wrench into the plans. Had Guillaume's son made his traitorous assholery known when Stavro first started working there, he'd have cut bait and hit the road. But, at sixty-five, the quartz of his low-level criminality was succumbing to the cruel rock tumbler of age. He'd poured ten years of himself into that one last play, and he only had enough gas in his tank to make it to his final destination. No, he'd have to see his plan through to the end. He'd either ride off into the sunset with enough money to sustain him for the years he had left, or he'd wind up in a state-run nursing home.

Yes, Thomas was going to be a problem. A solution for that hadn't revealed itself to Stavro yet, but he knew it would. It always did when you were the good guy.

PRESENT DAY

"THE SURGEON WILL BE in soon to give you more detail. For now, just rest. You want some ice chips?"

His grogginess lifting slightly, Stavro glanced down at

himself. He was in a hospital johnny. His right arm and right leg were both swaddled in a thick layer of ace bandages.

"Whaaaa…?"

A young man in a white coat approached and rested his clipboard on the foot of the bed as he inspected Stavro's bandaging.

"I'm Dr. Grambleton. I performed your surgery just now. How are you feeling?"

"Like I got hit by a fucking snow plow. What's the damage, Doogie?"

Dr. Grambleton and the nurse laughed. Stavro knew they assumed his waning anesthesia was guiding his speech, when in reality it just made it impossible to maintain the veil of congeniality which separated innocent strangers from the insufferable asshole lying before them.

Stavro stared at the x-ray film on the backlit viewer as Dr. Grambleton explained the extent of his injuries. Titanium plates and screws contrasted brightly against the wispy gray bones of his right arm and leg.

"Well, thanks for piecing me back together, doc. Now if you don't mind, I'll need to use a phone to coordinate a ride home."

"Sounds great, Stavro. Someone can come grab you any time after eight tomorrow morning."

"No can do. I need to get home and finish packing. I have a flight to catch tomorrow."

"Oh, that is a real bummer!" The nurse moved to the side of the bed, gently placing her hand over Stavro's. "Unfortunately, you've just come out of a major surgery. We need to keep you overnight for observation. I'm sure you can understand."

"No, I can't understand." Stavros attempted wriggling himself into an upright position. "Didn't you hear me, you dumb floozie? I have a flight to catch."

"Sir, I'm going to need you to speak more respectfully to Susan here, and please stop attempting to move. You're risking severe damage to that leg of yours." Dr. Grambleton's easy demeanor gave way to a practiced sternness that belied his age.

Stavro thrashed on the bed, wincing with the effort. "I don't give a steaming burlap sack full of fuck! Get me out of this place!"

"Susan, please get Stavro something for emergent delirium. Five milligrams of droperidol. Our patient is getting a bit confused. He's had a big day."

Two more recovery nurses gently pinned Stavro to his bed as Susan injected the strong sedative into his IV drip. His panicked protests grew softer and softer as the drugs kicked in.

"No, you don't understand. The circles will…get me…"

Stavro's glazed eyes blinked heavily, fixating on the heart monitor after one of the nurses pressed a few buttons on it. On the screen, a handful of dots spun in a circle as the machine recalibrated.

FIVE YEARS EARLIER

SUNLIGHT GLINTED on the polished handrails of Guillaume's hospital bed as he watched a Red Sox game on TV. They were up two runs against the Blue Jays. Stavro had pulled up a chair and was watching with him. He had a hundred dollars on the Jays losing by three.

"You heard from Thomas? When's he coming to visit next?" Stavro asked.

"He'll be up in a few weeks. He's been busy with some important things at work."

Stavro sighed dramatically. "What could *possibly* be more important than taking care of your old man and his business? I just don't get it."

Guillaume looked away from the television and out the window. Stavro had trampled into painful territory.

"I know, bub. He says he's gonna come live up here full time as soon as he can get cleared to work remotely."

Stavro made a clucking sound with his tongue. "He's been saying that for years. You know that."

"I do, but he means it. He's a good boy."

"Hey, who's better than your Stavro? Nobody, that's who!"

"You're a good boy, too. I'm grateful for everything you do, bub."

The two sat in silence for a bit. The Blue Jays scored a run.

"He's busy with his work, and lord knows what else down there. Maybe..." Stavro paused for effect. He'd practiced this delivery in front of his mirror for weeks.

Guillaume looked at Stavro. "What's on your mind, bub?"

"It's nothing. Don't worry about it."

More silence.

"You know it's OK to tell me anything, Stavro. Even if it's bad."

"Oh, it's not bad. It's just..."

"Out with it."

"What if Thomas doesn't even want the Chevalier? I already have the place running smoothly. I don't want to overstep, but what if... What if you left the Chevalier to me? You know... when you..."

"It goes to Thomas, Stavro. I promised it to him ages ago. He's my only son. You know that."

"I know. He's your son. It's only right. It's just... He has a job. A life. A family and friends. And he's never here. I don't have any of those things, but I'm the one taking over his responsibilities. Cleaning up his messes. Taking care of his father. He doesn't need this place, you know? I don't have anything *but* this place."

Guillaume blinked, and a single tear rolled down his cheek.

"Listen, we don't have to talk about it. It's no big deal. Let's just enjoy the game."

And so the two of them turned to face the television. Stavro grinned. He wasn't trying to get Guillaume to sign everything over that day. He just wanted to plant the seed of the idea in his head, and that tear told Stavro everything he needed to know.

The Blue Jays scored another run. The game was tied.

PRESENT DAY

"HERE YOU ARE, sir. Would you like us to wheel you into the building?"

Stavro grunted as two EMTs pushed his wheelchair down the weed-choked path from the boarding house's driveway to the door that led to Guillaume's living quarters.

"I live upstairs, you idiots. Use the other door."

"Oh, we called ahead before we loaded you up. The bottom floor is the only one that's wheelchair friendly, so you're gonna rest down there until you're healed enough to use crutches."

Stavro frantically used his one good hand to pat his

hospital pajama pockets as the EMTs pushed him up the wheelchair ramp toward the door.

"My cellphone! I need to call the airport."

"Yeah, looks like that plow blade hit your phone before your bones. I'm a poet! But yeah, that thing is completely shattered."

"God dammit!"

Inside, Guillaume was sitting in his high-back chair. Linda, the young visiting nurse Stavro frequently harassed, was washing and wrapping the stump of the old Frenchman's left leg, a casualty of diabetes.

Guillaume frowned as the broken Stavro was wheeled into the room. "Oh, look at you. I hate to see you in that state, bub."

Stavro instantly drained his energy reserves to maintain the pleasant facade he always used with Guillaume. "Look at us. Two broken old men."

The EMTs parked Stavro next to Guillaume and went over his medication schedule with him before they left.

Linda finished with her gauze and turned to Stavro. Her eyes radiated with the promise of revenge.

"I hear you'll need help using the shower and the toilet for the next month or so. Guillaume begged me to help out, and you know what? I just couldn't say no."

The shift in power dynamic between Stavro and the woman he perpetually solicited made him shrink in his wheelchair. "Oh, you don't have to worry about me, ma'am. If you can just wheel me over to the phone, I'll make a call and be out of your hair before you know it."

"Ma'am? Well, that's certainly new."

Linda wheeled him into the sitting room, where a black rotary phone sat on an old desk. She whispered into his ear before leaving to attend Guillaume. "If I'd known all it would've taken to turn you into a polite gentleman was a shattered leg…" And with that, she left the room.

Stavro shivered and quickly dialed zero to have an operator connect him with a ticketing agent at Burlington International Airport.

"I'm sorry, sir, but in your condition, you'd simply take up too much space, and we have to take aisle obstructions into consideration. You'd have to purchase a neighboring seat to accommodate your arm and leg, and the flight is fully booked."

"What do you mean?!"

"You're more than welcome to sit at the gate to see if someone drops out, but that would be extremely unlikely so close to the holiday. Otherwise, I can help you pick another flight later this week."

"But I need to leave tonight! What part of this don't you understand, you dumb fuck? I can't be here!"

Stavro slammed the phone down, sending up a small mushroom cloud of dust, and began to cry.

THREE YEARS AGO

A HEAVY SNOWSTORM had blown into northern New Hampshire, dashing Thomas's children's plans to drive up that Christmas Eve. What was supposed to be a wonderful family holiday had devolved into a depressing bachelor gathering. A Christmas-themed episode of *Murder, She Wrote* played on the television as Guillaume settled into his post-dinner living room nap. A thin stream of drool glistened in his silver chin stubble. Stavro and Thomas sat at the kitchen table, each nursing a pour of Canadian whiskey as they begrudgingly played a hand of gin rummy. Both of them wore undershirts, as they had no company to impress and the thin-skinned old Frenchman had the thermostat set to a sweltering eighty-six degrees.

"I'll help you shovel tomorrow morning," Thomas said.

"No need," Stavros responded, laying a card down. "Plow comes at sunrise."

"Yeah, for the driveway. We still have to shovel the path to the side door from the driveway, and the one to the front door from the sidewalk."

Stavro, in an effort to keep himself from flipping the table in a fit of impotent rage, drained half of his juice glass full of whiskey. "Sure thing."

"Just want to make sure they're not all icy again like the last time. Took forever to convince that guest not to sue us when she slipped. It's a safety thing, is all."

"I said sure thing, boss man."

Thomas glared at Stavro, who refused to look up from his hand of cards to make eye contact with Guillaume's son. "Alright, then."

It had been two years since Stavro learned he was on thin ice at the Chevalier Boarding House, more specifically with the man who stood to become Stavro's boss when his dad kicked the bucket. Stavro still hadn't come up with a plan to get rid of the interloper who constantly had something bad to say about his performance. The sidewalk in front was never iceless enough. The rooms were never clean enough. The ledger sheets never seemed to balance. Money was somehow always missing.

After winning the last hand, Thomas began shuffling the cards again to play another. He cuffed them together in his palm, bridged them, and reconstituted the deck in a practiced flourish. Stavro refilled his glass with whiskey as Thomas went shuffle, riffle, shuffle, riffle.

And then, without warning, the cards sprung all over the kitchen table. Stavro paused mid-sip. He'd been playing rummy with Thomas for years, and he'd never seen him screw up a shuffle before, not even at his drunkest. Thomas said "shit," which came out like *sheet,* and moved to recollect the cards. Stavro chuckled. The whiskey must've snuck up on Guillaume's golden boy.

"Shumthing'sh wrong," Thomas said as he tried to gather the playing cards with his right hand. His left arm remained at his side. "I can't move my left arm. Shumthing'sh wrong."

Thomas suddenly dropped the cards on the kitchen floor and stood. Stavro laughed as Thomas's chair toppled over.

"My leg won't move. Shumthing'sh wrong." Thomas's left leg pinned him where he stood. His right shuffled him in a tight circle. "Call 9-1-1. I think thish ish a shtroke."

Stavro stopped laughing and put his glass down. He watched the man babble incoherently and shuffle in circles as the grim reality of Thomas's situation finally dawned on him. The greedy gears of Stavro's brain slowly ground to reveal the opportunity that had presented itself, but he had to act fast. "Oh no, you're just tired. Here, let me help you to bed."

"I need an ambulansh. Pleash, Shtavro. I need help."

Stavro stood behind Thomas, draping the dead arm around his neck, slowly guiding him toward the bedroom door on the opposite side of the kitchen.

"No! Shtavro! Call an ambulansh!" Thomas protested as Stavro opened the door with one hand and shoved him inside the small wood-paneled bedroom with the other. Thomas's eyes bulged with terror as the door closed, blanketing him in total darkness.

After turning the kitchen lights off, Stavro crept past the snoring octogenarian in the living room just as *Murder, She Wrote* was wrapping up with a whimsical flourish playing over a frozen frame of a smiling Angela Lansbury. He glided through the dimly lit sitting room, but before he opened the door that separated Guillaume's home and the boarding house, he turned around and listened for the inevitable sound of Thomas's bedroom door opening, a foot dragging on the kitchen linoleum, a quavering voice on a phone calling for paramedics, anything that would prevent him from finally taking what was rightfully his.

But all he heard was the drone of the television and steam hissing from the antique radiators. And his own heart, pounding in his ears like a kick drum.

PRESENT DAY

"Merry Christmaaassss, Popop!!!"

Stavro was on the phone again, this time begging his drunken acquaintances from the Elks Lodge to let him sleep over, when the door burst open. Thomas's four adult sons exploded into the living room, carrying luggage and wrapped gifts and electric fans to combat the stifling heat of Guillaume's house. And then came the children's children, tottering in with their stuffed animals and action figures.

"Hey, Stavro. You're not looking so hot, my man."

As soon as Thomas's son said it, the family turned to regard the sweating, shivering old man, his once perfectly pomaded hair now a chaotic mop.

Linda blotted the sides of her mouth with a napkin and scooched out from the table. "I think it might be time for our very own Evel Knievel to have himself an early beddie-bye. He's had a big first day back."

The family all nodded in agreement and wished Stavro

goodnight. Thomas's grandchildren kissed Stavro on his cheek, making him grimace. Linda grasped the handles of his wheelchair and deftly navigated him across the linoleum floor.

"Thank God I don't have to haul you upstairs to your room! Lots of people staying over tonight, but luckily there's one bedroom left on the first floor, and I saved it just for you."

Stavro's jaw went slack as the nightmare scenario unfolded before him. He wasn't sure if he'd wet himself or if the sweat trickling down his back had pooled at his crotch. He wanted to scream, but his vocal cords were paralyzed by fear. Tears cascaded down his face as they said goodnight in unison, and then turned back to their familial revelry.

A scratch-and-sniff Santa sticker stuck to Stavro's left tire orbited the wheel's hub in perfect circles as Linda slowly pushed him toward Thomas's old bedroom.

ONE YEAR AGO

"You've got this. We're at the end zone, baby. Hold your shit together for a few minutes, and it's easy street from here on out."

Frosty December winds whipped past the warped leaden glass of his window as Stavro stood in front of the dirty full-length mirror, giving himself a vigorous pep talk. Dark circles that screamed of sleepless nights were parked snugly under his stinging, bloodshot eyes.

When asked by the doctor, who refilled the sleeping medication he ate like Skittles, Stavro said he had no idea what brought the insomnia on or when exactly it started.

But he knew when. And he knew why.

It was a year after Thomas's funeral. He was kicking beers back at the Elks Lodge the week before Christmas, watching the bartender install a new frozen drink machine.

Stavro sipped his Coors Light as the bartender turned the machine on, the steel augers whirring to life behind a glass chamber, churning ice and eggnog into a frozen slurry. He stared at the spinning blades, first entranced by the slow circles they made, and then, as his eyes relaxed and his beer grew warm in his hand, became nauseated by them. The motion of the machine caused his brain to ache and his heart to flutter. Deciding he needed a nap, Stavro threw a handful of ones on the bar and left.

On his walk to the Chevalier, the feeling of wrongness forced beer and bile to well up in the back of his throat. He couldn't tear his eyes away from the hubcaps on a moving sedan or a spinning barber's pole, despite how awful they made him feel.

Back in his room, he had to unplug his bedroom fan. He flopped on the bed, clamping a pillow over his head to create a barrier between himself and the horrible rotating circles of the waking world, but sleep never came. It didn't subside until the following day, while he was on a flight bound for Key West to spend the holidays at a seedy singles resort.

It had taken Stavro a couple years to discover the connection between his episodes and his proximity to the Chevalier around Christmas. It was why his annual holiday travel started—not to visit family or see the world, but to escape bouts of circle-derived nausea and vertigo accompanied by a sense of foreboding that squeezed his guts so hard it turned every trip to the communal boarding house bathroom into an ordeal. Over the years, the weeks leading up to his Christmas excursions became more excruciating. His paranoia deepened. His insomnia left him exhausted and scatterbrained, incapable of reasoning out why he was being haunted by circles—of all things—every December. He'd tried to piece it together once he returned from vacation, but he always found himself distracted by his little schemes. Skimming money from the boarding house's books. Showing a young woman down on her luck there was another way for her to make that month's rent. When it came down to it, Stavro was a deeply uncurious man who was only interested in catering to whatever vile impulse he felt at any given moment, even at the risk of his well-being.

That was all about to change, though.

Withered and gray, the owner of the Chevalier Boarding House lay awake in his bedroom, a lone lamp staving off evening darkness. A collection of orange prescription bottles rested on the nightstand like a small orange cityscape.

"Knock, knock," Stavro said in the doorway. "How are you feeling tonight?"

"Not so hot, bub. I got the aches in the leg, even though there ain't no leg."

Stavro walked over to the nightstand and shook out exactly twice the number of pills Laura said were okay to have. He'd been doing that for weeks to make the man more pliable. Less resistant to what he was about to ask.

Guillaume swallowed the pills with a mouthful of Ensure.

"You must be getting ready to leave soon. Where are you headed this time?"

"Hawaii. Umbrella drinks and girls in grass skirts."

"That sounds nice, bub. Once of these days, you should stay here for Christmas. The kids still come up, but it's been hard since Thomas passed. You know I think of you as my son. Maybe next year you'll stay?"

"Sure thing, boss man." And then, "Dad."

Guillaume smiled weakly. He'd gotten so frail over the

last few months. The extra pills weren't helping his constitution, either.

"Before you leave, I want you to know I spoke with the lawyer. I told him since Thomas was gone, I had to change the will."

Stavro summoned every ounce of self-preservation to keep from grinning like an idiot. He couldn't believe his luck.

"Oh yeah?"

"I told him I want this place to go to you when I die."

Stavro hugged Guillaume. "I don't know what to say.

"The lawyer said I can sign the papers next year. He said they gotta make sure my brain is good, and that I'm not being bamboozled by anyone to change the will. I said that was fine. I know you'll keep this place in great shape when I'm gone."

"I… That's more than fine. It's good he cares so much about you."

"Merry Christmas, Stavro. Now get out of here. Don't miss your flight on my account."

"Merry Christmas, Dad."

PRESENT DAY

STAVRO BLINKED AWAKE.

Early morning sunlight peeked from around the vinyl roller shade that covered the only window in the bedroom. The welcoming smell of coffee percolating just outside his door gently separated him from his morning grogginess.

His eyes bulged, reality dawning on him. He used his one available hand to feel his face and pat his body. No carving knives sticking out of his chest. No pools of coagulated blood. No circles driving him to puke or shit himself.

He made it. He'd survived the night.

Linda situated him in his wheelchair and rolled him into the kitchen for breakfast. The family was stuffing their faces with scrambled eggs and leftover ham from last night's dinner. Once parked at the table, Stavro smiled and thanked Linda for her help. She raised one confused eyebrow at him, and then busied herself by making a plate for Guillaume, who had a self-adhesive gift bow stuck to his head. He looked much more alert after not taking Stavro's double and triple medication doses.

Stavro watched in amusement as one of Thomas's grandchildren graffitied his casted leg in marker doodles and tinsel. He chuckled. He was alive. He was sane. What had he been thinking all those years? He vowed to go see a shrink about it after he sold the Chevalier out from under the idiots in that room.

Thomas's eldest son placed a small box on Stavro's lap.

"The kids made this for you. Merry Christmas, Stavro. It's good to have you here."

One of the children spilled their hot chocolate, and a few folks helped blot it from the carpet with paper towels. Stavro opened the box.

Inside was a crudely crafted Christmas ornament: a green construction paper circle with STAVRO drawn on it in thick red crayon lettering.

Shumthing'sh wrong

The voice came from behind the Christmas tree. He slowly looked up from his ornament, his heart locking in his chest. His guts turned to ice. He knew what was coming, and he was powerless to do anything but watch it happen.

Shumthing'sh wrong

The quavering figure of a middle-aged man in sweatpants

and a tank top shuffled from behind the Christmas tree. Its left arm dangled by its waist. Its left leg dragged behind it as it staggered around the tree in a horrifying circle. Stavro looked frantically around the room. Somebody else had to be seeing it too, but no. The deepest vestiges of his humanity knew it was a show for one.

Shumthing'sh wrong

Shumthing'sh wrong

Shumthing'sh wrong

The ache in Stavro's chest careened into a lightning bolt of pain. He clutched at his pajama top as the spectral echo of the man he murdered slowly wheeled its way around the tree over and over again. Its blurred face shook like a paint mixer as it went.

"Circlesssssh..." Stavro slurred as the room went out of focus.

Stavro's eyes fluttered closed, and he slumped over in his wheelchair.

The last thing he ever heard was one of the children whispering, "Look Ms. Linda, Stavro's sleeping."

"Thanks for telling me!" Linda mock-whispered back. "I'll wheel him into his bedroom so he can finish his nap in peace."

MICHAEL BOULERICE (HE/HIM) is a lifelong resident of New Hampshire who spends his winters snowboarding in the White Mountains and his summers lounging by the coast. When he's not doing that, he's writing, acting as Mr. Fixit for a span of businesses and properties, tinkering on his ancient Volkswagen, or being held hostage by his two spoiled cats, Charlie and Sydney. He's had stories published in magazines like Cosmic Horror Monthly *and* Thank You For Joining the Algorithm, *in anthologies like* Monster Lairs *and* Your Flight Has Been Cancelled, *and adapted for audio by venues like* NoSleep *and* The Creepy Podcast. *His debut novella,* Feeding the Wheel, *is slated for release by Dead Sky Publishing in July 2025.*

For more information about Michael's works and whereabouts, please visit michaelboulerice.com

DISAPPEARING AT MY FEET

L.A. SELBY

When I looked over my shoulder, the shadows had gone. Like any good thriller, I felt if I walked where those shadows had been, it was not shadows I would be walking through but something more.

Until that moment, the sound of my tennis shoes on smooth, gray asphalt sounded the same as every day. The pat—pat—pat of my regular tread was familiar. As always, the sweet smell of damp air on a Georgia spring morning tasted almost as sweet as sugar from the new flowers and felt as wet as a humidifier in the hospital room of a pneumonia patient.

Loud mockingbirds sounded the same, by which I mean to say each call rang completely different, and the violent crackling calm of power lines next to the walking path made me consider how spirits travel like electricity through the air and might use them as a vast network of highways.

The air lay still, and that was different, because it made mockingbirds and jays and sparrows and crackling power lines that much louder. A cacophony rang with the combination of nature and man-controlled nature.

With humidity high, the crickets sang, and in the far

distance, woodpeckers struggled for food in the forest of dying pines stretching out on either side of my path in vast, unknowable arms, their brown pine needles fading to sickly green closer to the trunks that didn't have enough room between them. Thick and tangled underbrush grew as a barrier no one could pass.

Not for the first time, I wondered who laid this path, not a road big enough for cars, and a place without houses. It should have been a dirt road, or gravel, or track. I walked it because it was quiet of people. I had never seen anyone on it but me, until today.

What I had seen were shadows.

Sweat pooled between my shoulder blades, and it wasn't my usual sweat, not the kind from a humid Georgia morning, nor from exercise. My pace had been slow under the blue sky high above, a thin line overhead between dying pines like a river of bright, blue-white water in the sky.

Wherever the sun might be, it was not visible in that thin sliver so far above, and it was not enough to cast a real shadow from my body and force it to follow me on the asphalt. Light was diffuse and held the chill of missed sunlight.

That was why I sweated and the hair on my neck and arms stood up. Why my earlier breakfast of thick bacon and hard eggs changed from a pleasant leftover in my mouth into a ball of something unwanted in my stomach, pressed hard by the contraction of gut muscles.

I sweated because the wrong shadows had come. And then gone. They should not have been on that road in the first place. They had appeared when I turned, naturally, at a rustling near the ground and hidden in the trees, the kind that could mean a rabbit or opossum. In the gloom it might be anything.

When I turned, what I saw behind me, twenty of them,

maybe thirty, were the shadows of other walkers, even though I cast no shadow myself.

I blinked, I sucked in air, and stood with hands on my hips, too stunned and even too excited to feel fear.

They moved in the same loping stride as walkers on their daily walks. Some were shorter than others, with the vague shape of children; some that with the curve of their breast at certain angles would've been women; some larger and may I say quite a bit wider; some with shorter strides than others, all coming toward me.

Moments stretched. I experimented with my own sanity by turning away from them, by allowing my back to be exposed to whatever they might be. Then, fast, I turned right back to face them.

Just before they reached me, they vanished. Right when they might have been next to me.

Crows and jays and mockingbirds gave no hint that I was anything but a lone walker on an unmarked and unnamed asphalt path in a forest of dying pines still capable of sweetness and spring flowers somewhere close enough to the path to smell like damp sugar. Those shadows had been clear, and at age forty, I was too old for a new insanity.

It was like a New York Times puzzle played in a soft bed alone in the morning, matching groups of words into meaningful lists, until the last two groups were too complex and I just knew I'd never solve it. I'd have to go ahead and submit to see the answer.

Sharp shadows of people without the people who cast them, under diffuse light where I couldn't even see my own shadow was like that: a puzzle that needed a submit button. I knew I would not be able to think my way through what I had seen.

I considered calling out, to ask if anyone was there, and dismissed it as useless.

If they belonged to something physically harmful, the bad thing would have already happened.

I wiped damp hands on my pink flowered nursing scrubs. I did not know what to do. I could go forward with my daily walk and let the wonder of disappearing shadows stay on my mind, except I knew I would be turning to check behind me every few steps. Or, I could turn and go home to that one-room studio over my parents' garage, get in bed, and drink a glass of Pinot Grigio, mild and sweet, thinking about the meaning of shadows.

That would mean walking through where I knew they had been.

That stopped me. In the center of the asphalt path, and with a new wind stirring the tops of the trees and a light feathery crackle, I looked around for what wasn't there, in the midst of what I knew was there indeed.

My cotton scrubs were glued to my back with sweat, and I wiped a layer of salt from under my eyes. There was no loop to this road, just a straight path, mostly flat with a bit of slope.

My mother, not the kind to go out any more, asked me every morning if I really needed more walking. It's not like my calves weren't already rock solid from walking the hospital floors, but that didn't mean I wanted to push myself every moment of every day. But I didn't go out for that. I went out to be away from people.

I could stroll forward like every day, to clear my mind of pungent antiseptics, helpless body fluids, and constant clanging alarms. Or I would have to walk through whatever had made those shadows, as if I had a right to walk through them.

The pines were too thick for me to ditch the road by cutting my way through. At best, I might make it a couple of feet trying my way through thick brush. I didn't have a knife to hack a new way home like heroes did. I was no hero.

The shadows were gone. Whatever they were, I hoped they stayed gone, and I would never come here again. I thought that, but as soon as I did, I heard it for the lie it was. Of course I'd come back. Next time I'd bring a friend. Then we'd see together if anything was out here. And if we didn't see anything, I'd even come back alone.

Who could I tell without losing my reputation for being solid, upstanding, and reliable? I liked being that. I didn't want to not be that. Shadows might come and go and do nothing, but talking about them could lose me a lifetime of work and my reputation.

A jay screamed at me. I looked up.

"Please," something whispered, quiet and intense, from right in front of me, sounding as close as one hospital bed to another in a shared room, almost the same, as if a dangling cotton curtain was all that separated the speaker and me.

Now I was scared. More scared than just at the shadows.

"Who's there?" Now it made sense to ask. I could almost smell a tray of lean chicken, broccoli, and mashed potatoes being delivered and laid down with the clink of a plate on a rolling bed-desk. It wasn't there, of course. I was thinking of the curtain, and the beds, and the times peoples asked me, "Please."

The voice, recognizably a woman's, youngish with no tremor, whispered, "Please let us go."

"Mrs. Evers?" I asked of nothing but air and trees and loud blue jays. "Mrs. Evers?" Of course it was not her voice, as I'd been in the room three days ago when code was called and the sheet covered her pale gray skin for the last time.

"We can't go." That voice was different.

I dropped to my haunches in the center of the road,

unable to stay standing and unwilling to simply lie down and stare at the sky and hope this insanity disappeared.

The new voice was a man. Much older. Shakier. Breathier, yet louder than the whisper of Mrs. Evers. Light shifted on the asphalt, but it wasn't the clean and clear shadows of before. Any other day I would have thought it was clouds or the swaying of dying pines thick on either side. I concentrated on the voices.

The voices were more real than the shifting lights. My thigh muscles twitched, and my feet ached. I put my hands to the warm asphalt, its grit a whisper on my fingers. The voices wanted something. I was the type to want to help.

"I need more to go on. Whoever or whatever you are, your messages are too vague for me to know what you want."

Sometimes, medication made it too hard for people to tell me what they needed. It felt like that. Pressure rose in my chest. I rocked a bit from my crouch. I might be able to stand again soon.

I should stand in front of...whoever was talking. While they figured out what they needed to say, I grunted a bit; I wasn't as flexible as when I was younger, despite the solid leg muscles good for running. Back on my feet I took a deep breath of sweet flowers and pines. I let myself see the path clearly without avoidance.

The shadows were back, but not walking.

Thirty distinct shadows of men and women and children stretched like the kind seen in the early morning and late afternoon, not when the overhead sun cast blobs underfoot. The closest one's feet were talking distance from me, maybe four feet away, with the shape of its head farther back.

"I don't know what you want," I said to the shadows, as if that were a normal thing, because what else could I do? The shadows swayed in front of me but thankfully didn't come any closer.

The next thing I heard was sobbing, quiet sobbing from a child of maybe four or five. That made my heart hurt because I couldn't hear a child sobbing without feeling anything. Except there was nothing for me to do.

Who was I, what was I in this life, if there was nothing I could do? I had to find something I could do. I had to. I'd try again. Still, I didn't move from my spot, and even though the day was warm and humid and sweat-worthy, something cold went through me. My emotions were so intense, they made my chest hurt.

Crying would not help them or me. I wouldn't. I had to find a way to keep myself together enough to try and do the right thing for those in need.

"We can't leave the road."

That was something. It was an instant relief to have more information.

"Why not?" I asked.

"We're trapped." Mrs. Evers was the one who answered. I was grateful for that, because I'd known her.

"How?" I grasped at a familiar voice as a way out of my craziness.

"You have to let us go."

The sobbing from the child grew louder. Reacting to emotion could stop action; I could not allow that.

The whispering man's voice became stronger and sounded almost familiar, though wheezy, like a voice that used to be deep before age and failing organs ripped away the sound. "We started on this road, but we were not meant to be this far. We should have been days, weeks, months away from here. For some of us maybe years. She put us on this road too soon, and we can't leave it."

I closed my eyes to try and understand, as if cutting out the overcast sun and the swaying shadows would give the clarity I desperately needed.

"Who are you?" I needed more information.

Literal or metaphorical or metaphysical, I thought I heard something like hospital alarms high above the trees, up with the sun. I smelled bleach. I hated that out here. This was not the place for it. This was a forest. It was. The pine forest with its dying trees was completely and totally real, and it was where I was able to let all of them go. Except they were here.

"Carl Dever. My name is Carl Dever. Tell my son it was not his fault. He blames himself. It wasn't him. He wanted me gone, but the pillow did not work. I was going to make it, and I would have forgiven him. No, it was the charge on midnight rounds. She was the one."

"What?" I exclaimed and opened my eyes. Cold deepened under my skin.

Such betrayal. Under the florescent lights I understood in my gut more than I understood under the sun of the planet where I'd lived my whole life. He'd said "charge." There were plenty of records to show who was the charge nurse the night he died.

The names of who it could be ran through my head. I couldn't help it. My own mother had worked twice in the last few weeks. She wasn't a nurse, only working the charge desk phones, but she had to know who it had been. I was still reeling from the idea he could forgive his son.

I shivered. "How am I supposed to do anything?"

Carl said, "You can. You can set us free, if you get out of here."

"You mean after I get back from my walk?"

"No," he said. The shadows expanded and contracted, just like candle flames made of darkness. "If you get out of here, you can tell everyone the truth, and we can go."

What manner of philosophy or religion had created such a trap was too far beyond me. My only desire was to do as I had always done, and help. That was what nursing was. It was helping.

The sobbing increased, first the little child, then more weeping and a loud tapping, like a fist on a door.

The pounding was different than the wind in the trees so high above, the wind that sounded so much like the constant air conditioner hum on the fourth floor, the one with the empty rooms locked ever since the murders.

No one would stay in them after the newspapers made sure everyone knew about all the murders. Even when I tried to reassure people, when I explained to everyone in town how there were no ghosts there, that the rooms themselves were just as clean and sterile as any others, word had gotten around, and despite my perfect reputation, no one would agree to stay there.

Sometimes I opened those doors and looked inside, to make sure I was still telling the truth. I wiped the blood pressure machines and monitor tops. I dusted the keyboards. I straightened the paper on the bed or took it off and changed it. I double-checked the supply cabinets. Sometimes, when I had worked several shifts I should not have worked because they made me so tired I couldn't see straight, I unlocked the door and lay down inside. I lay flat on my back, arms crossed over my chest.

I would drift into dreams of doing other things in other places. One time when I fell asleep, my mother had been on duty, and she came in and found me. I knew she would wake me up so I wouldn't get in trouble.

She was not a nurse. She had always wanted to be one, but raising me had been her priority. She was so proud of how hard I worked.

It was getting hard to breathe. I shivered. It was too soon for the sun to be going down, yet it was. I could tell because there were no clouds in the sky, but everything was getting darker. Even the shadows were getting darker.

"Just tell the truth, if you make it back. Do you promise?"

"Why wouldn't I? Of course, I will tell the truth. Of course." I paused, feeling weaker than I should be, and asked any of them who would answer, "How did you know it was the charge nurse?"

Mrs. Evers said, "She said she was, before she put the air in my vein."

Carl said, "She said she was a nurse, and that I deserved to go with dignity."

A child whimpered somewhere in the growing darkness. "She said she was in charge, and I would not hurt anymore."

Another voice, familiar, whispered in my ear. It was not the shadows. It was not feet away, or up high or down low or hidden in the trees. The air of it tickled the edge of my ear.

"You know better than to sleep on duty," my mother whispered, and something soft pressed hard on my face. The path had gone, the forest, the cicadas, jays, and pine.

* * *

My mother was pressing a pillow over my mouth and nose. It panicked my lungs. She leaned her whole weight into it. I pushed frantically. I grappled with her thin and wiry body.

Her loose shirt caught on my fingers. My heels smashed against the bed. I had to throw her off.

I was stronger than this. The clean linen smell of the pillow choked me.

If I died, I helped no one. I freed no one.

My entire body twisted and bucked, a practical convulsion. As if strychnine filled my tissues, my mouth stretched in a scream for air. My head pushed back so hard I thought my neck would break.

When I finally reached a scream in the darkness, it powered my spine. My whole body shoved at her. My head swam. She was old. I was young. The strength of madness and obsession is inhuman, but the strength of my will was stronger than that.

It always had been.

One last shove. I heaved all of my self against her. Against failing.

The pillow dropped. My mother stumbled back in the deserted room. She landed on her tailbone with the kind of jarring shock I felt as if it were me.

I gasped and swung my legs off the bed, ready to run for help.

I didn't have to.

The shadows came. In the unlit abandoned room, they appeared like a mist rising fast from a lake, yet they became more solid, not less. Two. Then ten. Then twenty. By the light of one small square in the door, I watched them come. Men. Women. Children.

Silently, they surged toward my mother where she struggled to her feet.

They reached down for her, some of them. Others pointed, the shadows doing what they had never done on the forest path, stretching their arms forward, moving into the air, reaching for the destroyer, putting their coldness into her.

If I stayed, I would have to try to explain how she died in this room with me. There was no way I could explain, but I had promised them I would help, so I would do my best.

She clutched her throat while I watched by the bed.

Now she was the one twisting and writhing. Now she was the one whose body convulsed while her face turned blue.

I had promised to help her victims, but I was a nurse, and

I would not allow this, not even to a murderer. Not even to the one who tried to kill me.

I leapt to the intercom next to the door. The shadows parted for me. I called a code.

I knelt beside a murderer. I remembered their stories. How on earth could a man forgive his son for trying to kill him? How could anyone forgive anything at all?

I would save this woman because who I was was not determined by her guilt. I would decide who I was.

"Go away!" I yelled, "I've got this. Trust me!" and started CPR on a murderer.

* * *

A MONTH LATER, my mother still lies in the ghost-induced coma no doctor can explain. I did not let her die, but the shadows will not let her wake up. Her thin face is more gray than white, and her eyelids are almost thin enough to see through. Her lank gray-brown hair lies flat on her head, and the pillow under her head reminds me of her body in a coffin. Her room smells like antiseptic and is sour with old breath.

Though she is a human being, I do not touch her. I cannot go that far. When I look at her hands, wrinkled and spotted and thin, I see the hands of a killer.

When I look at my own, tan and strong, I see the hands of a healer.

The shadows watch her. They watch me too, and they do not smile or threaten. They are not free yet, but they will be. She is not eternal. Her death will come. They just need to wait a little longer.

Sometimes, when the hospital is quiet except for the constant beep of machines, I whisper to them. "I am sorry I cannot become what you needed, but I can wait with you. I am here with you. You will not wait alone."

L.A. Selby, a writer of dark fantasy, supernatural suspense, and horror, finds inspiration in gray skies and the kind of forests that swallow her shadows. She divides real life between coasts and enjoys traveling to abandoned and haunted lands. The first city she ever loved was Venice. Ten years ago, she fell in love with Rome. Her newest passion is Transylvania—all of it. For more information, please visit www.LASelby.com

A DREAM COME TRUE

SARA JORDAN-HEINTZ

"There is nothing like a dream to create the future." – Victor Hugo

IVYEET SILVERMAN JOLTED upright in bed. Her pulse was racing, and her head was swimming. She reached for the pill bottle on her nightstand. She was most likely hours late taking her beta-blocker. As she was swallowing the pill with stale water that had sat in the glass overnight, one of her roommates walked by the open door and popped her head in the room.

"Glad to see you're up, sleepyhead. Ricia made waffles for breakfast, or at least attempted to. There was a lot of scraping them off the griddle. DoorDash may be the more humane way to go, if you've got an appetite."

Ivyeet blinked several times then stared blankly at Edna, telling her she'd join them in a minute. With exaggerated effort, Ivyeet kicked the layers of blankets off herself and placed her bare feet on the cold hardwood floor. She tussled her long brown hair and felt around for her slippers. After locating them, she sloshed out of her bedroom down the stairs into the breakfast nook that adjoined the kitchen. There sat Edna and Ricia talking up a storm. It was just like she had seen it in her dream.

"Good morning, Ivy, your plate is on the counter."

She nodded at Ricia, still somewhat groggy, yet on high alert. Ivyeet took her usual seat across from Edna.

"As I was saying," Edna began, "he looked right at me and coyly asked, 'Do you come with the house too, babe? Because I'd never let you fall into foreclosure. What do you say?' Can you believe it? And his wife was standing right there!"

"No!" Ricia gasped in delight, tears of laughter streaming down her heavily made-up cheeks.

"And would you believe it?" She slapped her thigh. "They took the house—above asking price, too. You wouldn't even believe the commission I'll be getting." Fork suspended mid-air, Edna took a bite of her now soggy waffle.

Ivyeet was pleased for Edna. After all, she was the lowest-ranking Realtor, and this sale would elevate her standing as well as bolster her bank account. Sharing a house in this ritzy neighborhood, the gals could use the windfall. "Didn't you tell us about this yesterday? I can't quite remember."

"Couldn't have. I met with the clients around ten last night. You were asleep when I got back."

"Déjà vu again, my dear?" asked Ricia. "You've had it all week. And the week before last. Yes, I have the strangest feeling I have heard that complaint from you before. But when? Maybe in a past life..."

"Very funny," Ivyeet retorted. She threw her syrupy fork at Ricia, but not realizing her own strength, flung it hard against a nearby wall, where it landed with a clank.

Few people in her inner circle approved of the alternative medical practices she swore by. Sure, yoga had become mainstream enough to only illicit a brief eyebrow raise now and then, along with the healing crystals she kept under her pillow, but then there were the Tarot cards, Akashic records, and spell books. Ivyeet had experimented with it all—anything to bring her a modicum of sanity. Her maternal grandparents, who had hailed from Ireland, would regale her with tales about witches and fairies and how her mother Kathleen had developed the gift of second sight in her childhood. Funny, the things you remembered at inopportune times. Her dad, Peter, a doctor from a prominent Jewish New England family, used to scoff at the stories. A man of science, and all of that.

"I think you've been drinking too much of that tea Dr. Jorge Rico gets for you." Edna stood up, plate in hand, and walked toward the kitchen sink.

"You don't understand; I saw all of this, too. I knew how you'd both be dressed and that we were going to have waffles."

"Ah-huh," Edna said as she bent to load the dishwasher. "Like we never discuss our jobs. Or eat waffles. Why, it's uncanny."

"My own friends don't believe me. As we speak, you are about to pour yourself a glass of tomato juice, because your doctor said your blood is low in vitamin A."

A startled Edna emerged from the refrigerator door carrying a can of tomato juice. She bent down and picked up the fork, which had left a sticky residue from where it had landed near the stove. Edna looked at Ricia, and then walked to the sink to wash her hands. The two women knew Ivyeet suffered from bouts of anger. It was a common occurrence in an otherwise amiable household.

Ricia stood from the table. "Ivy, are you feeling ill? You look kind of pale, like Casper, but with hair and a better fashion sense. Maybe you should talk to Dr. Rico. Would you like me to call his office for you?"

Ivyeet hesitated for a moment.

"I hate to eat and dash, but I'm the first lifeguard on duty today. Edna, are you ready to roll? I'll give you a lift and drop you at your office on my way to the YWCA."

Edna's dark green BMW was in the shop. Ivyeet had driven it straight into the garage door a week prior, during one of her manic episodes. She hadn't even remembered the incident. Her roommates had found her passed out in the driver's seat, seatbelt on, with the car idling and smoke sizzling from the engine.

"Nah, that's okay. Thanks for the offer, though. You two have a good day."

After Ivyeet watched her roommates pull out of the driveway, she quickly threw on a lightweight blue sweater and slacks and slipped on her brown mules. She grabbed her tote bag, and her gold bangles jangled as she reached for the knob of the front door. Her amber eyes glistened in the sunlight of the cool Vermont autumn day. She proceeded down the porch steps and crossed through her yard on the way to the bus stop four blocks away. She'd see him in person.

* * *

HIS SMILE WAS friendly as he guided her into his office. "Good afternoon, Ivyeet, how are we doing today?"

"Well actually, not too hot. I've been having these dreams, and—"

"And you have been brewing the tea leaves I gave you?"

"Yes, but—"

"How many cups of tea do you consume a day? On average."

"Three to four, usually. Plus I take the beta-blocker twice

a day. Occasional aspirin. Vitamins. You said it was all right to take those together."

"I did."

"Anyway, this dream, it came true. I guess they all have—they all do. I just haven't been able to fully remember them until now. It's some kind of precognition. Second sight, Nan would say." She relayed the morning's events involving her roommates and knowing how the morning would unfold before it had.

He waited until she appeared to end her story then said nonchalantly, "Ivy, you're a very sensitive woman, but I don't think in the way your grandmother would have meant. Not everything that happens in life is a psychic phenomenon. Some things are coincidence, or gleaned from experience. Keep exercising, stay hydrated, try to get an extra hour of sleep every night, and stick with the tea. Remember the files I forwarded you? Remarkable breakthroughs in the case studies in Bulgaria using this herb."

She rolled her eyes. She had never been fond of tea, always more of a coffee drinker when she had the choice. "Breakthrough" was always the word the doctor used in describing the various success stories psychiatrists had in using tea made from this coveted plant whose name she never could pronounce.

"You understand why I put you on this alternative treatment, *verdad*?"

She nodded, used to him occasionally using a word from his native tongue. The young psychiatrist, who originally hailed from Cuba, had completed his residency at the same hospital where her father had been employed as head of psychiatric medicine. Jorge was one of the few people from her old life she remained in contact with after her parents' deaths. "Grisly" always popped into her mind when she thought of that night.

"The dreams are so vivid—so realistic." Ivyeet's voice turned from her usual soft, Jacqueline Kennedy-esque tone to one of clear agitation. "They scare me. Sometimes I'm not sure what's real, or where I am, or what I'm doing or why."

"Ivy, these are trauma-induced dreams, teamed with illusions, mania, and blackouts. There are a lot of mental health issues and stress responses going on here." He walked behind her and placed a hand on her shoulder—a cue for her to begin her diaphragmatic breathing exercises. "When your thoughts race, your speech pattern accelerates. Slow it down."

Boy, was it hard to talk about. Hard to picture in her mind's eye. A murder/suicide was a difficult conclusion to accept, but one the coroner's report had determined. It was a subject she'd avoided providing too much detail about, particularly to her closest friends and roommates.

"The tea takes time to work, but once it does, I know it will have a better effect than those antidepressants and antipsychotics that hospital hack put you on before you came to me."

"Okay."

She was treatment resistant, after all.

* * *

AFTER VISITING DR. RICO, Ivyeet ran a few errands, spent an hour on tech support trying to restore the Internet (damn the construction crew digging too close to the lines), and then finished writing an art feature for a local magazine. Freelance writing barely covered the bills, but Edna's and Ricia's rent money helped considerably with her mortgage payments. She had funds from her mother's life insurance plan, but it'd been a paltry sum of money compared to what her father had been covered for. Alas, no payout for suicide.

As she began proofreading the article one final time before sending it off to the editor, her vision went black, and she collapsed to the floor. The next thing she heard was the sound of Edna's voice. Ivyeet seemed to be in a catatonic state. It was 10:00 the next morning.

Ivyeet began to focus her vision and clutched Edna's arm.

"Ricia! Where's Ricia?! I have to find her. She's in danger. She's going to drown. I saw it in my—"

"Ivy, calm down. Ricia left for work hours ago. You just had a bad dream. I'll get you some orange juice. Your blood sugar must be low."

Edna fetched the beverage. The woman had seen her roommate, well landlady really, like this after a prior blackout. Edna made her finish the juice then said, "If it will make you feel any better, I'll give Reesh a call on her cell. Okay?"

The phone rang several times before someone came on the line. "Is Ricia Seymour there? May I speak to her?" Edna asked. There was long pause. "What?… When?… We'll be right there." She ended the call and put her cell phone in her jacket pocket. Tears streamed from her gray eyes as she gathered her thoughts and found her voice. "Ivy, get yourself together. We're going down to the aquatic center at the Y. There's been an accident."

"Did she…?"

"One of her coworkers found her face down in the pool about an hour ago. He said it was almost as if she was intoxicated or something. She slipped and fell headfirst into the shallow end and was knocked out cold. Her lungs filled with water, and she didn't make it back up to the top."

* * *

IVYEET FLOATED through the funeral service as if she were watching a film and not sitting in a church in real life. The minster's eulogy was difficult to hear over Ricia's mother's sobs. She and Edna sat together two pews back. The autopsy report followed several weeks later. It claimed the deceased was four times over the legal alcohol limit and had ingested some pills left over from Ivyeet's stash of meds. Where had she found them? Ivy had tossed them out months ago.

Days evolved into weeks, and the calendar turned to November. Ivyeet woke one morning, heart pounding out of her chest. She ran to the hallway calling for Edna, flew out the front door, and ran down the driveway. Edna's vehicle had been fixed and returned to her weeks ago. Still, Ivyeet didn't want her to drive it. She ran to the car, barefoot and in her nightshirt, and made Edna roll down the window.

"Please stop. Get out of the car. I had a dream last night. You can't go. I saw it happen. I saw—"

"Sweetie, I'm running behind. I have to show a couple a house in ten minutes." Edna was dressed in a fitted black blouse and matching pencil skirt. Her dark hair was pulled back with a stunning antique silver pin. Always the professional. No-nonsense. Reliable. Stable. Her friend. "Tell you what, how about I take your Lexus instead? Would that make you feel better?" she asked kindly, but clearly irritated.

"It would," Ivyeet stammered.

Edna hopped out of the vehicle, reached in the back seat for her briefcase, and walked toward Ivyeet's car. Ivyeet walked back inside, then came out holding a key ring, removed the fob, and handed it over.

"Losing Ricia felt like losing my parents all over again. I was home on winter break my senior year in college, but out seeing a concert that evening. That was... gosh, nearly three years ago.

"I found them bleeding out on the bright white carpeting of their bedroom, gunshot wounds painfully visible. I knew they'd been bickering a lot. They seemed bothered by something but wouldn't share anything with me. And of course they owned a gun. For protection. Everybody in the neighborhood did, although crime tends to be nil in the type of gated community where they lived. Where we lived. Money problems, the police thought. And sure enough, the bank reported some abnormally large withdrawals and deposits. There was even talk Mother had been selling off some furniture and jewelry. I was aghast at the thought, but after that night, I searched and couldn't find her antique emerald and diamond necklace Dad had given her on their honeymoon.

"The police said there were no signs of forced entry, Dad's revolver had been used with only his fingerprint on the trigger, updated insurance policies were less than two months old, and they'd had a couple of fights in public—including at the hospital's holiday charity gala the weekend before. Ultimately, it was presumed the financial stress led to the deed."

"God, you poor kid. I didn't know any of that. Do you want me to stay home with you today? I can re-schedule my clients. Not a problem at all," Edna offered, making a motion to step out of the car.

"No. That's okay." Ivyeet wiped her damp, burning cheeks and tried to compose herself. "You need to work. We both do."

She reassured Edna there was no need to stay home and waved to her as she pulled out of the driveway on her way to the showing. Ricia's blue Buick was still parked on the street. Her parents hadn't wanted to drive it after her death. Edna's Beamer would soon provide it company.

* * *

ABOUT AN HOUR LATER, two police officers arrived at the house, informing Ivyeet that Edna had plowed her Lexus into the side of a city bus. In a mere six weeks, Ivyeet had lost both of her roommates. What did the cards have to say about that?

The police of course questioned Ivyeet about her roommates' deaths. Just protocol. They asked her if she thought Edna had drugged Ricia and then decided to kill herself out of guilt. Each time she went to protest and defend their honor, she faltered. How well had she known them anyway? They'd only been with her for a couple of years. Edna first, whose firm had sold the Silvermans' family home, and then Ricia had answered Ivy's ad in the paper. And the blackouts… well, complicated things.

Her friends and neighbors were sympathetic and sent over casseroles and pizzas and took turns phoning her throughout the day. Then of course, as time marched on, those niceties become less and less frequent.

An aunt from Topeka, Kansas stayed with her for a week. After some considerable wrangling on her aunt's part, Ivyeet decided to put her house on the market and return to Kansas with her. There was no way she'd be able to keep up with the mortgage payments and the high cost of living in the sugar maple state on her own.

The closing on her house was mere days away, and Christmas Eve was Friday. Tomorrow would mark the three-year anniversary of her parents' deaths.

* * *

IVYEET AWOKE in the middle of the night to frantic knocking on the front door. She glanced over at her oak nightstand. The illuminated face of her alarm clock said it was 2:20. Ivyeet wrapped a robe around her middle and crept carefully down the stairs. The house was pitch black, but the lightning from the thunder snowstorm helped illuminate her path in golden bursts. It was drafty in the house, and the floors creaked mercilessly as she tried to be quiet.

"Open up, Ivyeet. I've got something very important to tell you. It's urgent. Open up!" Dr. Rico demanded. She froze in her barefoot steps. What could he want at this hour? It was raining hard, and the wind was gaining momentum. But he refused to leave. A second later she heard the glass portion of the front door shatter. Ivyeet screamed and ran to her room, locked the door, and huddled on the floor beside her bed. She remembered only then that her cell phone was charging downstairs on the kitchen counter. After gaining entrance into the residence, he ran up the stairs and pushed his weight against her bedroom door a half dozen times before it gave way. He strode to where she lay cowered near the window.

"Now now, Ivyeet Agnes Silverman, is that any way to treat me? The only man who loves you? Will love you? Putting your house on the market and moving away? Without asking my permission? How could you?"

She looked up at him, arms wrapped tightly across her body, then at a baseball bat peeking from under the nightstand. She took one awkward swing at him, but Dr. Rico bent her shoulder back so deftly, she was on her knees in the blink of an eye.

"Now that your roommates are out of the way, we can finally be together. Don't you see what you're doing? You're ruining everything. So easy to get rid of them. Ricia, that *puta*. I invited her over to my house the night you blacked out. She'd wanted to discuss something important. You. Said she'd done some research on the tea and was concerned about some of the reported side effects. I had to put her mind at ease. Just a little drop of this, and a little drop of that into her drink, to take the edge off. Once she passed out, I gave her a time-release injection, just enough time for her to drive home, change, head to work, and then..." he chuckled and threw his hands in the air as if to say, "what can you do?"

"And Edna? Why hurt her? She was nothing but wonderful to me. They both were!" Ivyeet screamed in his face.

"Edna." He made a clucking sound with his tongue. "That really wasn't how I'd intended to kill her, or so soon after that *puta*. See, there are so many ways you can sabotage a car without it being obviously detected. I learned a few things while working at my uncle's body shop in Havana. Ivy, all I wanted was for you to have a bit of car trouble and for me to come to your rescue. I never meant for the brake cables to completely fail. And with the icy conditions and Edna always being in a hurry and all… well…"

"I saw it happen. In my dream. But I thought she'd be driving her car—"

"There wasn't anything wrong with her car, but I appreciate your help all the same."

Ivyeet tried to bolt, but the doctor grabbed her by the waist and slammed her head against the footboard. His strong body crushed her torso.

"The tea leaves are poisonous, aren't they?" Ivyeet spat.

"Now Ivyeet, I had to make you sick so I could take care of you. Who would have guessed those leaves would awaken psychic abilities?" he asked with a shrug.

"You think this is funny? You're a murderer and a psychopath."

"You're becoming such a pain in the ass. Like your parents were." He reached in his pocket, took out a long, weighty object, and wrapped it around her neck.

Her blood went cold. She stopped fighting back, and her whole body went numb at the realization.

"Ivyeet, I've been in love with you since I first laid eyes on you your senior year in college. You were twenty-two, so sweet and wholesome. Untouched. I was a young psychiatric doctor working at St. Luke's Medical Center. You were so beautiful." Dr. Rico looked at his captive, as if he wanted to bask in the beauty he saw in his twisted brain and not the image of the frightened woman with the tangled hair and eyes the size of full moons.

"I worked with your father. Fine psychiatrist, if not a bit full of himself. He had your portrait framed on his desk. So proud of his 'little princess.' I asked questions about you. Maybe too many. I even followed you and your father to the movies once. Then I began to just follow you. He gave me a little money to not ask you out. To go away, maybe back to Cuba.

"I swiped your dad's key ring one afternoon while he was flirting up his receptionist. Your mom deserved so much better. I made myself a copy of their house key. I visited several times—always wearing surgical gloves—so I could snoop around, go through your drawers, and memorize the floor plan.

"Well, of course, I couldn't leave things at that. I had to talk to Peter, but he wouldn't listen, and we got into a huge fight in the hospital parking garage. Big Man on Campus type of power struggle. I'm so glad you didn't have to witness it. He bragged that he had a gun and wasn't afraid to use it on Hispanic trash like me. He punched me as hard as he could, then got in his Mercedes and drove away. I followed him, discreetly, of course. The only way I was going to get to you was by eliminating my competition."

Ivyeet could feel his hot breath on her bare shoulder. She shuddered at the repulsion, and then kicked him in the groin as hard as she could. "That's for my parents." He winced in pain. She kicked him again. "And that's for my roommates." Ivyeet, disoriented, stumbled on the rug and fell to the floor. She got up quickly and staggered to the nearest room—the bathroom. She shut and locked the door, planning her escape. She had to remove whatever was around her neck; it was starting to choke her, cutting into her warm flesh.

A choker.

Her sweaty fingers fumbled clumsily with the clasp.

"Your mother begged for their lives. She was such a pretty woman. She had on the most stunning necklace that night. I had to make sure no one walked off with it. Looks a lot nicer on you than it did on your mother. And now it's yours."

"Go to hell," Ivyeet yelled through the door.

"And once they were dead? Pretty easy to set the scene just right. Any true crime junkie could have done it. Certainly helped that they were having money troubles and marital woes. Never did quite figure all that out, but the cops never probed too deeply, did they?"

As Ivyeet was poised to climb out the bathroom window and land God knows where, Dr. Rico forced his way in and grabbed her by the nightgown with meaty hands. The lights flickered, the power lines likely buckling under the weight of the ice. The neighborhood was plunged into total darkness. She used the brief moment of confusion to barrel past him. She was halfway down the stairs when he jumped her from behind, their bodies tangling the rest of the way to the floor below. She made a grab for his gun.

* * *

THE SOUND of the gunshot's blast catapulted Ivyeet to a sitting position in bed. She grabbed at her throat. No emerald and diamond necklace.

The wind howled, and rain pelted at her windows. She breathed heavily and reached for her beta-blocker. "Just a dream. You're safe." She laid her weary head on the pillow, then glanced over at her clock. It was 2:19 a.m.

At the sight of the time, she bolted to her feet, fumbled to put on jeans and a sweatshirt, and dug frantically in her purse for her key fob. One minute later, there was incessant knocking at the front door.

Sara Jordan-Heintz is an award-winning newspaper journalist. She is also a twentieth century historian with an interest in popular culture, the Golden Age of Hollywood, the Cold War and the JFK assassination. She is the author of the biographies Going Hollywood: Midwesterners in Movieland *and* The Incredible Life & Mysterious Death of Dorothy Kilgallen. *She has written hundreds of articles for newspapers and magazines, many republished through the Associated Press and USA Today Network.*

Her novella A Day Saved is a Day Earned *was published in the inaugural anthology of Rod Serling Books',* Submitted For Your Approval, *edited by Anne Serling.*

Her fictional stories, heavily inspired by film noir, The Twilight Zone, *and everyday observations, have appeared in* 101 Words, Red Planet, 365 Tomorrows, Friday Flash Fiction, Blink Ink, The Mambo Academy of Kitty Wang, Better Than Starbucks, Potato Soup Journal, *and* Shady Grove Literary. *Her work has also been published in the Brilliant Flash Fiction anthology* Branching Out, *in Inkd Publishing's anthologies* Hidden Villains *and* Hidden Villains: Betrayed, *and in Savage Realms' horror anthology* Symphony of the Damned. *She serves as editor of Inkd Publishing's horror series* Behind the Shadows.

She most enjoys writing speculative fiction, human interest stories, and pieces meant to provoke deep feelings and opinions in its readers. She lives in Iowa with her husband Andy Heintz, also a writer, their young daughter Louisa, and their tuxedo cat Madeline.

ILLUSIONS OF PRIDE

RORY THOMASSEN

The UCS Acheron had one too many ghosts on board. As the captain and a loyal man, Karrin blamed himself. After all, the ship was under his care and the responsibility to keep her afloat in the rivers between stars was his duty.

No matter the cost.

Synth whiskey dribbled past Karrin's lips and left a trail down his chin. He gulped with no satisfaction. It made for a terrible breakfast, and it settled in his stomach only as well as it had for dinner. Real food had run out two days ago. "We are still three nights from the nearest system, and I am starting to think we might not make it," he said with a wry tongue. "There's nothing left but cheap, synthetic alcohol and urine recycled so many times it's starting to taste like tequila. Usually, that would sound like the end of a great party, but the prospect isn't all that fun when mortal peril is involved."

Nix chortled. "Why Captain, what an insightful glimpse into your past." She kept her good hand on the helm as she sat on her only leg. "Were you a rowdy ensign? I'm having a hard time imagining it."

"When the situation called for it, I was."

The navigation computer sputtered to life with another proximity warning. Neme shook out of his nap. He furiously wiped his eyes as he struggled to focus on the dull glow of the screen. He reached out with a bandaged nub before he remembered the limb was gone. He sighed a mighty punctuation of annoyance. He lifted his last finger on the other hand and poked a few commands that silenced the beeping. "In the vastness of space, we happen to sail through the one stretch with an overabundance of debris," Neme bemoaned as he tried to settle himself again. "I suppose that's why most direct routes aren't advised in this sector."

"Is it going to be a problem?" Karrin asked.

"No. Just a few scattered asteroids. The hull is galvanized iridium, so it won't make a dent."

"Less chance of a dent if the shields were engaged." Thane piped up for the first time in a long while. He was lying beneath his workstation, and Karrin had almost forgotten he was there. "And don't worry, Captain, that wasn't a plea to divert power from life support again. It was just a fact. A point of pride. This ship is my baby, after all."

Thane had sacrificed more of himself than anyone else when the time came. The first to surrender flesh. The first to suffer. Both legs were taken up to the sockets. One arm was lost to the shoulder, and if any of the crew were qualified to perform the operation, he would have given a kidney, his heart. Shame was a great motivator for the man.

Everyone else had given their blood merely to survive. The greatest motivator.

Eris remained by the bulkhead, wary of what was on the other side. "Well, your baby is the antichrist," she attacked. "I don't want to be the cynical scientist in the room, but the engine you crafted is a work of evil." The side of her head still had dried blood caked to it. When she lifted her ear from the cold metal, it left a stain. She hopped back to her workstation on her last leg. "I admire the genius it took to engineer, but I hate the cost to power it."

"The progress of new tech always has a few snags," Neme argued for Thane. "It is good to know that the engine can process any biofuel we feed it, although I imagine body parts are a poor substitute to the fuel it is used to."

Eris didn't want to start another heated back and forth. Karrin would have to intervene again. "I understand that. I just wish I wasn't part of it. Did you know half my leg only powered us for two days? Two days!" She waved the stained bandage at the nub of her knee.

Nix giggled. "Better than mine. Yours must have tasted better."

"My God, do you have to be so morose, Nix?"

"I am just trying to bring a little levity to the—"

"Cut the chatter," Karrin cut in.

A silence fell as sure as the vacuum outside the windows. Solemnity hung thick. Conversation was a necessary distraction, and Karrin could appreciate that, but its tendency to wander into a lane that ruffled feathers was easy. Sometimes quiet was better.

BOOM!

The bulkhead suddenly clanged with a shattering crash. The door's metal shuddered and vibrated. It punctured the quiet room, sharp as sin. It struck again and again, growing louder with each successive strike. Something on the other side wailed. Something on the other side wanted in. Thunderous pounds enveloped the modest control deck with a harsh resonance.

The UCS Acheron had one too many ghosts, and they hated the quiet.

Neme put a nub to one ear and his last finger in the other. He put his head between his legs and tried to tap his toes on the ground to mask the sounds. Nix put her crash helmet on, which reopened the wound on the side of her head; it began to bleed anew. Eris wrapped her spare fatigues around her ears, and Thane just lay where he had been since yesterday. Karrin didn't try to avoid a single knock. He listened, staring at the darkness of space.

"Why?" a voice yelled. The tone was shrill and unyielding. "Don't do this. You can't do this."

"There must be another way!" a second voice followed. "Nooo!"

The ghosts always got chattier before the engine shut down.

Another cry rose above those laments. There were no words, just a tortured wail that battled against a slow, agonizing pain. A hoarse moan that grated without hope of reprieve bounced between the walls. The attacks on the bulkhead were becoming more frequent.

Screeches echoed.

Nails dug into metal.

Slaps of skin pummeled the walls.

"Oh God, no!" the chorus bellowed.

It was a crowd, a mob, a massacre.

The ship's power flickered. The deck lights went out, and all the noise, turmoil, and violence outside the bulkhead went away with it. Only Nix's hyperventilating and Neme's toe tapping remained. The last sputters of backup life support clicked on, and the cabin regained its pale lighting. The tinny hum of recycled air started to pump again.

The captain stood and walked back to the window. He put his forehead to the glass and measured the spaces between stars.

Karrin sighed. Thane was the last to feed the engine, and it would be him next. He should have given all of himself from the beginning.

Guilt has a way of following honor like a wake in water.

"Is it me, or is your baby gaining more and more of an appetite?" Nix asked Thane as she took off her helmet.

He didn't respond.

"Feels like we're giving more and getting less," Neme added.

Eris pulled the clothes from her head. "Nope, it's the same. I've been keeping track." She scribbled numbers on a sheet of paper. "It just feels like diminished returns because of our depressing disposition." She looked past Karrin. "You're up next, Captain."

Her head wound had started to bleed again. It dripped down her temple and over her cheek, where it fell to a dark stain on her shoulder.

Captain Karrin had given only his left arm to the ship. It had been his index finger at first, the initial test. They checked to see if the engine would accept the sacrifice and convert the flesh to propulsion, and the positive results were met with ambivalence. Yes, they could finish their mission, make it to an outpost for damage control and repairs, but not one of them would be the same for it. They would be given accommodations for bravery in the face of terrible odds, but the medals would hang on broken bodies and shattered spirits.

The oxygen generator gave out. The last drops of power were gone, and the lights dimmed, dying to near darkness.

In truth, they didn't need the engine for the guidance systems or for thrust—they were heading in a straight shot to their destination—but they did need the power. Life support was key for the mission. General Erebus and two hundred decorated officers were on board, sleeping in cryo. They were the first passengers in the triumphant, experimental craft they sailed on. Captain Karrin would do anything to make sure they would not be the first victims. It's not like he could say "no" anyway. He had to save them. There was no way to fight against it.

"No need to stall, sir," Nix said as she stared at the great beyond. Her own head wound continued to drip to her shoulder. "The chip will force your feet in time. Best to get it over with."

Military ships meant military contracts, and those had the unfortunate caveat of a dereliction inhibitor chip shoved into the prefrontal cortex. Mutiny was impossible. The technology would compel action to the greater good of the United Navy. Sometimes that meant helping a fallen soldier instead of making a tactical retreat, and other times it meant cutting off your own body parts to an engine that converted organic material into power. They don't put that part in the fine print of the contracts. The devil is in the details after all, but a greater demon was waiting for the captain at the aft of the ship.

Eris was back at the bulkhead, inclining her ear. The terror on the other side would start coming in waves, and she was good at sussing out the best times to make it through safely.

Karrin left the window and walked to the back of the deck, never giving a second glance to those who had given all they were before him. They gave no looks of respect back. Grizzly sacrifice did not bring a crew together as other trauma did. It created a divide as gaping as the abyss. Resentment was a strong substitute for nobility when there was no choice in the endeavor.

Thane lay on the floor with his eyes closed. A small pool of blood was slowly building around the side of his head. If not for his erratic breathing, Karrin would have counted him dead. But that was the case for all of them, wasn't it? There was no coming back from this.

Eris hopped back to her seat, and Karrin put his hand to

the wheel on the door and started to spin the mechanism. Steel latches and locks undid themselves. The ghosts weren't there when Karrin pulled the way open. He stepped across the threshold and pulled on the heavy steel bulkhead until its automatic system reset and the door closed on its own.

Pushing forward, Karrin grabbed the synthetic whiskey from his belt and took a swig. The dark gantry muddled his balance, and spills of musty alcohol dribbled out the sides of his mouth. He was well into a few drinks. They helped against the noise, the shouts, and the banging. Everyone had their own way of coping; Karrin just employed a longstanding, traditional means of masking the pain. Didn't help with the bleeding, though, and gauze was running short, but that didn't really matter now, did it?

No. None of it did.

The crew's quarters were cast in the shadows of emergency lightning. They opened wide on either side of him. Two-man berths, the galley, and the observation room all spread out with the faded warmth of kinder memories. Simpler times. Back before the dread took hold. Now they were dark places for specters to haunt. Every corner was a dangerous nook for predators to leap forth.

The ship shook. Glasses sitting on the table rattled and fell, smashing on the ground. Darkness thickened. Karrin looked from side to side, ready for an attack. He stopped, whiskey held loosely in his hand.

Something was there.

He could feel it. Eyes. Watchers in the shadows spied with ill intent. Karrin tried to hurry the whiskey back to his mouth, but it fell from his fingers and clamored against the ground. He was distracted by his fumbling for only a moment, but that was enough of an opportunity.

The darkness charged.

Karrin ran. He barreled down the hallway, and the

shadows came with him. He thumbed the clasp of his holster and gripped his pistol feverishly. Sweat began to pucker on his cold skin. He sprinted, tired and achy from malnourishment.

Feet slapped to the ground in pursuit. The clatter of furniture being thrown and plates crashing cut into the thin air. Screams bellowed behind him. Karrin could almost feel the heat from their lungs. Their growls were gargled with saliva, bubbling in their throats. Silhouettes bobbed and weaved from side to side, dashing low to the ground. They were animals keeping close to the heat of prey. The smell of decay was heavy, and Karrin struggled to catch his breath in it.

A mess of debris was strewn just before the stairs leading down into Acheron's belly. Karrin had no balance anymore; the liquor saw to that. His feet caught on some loose ends of cloth, and he tripped, taking to the air. He couldn't see where the stairs began, but all the luck in the universe showed up to have him land on his feet. A loud crack sounded above the screams, and fire rose from his ankle to his knee. Karrin tumbled further, spinning again and again as the hard edges of metal stairs jammed into his arm, back, and hip. When he finally made it to the bottom, the adrenaline was in such a furious flow that he stood right back up and kept running on the fractured bones of his foot.

Those that hunted stayed their course. The stairs shook. They banged with the weight of empty stomachs, ravenous to satisfy their starved maws.

Karrin made it past dry storage and down the halls leading to cryo. He just needed to make it there. Beyond cryo was engineering and the beast's room. They wouldn't follow him there. They would never return. Not again.

The yells took shape. They changed. Words were forming, following Karrin through the darkness. Pleas. Accusations. Vitriol. All the anger was well deserved, and the captain had no energy to defend himself. He just gripped his pistol tighter. White knuckles answered their hard words. Karrin turned and fired a few shots into the shadowed mass. Metal sparked and reflected the drained, empty eyes behind him.

It was a foolish thing. He had to conserve the ammo, but he hated them. They spoke the truth, and it stung all the more. He couldn't handle it.

He would let them sink their claws deep if it weren't for the inhibitor chip. It gave him the drive he needed to carry on, to run on the crunch of a spent ankle. Karrin had to get to that terrible engine. It was for the greater good, whether he was there to be part of it or not.

Another bulkhead kept cryo separated from the middle of the ship. Karrin slammed into it and fumbled on the wheel. The pistol fell as his shaking hand struggled to unseal it. In the shallow gloom, the voices, the wild specters rushed. The wheel spun, and the latches unclipped. Karrin shouldered the door open. His ankle finally succumbed to the hairline fractures and snapped beyond usage.

Spinning into the room, Karrin leaned his back against the door as it automatically sealed shut. Hands slapped against the metal at the captain's back. Muffled screams tried to wound him a few more times before he sacrificed more of himself. Salt on the wounds. He hoped they would be satisfied with his pain.

The waiting was finally over.

Karrin scrambled to stand, to get away from the door. He grabbed at the nearest cryo pod and pulled himself up. The glowing, milky liquid lit his gaunt cheeks and sleepless eyes. A body parted through the nutrient-rich fluid. General Erebus loomed above Karrin. He took in a shocked inhale before his addled brain realized what was happening. He rested against the pod and took a few moments to catch his breath and compose himself.

The captain looked at Erebus. He wanted to blame the man for everything, all the carnage and sadness. He wanted to, but even that was too much insolence for the chip in his head. Such dissent was mutinous. That blame turned to admiration, a falsehood that dug deep into belief.

All the noise stopped as the general came into the dim light. The screams, the clawing, and the pointed words were drowned before the authority of Erebus.

The UCS Acheron had too many ghosts, and even they couldn't lift a hand to the general.

Unable to look away, Karrin gave the last of his resentment to the pod. The general floated in benign ignorance. He would be blissfully unaware of any monstrosities until the outpost woke him three days from now.

Karrin regarded the cryo liquid lustily. All of the fluid inside was potent enough to keep the occupant sustained until most suns lost their light, but not a drop could be used to keep the Acheron going. It was the first fuel they thought of using. They even tried a few times, but flushing a pod too soon could harm the subject within. Their chips would not let them. Even with the best intent, the chips denied the simplest answer to the problem they faced.

Erebus was smiling. "Have fun, Captain. Your sacrifice will mean more than you know. Glory to the United Navy!"

Karrin scowled. "Suck on nutrients, old man."

He turned away, and his first few steps were agony as the rubble of his ankle crunched. The torment was a close friend now, but the relationship did not numb the pain. There was much more to come, and it would not be over quickly.

Rows of officers saluted as he stumbled by. Their faces showed reserved admiration. They marched in place as best they could, floating in their pods, as Karrin shuffled on to meet his fate by the aft. The anthem of the United System Colonies began playing over the ship's speakers. A sliver of pride spurred his steps, but it was an illusion created by the technology deep in his brain. It was not a subtle song, but it worked. He was almost excited to brutalize himself for the engine.

Karrin reached the last bulkhead, and an unnerving silence was present on the other side. The beast was asleep. It did not wait—it never waited; it merely took the scraps it was given and was content by the offerings. It was not thankful. It was not angry. It simply was. If it had been some terrible, gluttonous villain, it would be easier to hate, but it was just a machine. A necessary burden.

Karrin turned the wheel and passed through the doorway. The bulkhead closed behind him, and he gritted through the last steps forward. The engine room was a tangle of tools, circuitry, and tubing. The structural plating had been removed and thrown to the floor; she had been undressed in the days when there was hope. They looked for a reason why this happened. If Thane had the time, he probably could have figured it out, but as it passed and reality got darker, there was no chance. They had to act.

Karrin lowered himself into Acheron's skeleton. Loose wire and cooling circuits led the way through her body to an altar of sharpened blades. More uprooted grating was beyond that, which led through a small passage where no one was meant to crawl. Karrin's destination was there, a secluded space where he was barely able to stand. The floor was painted in blood and lingering cuts from sawing blades and knives, the reminders of their worst possible passions.

At the foot of the space was a small opening that had all the charm of a meat grinder. Karrin looked down into the thick, spiked cogs as they rotated into each other. Her teeth were ready. Always ready. He could see himself in the unstained cogs as they passed each other with seamless gaps. It made no noise until blood and bone were lowered in. The noises thereafter could never be forgotten.

"It's not as bad as it looks," someone said from behind. Karrin didn't need to look back; Nix was always soft spoken. "It's over quickly if that is any consolation. Well, it was for me."

"Not for me," Neme butted in. "I gave the captain hell."

Karrin turned around to face the command crew.

The UCS Acheron had too many ghosts but was always short of a full complement.

Eris nudged Neme in the shoulder. "At least you didn't beg. I got on my knees, but that only made it easier for the captain to get a better shot on me."

"I branded him a coward," Thane pointed out with no delight. "He wasn't going to do it, you see. How could he again? Not after you three. I had to push him to the very limits to pull that trigger."

The sides of their heads, the wounds that wouldn't heal, had a flow that added to the soiled floor below.

"So, what are you gonna do, Captain?" Nix asked. She was always thinking of others, kind to a fault. Her concern was a gift amid the gloom.

She was talking about the gun. Karrin looked down at his empty holster. He had dropped it just before the cryo bay. In the hurry, the panic, he had tossed away his last salvation. The easy way out he planned for himself was gone. Honestly, it was a wonder he had made it to this point at all.

The captain was a loyal man. It used to be his only point of pride. That dignity had since been compromised, having left without hope for forgiveness. He was a butcher, deceiver, all of which was for a military and a ship he did not care for. The only pride he felt now was an illusion created by the inhibitor chip. It told him there was no greater duty than to give his life for this mission. Karrin wanted nothing more than to believe it. Otherwise, what he had done was as shallow as his honor.

"You are a good man," Nix offered. The chip was a compelling liar.

"Doing this makes you a hero," Thane added. "That fact alone absolves all past sins."

"It was honestly an honor, sir," Eris said with a smile.

Karrin stepped back to the lip of the engine's intake. He nodded as the cogs rotated below.

The crew spared what smiles they could. For a moment, the missing limbs, the gunshot wounds, and the blood were gone. The illusion was delightful. It burgeoned with lights and feelings of satisfaction. It swelled deep within. The pride it conjured was not his own, but Karrin accepted it wholly as he leaned back and fell into the waiting maw. There was a sudden crunch and then nothing at all.

The UCS Acheron had one too many ghosts and hopefully, by the mercy of passing stars, she had claimed her last.

Rory has been weaving worlds since he could hold a pencil. A consummate dreamer, a massage therapist by trade, and an author by passion, he will never stop endeavoring to create places for people to lose themselves in. When he isn't lounging about with his wife and three cats, he can be found skateboarding and hiking around the beautiful Rocky Mountains.

Making content on YouTube and Tik Tok has also been a treasured pastime since finding an audience during the pandemic.

If you like video games, nerd culture, and adult crafts, Rory can be found at youtube.com/rorysbrainworks,
tiktok.com/@xfinalgambitx,
and instagram.com/author_rory

IT'S EASY TO FORGET

L.N. HUNTER

Phillip picked at a paper tissue while Dr. Morton explained how blue nano worked. Phillip already understood the gist of the process, but still, it was *his* brain they were going to be burrowing into. His brain and his memories—but that was the point, wasn't it? He was paying them a lot of money to make him forget everything about his wife.

"Biomedical nanotech," Dr. Morton said, "the so-called blue nano, has been very successful in the treatment of severe phobias and PTSD for several years. We inject the brain with nano and then show subjects images of, say, spiders. Blue nano acts to suppress neurotransmitter absorption at active synapses, weakening and eventually breaking the connection between the fear stimulus and strong emotional responses. And then there was Professor Laker's breakthrough."

In just a few days, if all went well, Phillip wouldn't be able to remember meeting and marrying his wife, the good times and the bad, the quarrels and the make-up sex... and murdering her.

Of course, Dr. Morton and the rest of the staff at Laker Memories ("We forget, so you don't have to") didn't know about the murder. No one knew about it, though they soon would. By then, it would be too late for them to do anything about it.

Phillip had told everyone she'd left him, ripping his heart in two. Tearfully, he described his distress to Dr. Morton, explaining that he just couldn't live with the memories of his darling wife. He handed over psychiatric reports supporting his claim that he was a danger to himself and blurted that his final—his only—hope was to excise her from his memory. Completely.

Dr. Morton had nodded. "We understand. Laker deals with a lot of cases like this, Mr. Anderson. We can certainly help you."

Phillip forced himself to at least give the appearance of paying attention as the doctor droned on, while remembering to dab at his eyes every now and then. He really didn't care how it worked, as long as it did.

"Were you aware that the memory-erasing process was discovered by accident?" Dr. Morton asked, a look of fake outrage on his face. "Professor Laker won his Nobel Prize—did you see the medal on display in the foyer?—for a simple mistake. Serendipity plays a bigger role in scientific discovery than people expect. Anyway, usually, the data set used in the treatment would include positive images as well as those for which we want to break the association, so that the nanotech will target synaptic firings related specifically to the fear response. For one particular treatment, the data set had become corrupted, upsetting the ratio of positive to negative stimuli. The result was not only that the subject lost their fear of spiders, but she also forgot everything else about spiders—she genuinely didn't know what a spider was. Fortunately, it was quite a simple process for her to learn about them again." Dr. Morton laughed. "And without regaining her phobia."

"And this is what you'll be doing to me, right?" Phillip asked, with a tearful sniff.

"Yes." Dr. Morton adopted a more serious and sympathetic expression. "That's pretty much it, though the process has been refined since then. We need you to bring in representative images of your wife—"

Phillip forced himself to produce a loud sob, and Dr. Morton grimaced.

"I know it's going to be difficult, but I can promise—hand on heart—that this will be the last time you have to even think about your wife. As I was saying, representative images. If you have videos, phone messages and so on, as well as photographs, all the better—any sort of digitized content. Also include pictures of items that hold a special association with her, such as a favorite perfume brand or jewelry—anything and everything that defines your wife to you."

Phillip thought that the pillow he'd smothered her with should *not* be on his list, even though that was one of the more pleasant memories.

Dr. Morton continued, "We have a library of generic neutral stimuli here at Laker, but do feel free to provide anything else you can think of as contra-stimuli—material that excludes your wife but showing people, objects, or events which also cause you to feel strong emotions. Such stimuli will help improve the specificity of the process by allowing us to fine-tune the erasure boundary between your memories of your wife and other important memories."

He glanced at his notes again. "Usually, we give people a week or two for this data gathering, but I can see that your case is rather urgent, so we can start much sooner. Do you think the material we need could be ready by tomorrow? Bring at least three hundred images, videos, and the like relating to your wife, as distinct and distinctive as you can make them. Now—and this is important—you will also have to remove all physical traces of your wife from your life. No joint accounts or names on various contracts—will you be able to arrange such things in time? Hopefully, it shouldn't be too difficult with everything being electronic nowadays. Also make sure there's none of her clothing left in wardrobes, cosmetics in the bathroom, and so on."

He looked at Phillip over the top of his glasses. "And it's worth priming your friends too, so that they can avoid mentioning your wife afterwards."

Phillip nodded to show he understood.

Dr. Morton took off his glasses and absently tapped them against his chin.

"Now, there is one other thing. We recommend that we also erase this visit. Remembering that you engaged Laker Memories can cause mental stress, as you can't help but wonder what it was you desired to forget. We do acknowledge that it's only natural for people to want to forget as little as possible, if you see what I mean, but I do suggest that you choose to include Laker."

Phillip said, "Yes, that makes sense." He rubbed at his eyes, and trying not to sound too eager, asked, "Is there anything else I need to do?"

Dr. Morton stood and stepped around his desk. "Well, you need to fill in some forms and sign the standard disclaimer—there's always paperwork, isn't there? Then send the data to us as soon as you can, and come back here on the day after—if you can get us the material by tomorrow, let me see, that's Thursday, right? Our technicians will validate the data—don't worry, we have very strong confidentiality processes here. As long as everything's okay, we'll inject the blue nano and pop you in the machine. Two hours later, it'll be as if your wife never existed."

Phillip wondered what it would be like to know nothing about his wife or the murder. He hoped that future Phillip could cope with whatever was going to happen when the killing was discovered.

Dr. Morton ushered Phillip out of his office and into the reception area. "Jenny, here, has the forms and will give you all the details. You're making the right decision, and you'll feel much better afterwards. You have my word on it." He patted Phillip on the shoulder. "Well, good day, Mr. Anderson."

* * *

ON THURSDAY, Dr. Morton looked on as a nurse helped Phillip get positioned on the bed of the MRI scanner that would be used to monitor and control the process. He held up a syringe containing a blue liquid. "Amazing to think that something as small as this can have such a dramatic effect on one's memories." He sighed. "On one's whole life. This syringe contains tens of thousands of blue nano units in saline. Once their job's done, we switch them off, and your kidneys will flush them from your system within a day or so.

"We used to keep our clients fully conscious during the erasure process, but we've found that it's both faster and more robust if you're unconscious—we can present the stimuli more quickly, and the emotional signals are more pronounced without consciousness muddying the waters, so to speak. You'll wake up back at home, with no memory of your wife or of us."

Phillip swallowed, but calmed himself with the thought that it would soon be over.

"Are you ready, old chap?" Dr. Morton asked.

Phillip attempted to smile back, but his lips seemed too

dry to move. He nodded, causing the nurse to tut. She had told him to keep perfectly still.

"You'll feel a little jab," Dr. Morton said as he injected the anesthetic-laden blue nano.

Phillip felt himself drift off as the table slid into the scanner.

* * *

A WEEK LATER, Phillip sat in his kitchen, wearing paint-splattered overalls. He sipped a mug of strong black coffee and ate a croissant while he flicked through the morning's news stories on his phone. His "staycation" was almost over, and he'd have to get back to the office soon, but the next couple of days were to be occupied with painting the rest of the walls. He knew that the only way he'd get big jobs like that done was to take a solid block of time off work and disconnect from email and all his socials—a daily news check was all he allowed himself.

He'd just picked up his paint brush to get started when someone hammered on the door.

"Police! Open up."

Still carrying the brush, Phillip opened the door. "How can I help you, officers?"

"Phillip George Anderson, we are arresting you for the murder of Annette Roberta Anderson."

"Who?"

"Your wife, Mr. Anderson."

Frowning in confusion, Phillip said, "Wife? I'm not married. There's been a mistake."

* * *

THE CASE TIED up the courts for months, making several lawyers very wealthy, and occupied the media for longer still.

Prosecution lawyers had physical evidence on their side. Annette's red VW convertible had been found submerged in Lake Louie, her body in the driver's seat. An accident had been ruled out because of the lack of water in her lungs, which indicated she was dead when the car entered the water. CCTV footage in several locations on the way to the lake showed two people in the car. Although Phillip had no memory of his wife, friends of the couple provided a good many photographs of the pair as well as personal testimony.

Phillip was trapped in a nightmare. He saw the evidence but couldn't recognize the woman. "It can't have been me! I'm being framed—no, I have no idea why." Even when his visit to Laker Memories was discovered and their records subpoenaed, he still denied everything. "I must have a doppelganger." Lie detectors confirmed that he truly believed this.

The prosecution acknowledged that Phillip's memory had been—in their words—tampered with, but he had committed the crime. He was guilty.

The defense did not deny that the Phillip Anderson who existed before the memory wipe had killed his wife, but they argued that the Phillip Anderson of right now could not be considered the same person. Memories made a person, their expert witnesses stated; today's Phillip had never been married and knew nothing of the events of this stranger's death. It would be unjust to punish him for something he knew nothing about.

They drew similarities between this case and the 1987 sleepwalking defense employed in Regina v. Parks, whereby the accused was declared not responsible due to being unconscious. If, Phillip's lawyers said, having no conscious memory and intent was a viable defense in that instance, surely the same held here.

The jury failed to agree on a verdict, resulting in a mistrial. Two more trials similarly foundered, so in the end, the case was decided by senior law enforcement officials. They were worried that a not guilty verdict could open the floodgates for copycat murder defenses, so Phillip was declared guilty. However, public outrage led to him receiving no sentence, so he left court a free man, which did little to assuage the worries about copycat crimes.

Phillip was grateful to avoid prison, but he wondered what sort of despicable person he'd been before. *What was going through old me's head when I planned all this, and what made me want to kill my wife? What had she done?* He knew he would need years of therapy to be able to process all that had happened. The wry thought crossed his head that he could pay Laker's to erase the past few months for him—he shuddered and dismissed that notion.

Laws were hastily passed to prevent companies like Laker Memories from manipulating memories in cases of disappearances like that of Phillip's wife.

* * *

BEHIND THE SCENES, beyond the scrutiny of the media and indifferent to any court decision, military officials were intrigued by the possibilities of this technology. Could it make assassins forget anything that could connect them to their crimes, and more importantly, obliterate all links to the nation state controlling them? Perhaps a portable blue nano device could be developed for an operative to use in the field.

Could the technology, they asked themselves, be extended to implant memories, to prime unwitting stooges to take on the role of assassin?

Several dark-suited men from a certain agency eventually approached Professor Laker, inventor of the memory-wiping process, and quietly asked him that same question.

Professor Laker scratched his head, wondering why the words coming out of his mouth seemed familiar. He had a feeling he'd already researched the use of biomedical technology to create false memories, but the details eluded him. Perhaps he'd merely read about it, or was it just a conversation about the ethics of such a process that he vaguely recalled? Surely, no one in their right mind would carry out such a procedure.

Maybe he was being fooled by simple déjà vu.

But still, he just couldn't shake off the sense that there was more to it than that. It was as if he'd forgotten something important.

Or as if someone had forgotten it for him.

L.N. Hunter's comic fantasy novel, The Feather and the Lamp *(Three Ravens Publishing), sits alongside works in anthologies such as* Best of British Science Fiction 2022 *and* Hidden Villains: Arise, *as well as several issues of Short Édition's* Short Circuit *and the* Horrifying Tales of Wonder *podcast. There have also been papers in the IEEE* Transactions on Neural Networks, *which are probably somewhat less relevant and definitely less entertaining. When not writing, L.N. occasionally masquerades as a software developer or can be found unwinding in a disorganized home in Carlisle, UK, along with two cats and a soulmate. For more information, please visit https://linktr.ee/l.n.hunter or https://www.facebook.com/L.N.Hunter.writer*

LAST SONG FOR LISSANT

LANE ROBINS

When she knocked on my door, it was without an appointment, well before office hours, and I was suffering a stinking hangover. Not my usual practice, but I'd had some bad news a couple weeks prior and was still working my way through it with the help of whiskey bottles.

I opened the door anyway. I'd been expecting her; her name had been in the tabloids recently, and not in a good way. My specialty: solving problems for the rich and successful.

Rain pelted outside after a few dry days. She shook her umbrella, spattering my doorstep with acid-smelling water. LA smog meant rain that stank.

"Simon Hanover?" She sounded like she wanted me to say no.

I don't look like much, even on my best days when I'm shaved and not smelling of sweat, tears, and metabolized alcohol. Firmly middle-aged. Middling height and weight. Fit but not flashy. More Q than James Bond.

As she entered, her shoulders eased. I owned a tiny bungalow, and significant funds had gone into the home office. I needed my clients to feel comfortable, which meant luxury.

"You have a problem," I said, opening the conversation.

She flinched as if she would rather have wandered around the topic a while longer. Most times, I let the clients dance as long as they wanted, but today I lacked patience.

"Yes," she said, settling into her chair. "My daughter's beside herself, and I'm…I'm very afraid."

She folded her hands—diamond rings crusting her fingers—over her knees and said, "You know who I am, who my daughter is?"

"The whole world knows your daughter."

Lissant LeMarchant.

For her first show, she opened for Dua Lipa, and the restless crowd had turned attentive by the third song. Her voice bespelled them; her songwriting even more so. And of course, Lissant was beautiful—a golden girl, a golden voice, a golden goose. She'd earned millions on her first album, double that on the second.

"Tell me what's happened," I said. I fiddled with the coffee maker.

"Lissant was attacked three nights ago. In our own house."

I handed her a tiny cup of espresso. She stared at the slide of dark foam and wouldn't meet my eyes. She had more to tell, and she didn't want to tell it.

"I hear lots of stories," I reminded her. "Nothing you say will shock me."

Her chin came up, challenged and indignant. "Lissant was attacked by a monster made of mud."

Yeah. Not shocked yet, though Mrs. L thought I should be. The thing is, LA is full of magic. Most of it—ninety-nine percent of it—is good, old-fashioned human magic, the cult of celebrity and money, but that other one percent… Witches exist—love spells, curses, resurrections, and all that—and their schedules are even busier than mine. A lot of people don't care about the metaphysics or the cost if they can just curse their enemies. It's not openly talked about, but word does get around.

"Go on."

"It happened while she was sleeping. Ryan, our head of security, couldn't stop it."

"*Something* stopped it." Otherwise, the tabloids would be reporting Lissant's death. A spurt of anger. Lissant was the kind of girl who'd be missed.

"We rushed Lissant into the safe room. It's sealed. Guaranteed to survive an earthquake."

"And the mud monster—the Sending—was gone when you came out?"

"You know what it is?"

"Big trouble is what it is. It just left?"

"We have a security feed," she said. "We saw it collapse, become mud again."

"I'll want that footage," I said.

"You'll help us?"

I led her through a few other questions. Magic, on this scale, meant bad blood. I would lay bets that Mrs. L knew exactly why someone was attacking Lissant.

Getting her to admit it? Impossible odds.

"What about Mariel?" I challenged.

"Mariel?" she echoed. Like she didn't know Mariel.

Mariel LeMarchant. The other daughter. Mariel was never in the tabloids, never caught in a candid photo with Lissant. Never mentioned in interviews. Her existence boiled down to a single line on someone else's Wikipedia page and a dig from a scandal blogger—*Lissant got all the talent and all the pretty in that family. Have you seen her older sister? No? Good. You don't wanna.* But she'd finally made the news. Tabloids said she'd taken off after a fight with her family.

"Mariel split; that says there's bad feeling there."

"Ridiculous," she snapped. "She couldn't handle the lifestyle, couldn't handle being less important than her sister, so she left. Lissant's the one in trouble."

A lie, but I let it go. I took her through the spiel: my fees—expensive as hell if she wanted me to deal with witches; what she could expect of me—twenty-four hour exclusive concentration on her case, unusual but in this circumstance, unavoidable; and what I expected of her and Lissant—honesty, access to their lives, prompt payment, and obedience in any dangerous scenario.

She slid a check across my desk, and I took the job.

I forgot my hangover in the satisfaction.

* * *

THE LEMARCHANTS LIVED on a multi-million dollar estate, as isolated as it got in LA. Beneath the rain, the driveway looked like a glossy black snake. The house sprawled behind wet, green lawns. Security seemed solid: a keypad entry gate across the drive and a fence that was less about show than it might have been. I'd seen houses that had four-foot-high fences and a beagle and called that "security." The house appeared all glass—enormous windows flaunting opulent rooms—but that was only an exterior layer. The rooms beyond that were less open, more able to be locked down. People could see in only so far. I'd known some of this already; I had friends in various security firms. The LeMarchants' home got rated as *Decent. Nothing special, except for the panic room.*

I dripped on the foyer's marble floor, took the towel that a maid handed me, and blotted myself back to civility. Mrs. L, who had entered the house beneath an umbrella held by her driver, waited with a tapping toe.

"Have you called the police?" I asked.

Mrs. L's mouth twisted. "Half the cops are in the pay of the tabloids, and we've had enough problems with paparazzi. Plus, what are they going to do about magic?"

There were a few cops I knew who dealt with magic, but overall, I preferred them out of this loop.

The cloudy day lifted. A light came into the room. Or, less poetically, Lissant LeMarchant joined us, a wash of rosy perfume and long golden hair, a professional smile on her lips. She held out her hands. "Mr. Hanover. Thank you for helping me. I've just been so frightened."

Practiced words, like something out of a movie—I'd heard she had acting ambitions—but pallor lurked beneath her tan, and her hands were restless, nervy.

"Lissant," her mother said, "why don't you show Mr. Hanover your room? He knows about occult things."

"Most spells are blood-borne," I said. "You might get lucky. There might be trace in the mud."

"Gross," Lissant contributed.

I supposed it was disgusting, someone else's blood giving life to a violent Sending. But I'd seen worse things.

As I followed Lissant through the long, wide halls of her home, I noticed mud everywhere—creating a snake trail over the carpets, splashed beneath the doors, spattered along the walls. I saw structural damage too—dents in the walls, cracked furniture, pictures hanging off kilter.

Nearly all of the pictures featured Lissant. Smiling, pouting, singing, posing with her mom, with other musicians, with movers and shakers, and boyfriends-of-the-week. Only one showed the full family—the two sisters, Mrs. L, and the long-dead Mr. L—and it predated Lissant's career by years.

"Not a lot of pictures of your sister," I said.

"She wasn't worth photographing," Lissant responded, scowling at the muddy stains on the carpet. Her head snapped up at my silence. "Oh, that sounded terrible. I didn't mean it. She said so herself. She always said, 'no point wasting pictures on the unattractive.' God, Hollywood's hard on the ego. She wasn't that bad."

In that long ago picture, Mariel had braces, a round face, and an acne collection—all in all, a regular teen. Eclipsed by Lissant, of course. Even preteen Lissant was spectacular.

"So where do you think she went?" I asked.

"How would I know? She kept things from me." Lissant shrugged. "Why do you care?"

"Do *you* think she might be behind this?"

Lissant shook her head.

"Any idea who might be angry enough to hire a witch? They're not cheap."

A new voice, male and irritable, said, "Isn't that what you're here to find out? If asking Lissant would solve this, I'd have done it myself."

Mrs. L had rejoined us, a stone-faced man in her wake. He wore fatigues, a tight black shirt, and a gun at his hip. Early forties, just enough silver in his hair to be authoritative. The security guy. Ryan Draskovich. An up-and-comer in the private bodyguard field who'd been wooed away from his previous starlet by the LeMarchants. A man with an impressive reputation for making troublemakers vanish. A man who wasn't happy that I'd been called in.

"I work best with access to information," I told him. He shrugged.

I loathed dealing with security.

"Lissant's room is this way," Mrs. L said. I followed politely, though I wanted to get a better idea of the house layout. So far, all I'd seen were hallways, pictures, and air handling vents.

Lissant's suite was opulent even in disrepair. A lilac carpet sighed under my feet like velvet, where it wasn't crunchy with cakes of dried mud; an enormous four poster bed held torn gauzy hangings; and a muddy imprint crushed the satin pillow. A broken lamp lay beside the bed, testimony to a terrified Lissant flailing for the security buzzer.

Mirrors filled the suite: angled mirrors at her dresser, old-fashioned easel mirrors in the corners, a mirrored wall beside the shattered grand piano, and a walk-in closet bristling with mirrors. Everywhere I looked I saw my reflection. I looked tired, my hair thin, my expression bitter.

"Seen enough?" Ryan asked.

I didn't let him rush me.

I scooped mud from the thickest area. I found it gritty with ground glass and stinking of diesel. Run-off mud from the highway.

Mrs. L's phone rang. "Bart," she trilled. "Lovely to hear from… Oh, I know, I know, she's working so hard, right now—"

Tabloid gossip said Bart would be Bart Whistler, and he was likely calling because Lissant's new album was months overdue. Her third album was slated for release in December, and nothing had been recorded yet.

"This way," Ryan said, a hard hand on my shoulder. "You wanted to see the security feed?"

We left Mrs. L arguing with Bart and Lissant leaning close to listen.

* * *

APPARENTLY, I could only see the security feeds of the Sending the same way they had: from the safe room. My request to take the discs home got me a brusque, "No way in hell."

"Don't trust me?"

Ryan paused. "I looked into you. You own a string of bars.

You're not hurting for money. I don't know why you work as a PI."

"Sometimes there are cases that just need working."

I annoyed him by peering into every room we passed. Kitchen, splattered with mud along the edges; home cinema, muddy; guest room, sitting room, dining room, muddy, muddy, muddy. The Sending had made itself at home during its search for Lissant. A closed door drew my attention. I opened it.

"Are these Mariel's rooms?"

"Before she left, yeah," he said. He reached around to close the door, but I stepped inside before he could.

"No mud here," I said. She had her own suite. Bedroom, fancy bath, living room, kitchen. Opulent here, too, but with the pastel shades that suited Lissant's vivid coloring; Mariel, sallower, probably had looked ill.

Where Lissant's room glinted silver with mirrors' faces, Mariel's bloomed with colorful guitars. Collectibles hung on the walls, one unstrung beside the couch, and one well-loved one in a battered leather case studded with bar stickers—Rooster's, The Taproom, Herlihy's, and Marlowe's.

"She was musical, too."

Ryan shrugged. "She dabbled. Hard not to when your family is in the industry." Another lie. That sticker-covered case was a gigging case, places she'd been, places she'd performed.

"Look, I've got things to do," Ryan said. "You want to see the feeds or not?"

When I thought of safe rooms, I thought of exactly that. A human-sized safe. But this safe 'room' consisted of a living room with couches big enough to sleep on, a bathroom, and a stocked kitchenette. The only things that betrayed its status were the bank of LED screens along the wall and the muffled acoustics. Currently, personal belongings cluttered the rooms—Lissant and her mother had been sleeping in here since the attack, Ryan told me.

Ryan passed me a remote and said, “It’s queued up.”

“Sure I can’t take it home?”

“Fucking paparazzi would probably mug you for it.

He left me alone in the safe room; it sealed tight around me.

I watched the video. No audio included, which only made it worse, somehow.

Dim lighting, the shadow moving through the halls, the rooms, then the beautiful blonde sheltered in the draperies of the four-poster. Like something out of a B-movie, except this was real. I saw the terror on Lissant’s face as she woke to the Sending bent over her. I saw the way the Sending moved, slow as the grind of the earth, but inexorable.

If Lissant had been sleeping more soundly, she would never have woken, smothered beneath fistfuls of mud.

Instead, she screamed and scrambled from beneath the Sending. The Sending’s blow left filthy smears along the drapes.

Ryan burst into the room, assessed Lissant’s position, and opened fire. He had a brute of a gun, and his aim was remarkable. Startled, in dim light, and facing an unexpected monster, he made every shot count—every one a chest shot.

It didn’t slow the Sending much, though mud spattered in a mockery of blood. Ryan dragged Lissant out and slammed the door shut. The Sending smashed the piano, sieved itself through the piano wires, and headed after Lissant.

The feed switched again, showing the Sending tracking the halls and beating on the walls, leaving holes. It cast its blind head about, searching, almost losing the trail until the safe room door closed. *Hunting by sound,* I thought.

It stalked nearly the entire house, one room at a time, then finally found the safe room door, the only door that didn't give beneath its fists. The Sending thundered like an avalanche, but the door held firm. The Sending liquefied and tried to feed itself beneath the door, but the safe room had been built with gas in mind—there was no entry there, either.

The Sending stalked back to Lissant's room and did the rest of the damage I'd seen today. Endless destruction, endless rage. The monster only stopped when it found itself reflected between two mirrors. It must have had some rudimentary sight, because it froze, then its featureless head…changed.

It grew a mouth, and it screamed.

I wondered what it had sounded like, that contorted wail of rage and agony, or if it had sounded like anything at all.

Then it shattered, exploding into muddy water that splashed the walls and soaked into the carpet.

I rubbed my jaw, profoundly unhappy. Not ready to face Mrs. L or Lissant, I poked around for a few minutes, checking out the security measures and figuring how the door seals and air vents worked. They had to have air from somewhere, or the safe room would be a tomb.

Lissant should have been dead. Sendings like the mud monster were powered by rage and betrayal, limited only by the parameters of their materials. They tended not to stop until they'd done what they needed to do. The Sending would be back.

If the past couple of days hadn't been unexpectedly sunny—the forecast had been for a rare week of rain—the Sending would have been back already.

It was raining now, soaking the earth. Somewhere, the Sending stirred, will and fury and mud coalescing into a whole. It would be back. Probably not tonight; it would take time for the Sending to regain its sense of purpose.

Ryan stuck his head in. "You done yet?"

I let him herd me toward Lissant and Mrs. L. Their low voices argued in the hall near Mariel's room, and I eavesdropped as we approached. The gist: Lissant couldn't find the songs for her third album.

Mrs. L stifled the conversation when she saw us, and I took my leave, though Mrs. L protested, "I paid for your exclusive attention!"

"I'm not your bodyguard. You've got Ryan for that. I need to talk to a witch."

"Should we leave? Find a hotel?"

"No," I said. "Sleep in the panic room again. You're safe there."

"I don't care where we sleep," Lissant snapped. "I just want it to be over."

"I'll see to that."

* * *

AFTER A BUSY AFTERNOON spent talking to people, I ended up in my favorite bar, Marlowe's. I had a half dozen, but this was my favorite: small enough to feel intimate, crowded enough that you could have a private conversation, plus a sociable bartender who had a remarkable knack for faces.

"Got your drink ready," Vangie told me as I sank onto a stool.

"Just give me the bottle," I told her.

"Not good for you," she said, but she set it out anyway. I agreed with her, but that security footage looped in my mind repeatedly—the Sending screaming. I needed that image to fade. I sipped my drink and studied the room. Piped-in pop music played in the background.

It was a decent crowd, mostly recreational drinkers from the middle class.

A man settled into the seat beside me and said, "Word is you got hired by the LeMarchants. Anything to tell?"

"Nothing for you today, Trevor," I said, without heat. No point in getting huffy. He ran the gossip site *All The Dirt*, and his skin was as thick as alligator hide. Besides, he had his uses.

"Nothing at all?"

I waved Vangie over and got Trevor a drink. "There you go. Don't say I never gave you nothing."

"Would never say that," he said, and faded away.

The music shifted—one of Lissant's mixes, bright and charming as the girl herself. I grimaced. "Change the station, Vangie."

"Not a fan?"

"Not even a little."

She ducked behind the bar and switched satellite stations. The crowd didn't even notice. Vangie cleaned an already clean glass and said, "Can I ask something without you getting mad?"

"There are better ways to start a sentence, Vangie."

She grinned, flipped her pile of bleached-blonde braids, and said, "Okay, but seriously. People are missing the live music. Do you think we should find another singer?"

My gaze jerked over to the small stage—micro-stage really. Just big enough for a girl, a guitar, and an amp. Now the stage was shadowed and empty, but for the past few months, every Thursday night had been live. I'd been a fan, then more than a fan, but I hadn't thought anyone else even cared when she stopped coming.

My mouth twisted; my drink tasted bitter when I swallowed.

"People don't know a good thing when they've got it. Let 'em suffer."

Vangie grimaced. "You're in a mood."

"You're smart and beautiful." I toasted her, and she left me alone.

I took the bottle when I left.

At home, I pulled out a thumb drive loaded with my favorite album, hooked it to my sound system, and wallowed in musical heartbreak—talented and fervent and *sincere.* Painfully so. Yet, someone like Lissant got all the fame.

Tomorrow, I'd end this.

* * *

I HEADED BACK TO THE LEMARCHANTS' house late the next afternoon, towing a trailer behind my sedan, racing sunset.

"What's this?" Ryan asked, peering through the drizzling rain at the trailer.

"I've got a plan," I told him.

He leaned against my car and said, "How 'bout you run it by me first?" Water beaded in his hair.

"In the house," I suggested. "That way I don't have to explain it twice."

Ryan opened the trailer, looked inside, and said, "Seriously?"

"Trust me."

He climbed into my passenger seat and rode up to the house with me. "This will really solve the problem?" He'd missed a patch of stubble, and his hand hovered near his gun. "'Cause I have to tell you, this is out of my experience. I went looking for a witch, but all I got was bullshit."

I wasn't surprised. The witch community kept to itself and was more conservative about new clients than bankers. But they knew me, and favors flowed both ways between us.

"That's why Mrs. L hired me," I pointed out. "Trying to cut me out, Ryan?"

"A bonus makes good retirement money."

At the house, I could tell neither woman had relaxed in the past twenty-four hours.

"Mr. Hanover," Mrs. L gasped, "this cannot continue. I barely slept."

"I have a plan," I said. "I need you to do a few things. Send the staff home. If this goes wrong, I don't want them involved."

"We already did that," Lissant said.

That did surprise me.

Ryan snorted. "Tabloids. We didn't need the gossip."

Color me less surprised.

"What else do you need?" Mrs. L asked.

"I've got a trailer full of mirrors. I need to get them inside."

"Let's do it," Mrs. L said. I had expected an unsubtle reminder that I was the help, that she and her daughter didn't do manual labor. But they were scared and desperate.

* * *

"WHY MIRRORS?" Lissant asked as we propped the sixth mirror against the hallway wall. I tilted it slightly, angling the reflection.

"We're going to herd the Sending," I said. Last time the monster had come through the front door, rising out of the rain-gutter wet soil; I had no reason to suspect otherwise this time.

Ryan glanced down the hall, past the safe room to the French doors I'd opened, and beyond. "You're aiming it at the pool?"

"Mud is mud, even when it's magical," I said. "That much water, it'll dissolve."

"And that'll stop it from coming back?" He sounded skeptical.

"There's more to it," I admitted. I explained it took a counterspell to dissolve the will of a Sending. But before you got that far, you needed to disable the Sending. It was too damned easy to get killed while you were standing there chanting paragraphs worth of tongue-twisting words.

"Tell me the counterspell," Ryan suggested.

"Not a chance."

"So why will mirrors work?" Lissant asked. She frowned at the glass. The mirrors were the cheap kind that college kids hung on the back of their dorm doors, and she didn't like the reflection they cast.

"A Sending's a thing with a human soul. How would you feel if you were shoved into a body made of dirt and water and then saw yourself unexpectedly? The Sending's got self-esteem issues. Like your sister, huh?"

"Mariel was such a selfish bitch."

"Lissant," Mrs. L chastised, two mirrors down. Her fair hair had come out of its updo, and she looked older by the moment. Stress could eat away at you like that. So could guilt.

These women had done something to have a Sending put on their trail. They had wronged someone, driven them to the point of magical homicide.

Mrs. L said, "Do you have brothers, Mr. Hanover? Sibling rivalry can be intense. Especially when the younger outshines the older."

I ignored her and finished the set-up.

I ushered them all into the safe room and closed the door behind us. Ryan asked, "Aren't you staying outside?"

"Let the mirrors do their work first."

Ryan threw himself before the monitors, flick, flick, flicking from one feed to the next.

We waited. Outside, rain slicked the cameras.

It grew dark.

In the room behind me, Lissant and her mother argued quietly, then less quietly.

"You're going to have to give Bart something he can tell the studios," Mrs. L said.

"It's his job to figure that out!" Lissant said. "I'm the artist! He's the manager."

"You could help him a little," Mrs. L said. In the reflection of the monitors, her mouth pinched tight. "Buy us some time."

"I just can't figure out where she hid the—"

"It doesn't matter now."

Lissant sighed, toying with her hair.

"I'm just not feeling inspired, Mother," Lissant said slowly. "I may be burned out. So much happening so soon, and of course, I'm worried about my sister—"

Mrs. L shook her head. "Leave her out of it."

Lissant said, "Burned out, and…I need to grow. I need to refill the well of songs within myself."

"Good," her mother said. "Bart can do things with that."

He probably could. Studios liked clichéd bullshit like that.

"Holy fuck!" Ryan shouted. On the screens, the Sending had made the scene, pouring through the front door, a churning mass of dirty water, a cresting wave that resolved into two legs, two arms, and a lumpy torso, topped with a featureless head. It slopped toward us, a skin of water soaking the carpet around it. The water kept coming.

The Sending seemed stronger this time; there was more rain, and the earth had already dampened, collecting more potential in its depths.

"What if it doesn't go down the hall?" Ryan asked.

The monster took its shape better this time. It became evident that the Sending, and therefore the soul attached to it, was female. Had been female.

Ryan licked his lips nervously. Lissant and her mother

huddled in silence, Lissant's face against her mother's shoulder.

"She will," I said. I felt confident. Things were going to work out. My hand fell into my pocket, tensing. "We just need to give her a little time."

"And we just wait?" Lissant wailed.

"You could go back to making up excuses for the recording executives. They're getting impatient, right? Beginning to talk about the money you're costing them?"

"It's hardly your business," Mrs. L said, "but yes, Lissant's having a little trouble getting inspired."

"Huh," I said. I took my hand out of my pocket. Mine wasn't a very big gun—not like Ryan's .45—but I was up close and personal. I shot Ryan as he turned, nailed him high in the chest. I kicked him out of the chair and took his gun away. He tried to get up, and I kicked him in the bubbling wound. His eyes rolled back in his head.

Lissant screamed shrilly, her famous voice strong enough to crack glass and my ear drums.

I said, "Stop that."

Guns were good for instilling obedience. She stopped.

"So your excuse for the execs is going to be lack of inspiration?"

Lissant's face shone with tears, slackened with shock. Mrs. L went as rigid as a statue, her nails digging into Lissant's arm in a way that would have been painful if either woman had been paying attention.

"What?" Lissant whispered.

"Why not just tell them the truth?" I asked. "You're not out of ideas. You're just out of talented sisters to steal from."

It seemed crazy that I could have any more of their attention than I'd gathered after shooting Ryan, but that got them.

"Mr. Hanover," Mrs. L said, raising her chin and shoulders, "I don't understand what you're doing, but if it's about money, we can—"

"*Mariel* was the songwriter. Lissant took the credit, over and over again, until Mariel couldn't stand it any longer. Until she refused to hand over another of her songs."

Lissant's gaze shied away from the first pair of mirrors.

"You're wrong," Mrs. L said, doggedly sticking to her story. "Lissant's the talent." Her fingers pushed at her cellphone, summoning 911, but the signal went nowhere.

"What I don't understand is why you didn't just give Mariel songwriting credit. Make them a duo."

Mrs. L let the cell drop, and said coldly, "And split the attention? Do you know how many girls have great voices? Thousands. Do you know how many girls have a great voice *and* that kind of songwriting talent? Very few. It made Lissant stand out."

"Mariel could sing as well as write."

"But she wasn't *pretty*," Mrs. L said. "You can't get anywhere in the business without being pretty."

"Mariel intended to try," I said. I felt breathless, my anger burning words out of me. "She wanted to keep her new songs for herself, and you two wouldn't let her. You've been looking for her songs, but she didn't trust you. She hadn't trusted you for a long time." My voice broke, went raw, a broken melody. "And when she wouldn't give you the recordings she'd made, you lost your temper and hit her—hit her too hard and cracked her skull. So, you had her dumped like garbage in a ravine."

Lissant looked like she might pass out.

"You can't prove anything," Mrs. L said.

"I don't care about that."

I looked over my shoulder at the monitors. The Sending was moving in our direction, funneled by the mirrors, and

Lissant bit her lip hard enough to draw blood. "What did you do?" Even in terror, her voice was musical.

But not like Mariel's had been.

I plugged my thumb drive in, and music rolled into the safe room. A melody that made your heart ache, a familiar turn of phrase made new, a desire to sing along. The stamp of all Lissant's songs, and just as obviously, not Lissant singing. An album's worth of new and perfect songs.

"Those songs belong to us!" Mrs. L said.

"She left them with me."

Mariel hit a note that rolled through my blood like electricity.

"Her voice might not be as smooth as Lissant's, but by god, these are her songs, and no one sings them like her." I controlled my anger. My finger twitched on the trigger, but shooting them wasn't the plan.

"You?" Mrs. L said. "You knew my daughter?"

"I loved her!" My words cracked, souring Mariel's song. Mrs. L flinched, and it made me furious and glad at the same time. "She loved me."

I forced myself back on track.

"Do you notice the sound?" I asked. "In here, I mean. The room's not as dead as it used to be. Not so muffled. I did a little remodeling yesterday. A few pieces of soundproofing torn here and there, so that she can *hear* us. So she can find you. "Can you smell that?"

Both women sniffed, automatically. Mrs. L went pale.

The air smelled like wet earth, like old oil and diesel, like burned rubber and glass and stagnant rain. The kind of smell you'd get in ditches along the highways.

"A few seals shredded…so she can *reach* us."

On the monitors, the Sending lurched away from the last pair of mirrors angled to drive her toward the air handling vents. Toward the sound of her own stolen voice. Toward her murderers.

Mariel splashed into a huge cresting wave and poured into the vents. The floor of the safe room began to grow damp, a dark trickle here, a flow there. The muddy water eddied around my feet like I was oil. A wavelet rolled over Ryan's face, testing the contours, then poured into his nose and mouth. His feet drummed, and Lissant shrieked.

"She's killing him!" Mrs. L cried. She made no attempt to help.

"Yes," I said. "You're next."

"We hired you," Lissant said. "We trusted you!" She made a pretty picture, and I'm sure she would have melted a heart of stone, but my heart had gone with Mariel.

I'd been a good guy my whole life, doing the right thing, believing in justice, following the law, never losing faith.

"Mariel hired me first. She wasn't dead yet, did you know that? When Ryan dumped her in the ditch, she was still alive. Barely breathing, not even able to crawl, but alive. She called me. Her last call. Her dying breath. She told me what you did. I found her, but I was too late. The only thing left was her vengeful ghost."

The two women were finally silent. Finally recognizing that I wasn't going to relent. I had been set on revenge the moment Mariel's ghost rose and screamed without a sound. They'd taken her music while she was living, then they'd taken her life.

They cringed on the couch as the water poured upward, past their kicking ankles and shins.

I'd brought Mariel's body to my witch-friend and told her what I wanted: Mariel should get her chance at life, the one they'd taken. Mariel needed her voice back.

It would take time, the witch told me, more than a week's

time, and it would cost me blood and money. So much money. And so much blood. I gave her two pints of my blood as a down payment and sold three of my bars to the coven for a dollar each. But not Marlowe's. Not where I'd first met Mariel.

She'd been staring at the small stage for most of an hour, and when I asked her what she was doing, she'd said, "Rewriting my future."

It took me an unforgivably long time to ask her out, according to her. Even longer for me to realize that she was Mariel LeMarchant, Lissant's sister. But after that, I figured things out quickly.

"The safe room was a problem. I was afraid it might be, until you hired me. I thought you might take longer, but I'm the only PI who's got an in with the witches."

It was the last sentence I thought they might hear. Mariel swamped her family, an animate mudslide, and they were kicking, screaming, drowning... Lissant took a long time to succumb, but then, her lungs were strong.

I turned up the music and waited.

Eventually, I heard their bodies fall, then a sound like a sigh, a sound I knew in my bones. I turned around. Mariel's ghost stood before me. Altered. Silvery, still mottled with mud, but human-like. Her cheeks were flushed with her killers' lives, her lips red as a car's taillights, her teeth sharp as broken glass, her eyes satisfied. And her voice...

"What now?" she asked. Harmonics echoed in ways that weren't quite human, and when I touched her hand, she swirled around my flesh like gelid water, barely keeping her shape. I thought of old stories, of sirens and undines and mermaids that could drown a man with their song.

"I've got your recordings," I said, "and I called some guys I know. They've got a studio we can use."

She smiled, bits of broken amber glass glittering behind her eyes. "You did that for me?"

"Let's go make you a star," I said.

Lane Robins (she/her) is a writer living in the American Midwest. Her books include the dark fantasy duology Maledicte *and* Kings & Assassins. *She is a graduate of the Odyssey Writing Workshop. Her short fiction can be found in* Nightmare Magazine, Strange Horizons, Daily Science Fiction, *and forthcoming in* New Myths. *She can be found on a rare occasion on social media, mostly liking posts about books and animals.*

LEON

BRYAN YOUNG

To Sam, every morning felt like a ritual. He'd awaken at three o'clock, long before the sun's warming rays. He'd shower again, bleary eyed, because the stink of the job never really left him. No matter how early he went to bed, three in the morning always felt too early. By three twenty, he'd have brushed his teeth, and the coffee pot would gurgle. The toaster would pop out his pastry, and he would eat as he zipped up his work suit. Then he'd sit on the couch his grandmother left him, where he would lace up his work boots beneath the landscapes full of ducks she'd painted by hand in her retirement.

By three-thirty, he'd be off to work on the tram.

By four, he'd be in his electric disposal truck, heading to his route, daydreaming about being one of those ducks flying through the reeds into a clear blue sky, and that would carry him through as sure as the thermos full of hot coffee and the promise of the sandwich he'd packed in his lunchbox. He wasn't a rich man and couldn't afford the cost to go grab lunch, and they really didn't give him the time to get takeout anyway. Instead, he ate in his truck. Sometimes, he'd sneak his reader in his pocket and read while he ate. Other times, when he could find one, he might bring an ancient paperback with crumbling pages. He liked those the best. The vanilla leather scent of disintegrating paper and book glue was intoxicating, a tonic for the soul.

For the most part, his truck did the work. The computer optimized his route, and he braked expertly in front of each house, letting the arm triangulate the distance to the garbage can so it could snag it, toss the contents into the belly of his whale of a truck, and place it neatly back on the street. Most of the time, he thought the computers could do the job all by themselves, but when things got unusual, he was pleased to be there and felt like he was good at his job. Or at least competent.

Sam enjoyed feeling like he was earning his pay.

Every so often, he'd have to reposition a garbage can that had been turned around or had been wedged too tightly between cars. More rarely, he'd get out to pick up a bag of trash that had fallen from a can. He'd put on his thick work gloves, pick up the refuse and whatever stray trash had been lost, stuff them back into the can, and let the truck finish its work. He'd been told repeatedly he didn't have to do that, but he took pride in what he did and would hate to leave his work undone.

He loved watching the sky change colors; it gave him a sense of satisfaction and of living life. He got to watch each day dawn and see the unique rainbow of colors each morning. Some mornings the sky would fade from black to gray and merge into the bold cobalt of his grandmother's paintings. Other days, purples and pinks would invade before the morning turned bright orange until it settled into a powder blue. Still other mornings, when the clouds were high and rain threatened, the two could mix, and who knew what sort of combinations could be made? Each new color made up the unique DNA of a day, and Sam loved trying to guess which shade would transform into the next right before his eyes.

The sky glistened pink with thin streaks of white cotton candy clouds on that particular morning. There was an unusual object leaning against the garbage can that required his attention. With a sigh, he pulled on his leather work gloves, opened the door and took in the cool spring air, then walked around his truck to the waste container.

Leaning against the can was nothing he expected to see: the torso of an android. It was gray in color, primed, but never painted. It lacked limbs, though the wires were exposed for such hookups. Curiously, it bore no head either. Sam opened the garbage can and found none of the missing extremities, but as he looked around, he saw an ovoid object next to the neighbor's trash can.

Curious, Sam walked to it.

His brow furrowed.

It was the head of a robot.

Its color matched the unpainted torso. It wasn't a model he recognized, and he knew a lot about android models. He'd obsessed over them. He wanted one badly, but knew he could never afford one. How could he on his salary? Androids were for the rich, and by the look of the neighborhood, it looked like these could have been the sort of folks who could have afforded one. But why would they tear it literally limb from limb and throw it away?

It didn't make sense.

Its eyes were unlit, and its nose and ears were merely lines to indicate the shape. The mouth was nothing more than the black box of a vocabulation speaker. It looked to Sam as though it would offer a waveform that looked like a mouth when it spoke, if it were powered up.

Sam looked in and around the nearby cans for other parts but found none. He figured it wouldn't hurt if he took the bits he did find home. If he could cobble together limbs somehow, maybe he'd be able to save on the cost of an android. He'd always thought of himself as a maker, taking a bit after his grandmother.

It could be a significant boon to him. Maybe he'd be able to offload some of his chores and mundane tasks to afford some free time, which was so hard to come by. Maybe he'd finally have just enough time to try to date.

Maybe not, but anything was possible.

He struggled to do it, but eventually Sam managed to lift the torso into the passenger seat of his truck. It was deceptively heavy—much heavier than what he'd have guessed a human torso would weigh. The head was heavier than a human head as well, but its smaller size made it easier to manage.

Sam spent the rest of his route thinking about the possibilities of his own robot and couldn't wait to get it home to tinker.

The whole time he ate lunch in his truck—a peanut-butter and jelly sandwich with the crust cut off like his father used to make him, an apple, a package of fruit snacks, and a stick of string cheese—he stared at the torso, imagining the possibilities. When he finally got off and the sun arced back toward the night, he began his trek home. Sam rigged straps from the warehouse to carry the torso like a backpack. He kept the head in his cooler, making it easier to bear, and rode the streetcar home in his usual silence.

By the time he got home, the sky had begun to change colors, and his eyes had gotten heavy, but he hadn't lost any of his excitement.

After setting his dinner tray to cook in the microwave, Sam went about soldering the connections between the android's torso and head. He knew the thick black and yellow wire was the one that connected the power supply—

at least according to the tutorial videos he watched between ads—so he waited to connect that one last, just in case something unusual happened or he electrocuted himself. He didn't even know if the batteries inside were charged, but better safe than sorry. Usually, androids and other less intelligent appliances could conduct ambient power from the recharge plates like phones and tablets did, but that usually came with a subscription fee, and who knew what the droid was registered as or who to and if they'd been up on any subscriptions? For those who couldn't afford a subscription, there were hardwire outlets or full-contact wireless options.

With the last of the wires connected, Sam tucked everything neatly into place, sealed the head onto the torso, and flipped the switch. He crossed his fingers, hoping the android would come quickly back to life.

There was a flicker of light in the eyes, but they sputtered back into darkness.

The microwave dinged.

After plugging the android into the hardline, Sam retrieved his dinner and sat on the couch to eat while he stared at his new robot on the coffee table, his eyes casting back and forth between the charging cable and robot. The Salisbury steak was rubbery, and since it was more of a hamburger patty in cheap gray gravy, he wasn't sure why they called it Salisbury steak in the first place. It was food and it filled a hole, but better than that, he could afford it—he knew a lot of people who couldn't afford to eat as well as he did, and he couldn't imagine what it would be like to do with less. He already cut things to the quick.

That's why he was so excited about the idea of having a robot.

By the time he chewed through his so-called steak, mushy peas, rehydrated mashed potatoes, and compartment of runny cherry pie, the lights of the robot's eyes lit up, and it tried raising its head.

"Where am I?" it said in a stiff, male voice.

"Hello," Sam greeted it softly. He wasn't used to talking much, other than to his supervisor.

"Repeat inquiry: where am I?"

"Oh, uh, you're at my place."

"Who are you?"

"You can call me Sam. What's your name?"

"I am Leon. You may refer to me as Leon. How did I get here, Sam?"

Sam scratched his head. "Well, it seems like you were taken apart and thrown in the trash."

Leon's eyes dimmed and narrowed. "I see. My deductive reasoning suggests that you found me and reconstructed my body parts."

"What I could find of them."

Sam found Leon's voice fascinating. It had an electronic buzz beneath every syllable but sounded utterly melodious.

"You were unable to retrieve my extremities?"

"That's right. I'll figure something out. I'll try to find some, or I might buy something if I need to. I always wanted a robot."

"I see."

Sam yawned and looked at his watch. "We'll talk again tomorrow, Leon. I need to hit the sack. I gotta get to work in the morning."

"Well met, then, Sam. Until tomorrow."

Tomorrow came, and Sam's routine varied only slightly. He showered, brushed his teeth, made his coffee, and ate his pastry. He laced his boots on the couch beneath his grandmother's duck-filled skies, but he stared at Leon the entire time, and Leon stared back.

"What is your function?" Leon asked.

"Me?" Sam said, his voice still gravelly. He wasn't used to speaking so early in the morning.

"Yes. What is your function?"

"I'm in waste management."

"A garbage collector."

"Well, yeah."

"And that is how you found me in the refuse?"

Sam nodded.

"I see."

"What's your function? You just a regular android? Or do you have a special function? What are you programmed for?"

"I am an experimental learning model. I take input from wherever I can, learn from it, and apply it. It is very simple, really. I take in input, reformulate possible permutations, and create new output to the financial benefit of my owner."

"Like AI?"

"Exactly AI."

"Do you know why someone would tear you apart and leave you in a garbage heap?"

Leon remained mute.

Sam stood. "Think about it and see if you can remember, but I gotta get to work. I'm gonna be late."

A week passed, and Sam's routine varied only slightly. He stopped by the android junk shops on his route home from work, hoping to source limbs suitable for Leon. He wanted to see the android whole again. There was something unnerving about watching him inert on the coffee table, unable to move, with only the view of the ducks above him to keep him company during the long stretches when Sam went to work. The paintings, at least, offered a window to the outside world, artificial though they might be.

Sam sort of wished he had a pet, electronic or otherwise, to keep Leon company during the long work days. At least then he'd have someone or something to talk to, even if it couldn't talk back. "What do you do all day while I'm gone?"

"Process," Leon said as though that were a complete and sufficient answer. Sam wasn't quite sure what it meant, but he didn't push it.

As ever, he was late.

Since Leon had arrived, Sam had a much tougher time staying on task and getting to work on time. He spent so much time researching how he could help Leon, how he could fix him, how he could get him working, and how he could find arms and legs for him, that his routine had started to slip. And the big mystery that plagued him was that he wanted to know why someone would have taken him apart and left him in the garbage in the first place—he was such a well-mannered android.

Three weeks and two limbs later, Sam managed to cobble together a mismatched left side for Leon from parts of children's play-bots. "Unfortunately, I am not programmed to stand on one leg," Leon said.

"I'm sorry. I'm doing the best I can."

"I do not mean to appear ungrateful. It is merely tiresome to be constrained to one spot when my programming would allow me to explore and grow and learn and create on my own."

"I know, buddy," Sam said, truly sorry for the robot he'd come to regard as his friend. "I know."

The grind of daily work took its toll on Sam, and he spent as much time as he could trying to locate suitable, compatible parts. But one night, after an exhaustive search in all the usual shops and on all of the usual sites, he couldn't do it. Sam needed a break—he had to do something else.

Sitting on the couch with Leon staring at him from the coffee table, he sat and watched streaming shows with a sketch pad in his hand. He wasn't a very good artist, but it helped him relax.

"What are you doing?" Leon asked, and Sam couldn't help but think there was an annoyed tinge to his voice.

"Just unwinding."

"There are more efficient ways of unwinding."

"Maybe, but this one works for me. I used to sit and do this with my grandmother. She was an artist, you know." Sam didn't look up at Leon from his sketch pad, tracing the gentle curve of a duck's beak in graphite on the textured sketch paper.

Each line felt good to lay down.

To Sam, there was something exhausting in the thought of getting his sketch pad out and sitting down to actually use it. Even more if he were going to break out water colors or acrylics, but he always found solace there once he knuckled down and did it.

"What are you drawing?"

Sam shrugged. "Just doodling. A duck, I guess."

"There are more efficient ways to capture images of ducks. Photographs, perhaps. Amalgamations of photographs and art could be pieced together into the desired pose and setting."

"I know, but that takes the fun out of it. That's not very relaxing."

Leon remained mute, and Sam couldn't help but feel like something was wrong. Instead of focusing on that silly worry, because really, who could worry about what an android thought, it wasn't even a real thing or person, Sam just focused on the rough lines of his duck. Jagged hash marks filled in for the feathers, and he darkened the outline for its outer edges and filled in the shading on its beak.

It wasn't great.

It wasn't even half as good as his grandmother could do,

but it had fixed something, released some bit of tension inside him, and he felt good enough to sleep and resume the search for Leon's limbs the next day after work.

Sam struck gold the next day. In a droid chop shop he found a right arm and a right leg from an older model butler-bot that seemed to have the same ports and hookups that Leon would take. They were longer than the other limbs Sam had sourced for him, but Sam couldn't imagine Leon would balk. Being mobile was probably more important than having matching limbs. At least, that's how Sam saw it.

"Leon!" Sam called when he came through the door. "Guess what?"

"You have been fired from your unskilled employment and will be unable to help me?" Leon answered.

Sam stepped into the room, confusion on his face. "What? No. Look what I found."

Raising up the arm and leg, one in each hand, Sam grinned. He imagined that if Leon could express pleasure on his face, he would mirror the same smile. The mute look on the android's face told him very little, though his silence told him plenty. The light actuators in Leon's eyes winked on and off, affecting a blink.

They stood staring at each other; Sam waited for some reaction. Then Leon burst to life. "Well, what are you waiting for? Put me back together. Do you think I like living on your coffee table in such squalor?"

Sam shook off the insult, remembering that Leon had been inert for a long time. He'd been torn apart and thrown away. If androids had their feelings hurt—though Sam wasn't sure that was possible—Leon had every right to feel anxious, betrayed, and emotional over his state.

"Of course, of course." Sam went right to work, attaching the arm first. Then, lifting Leon onto the couch and placing the new leg on the coffee table, he attached the leg to the proper connectors in the hip joint of Leon's torso. "I'm so excited to see what you can do now that you're all back together, Leon. I think we're going to be the best of friends, right?"

Leon stood, ignoring the question. And who could blame him? He was busy checking out the functionality of all his fingers. He tried going back and forth, tightening his right fist and releasing it, and testing the abilities of his limbs.

Sam could only imagine how strange it must have felt for him, to be able to move again after so much inertia. "How does it feel?"

"Invigorating."

"I was thinking," Sam said, "why don't you take a day or two for yourself, to get used to your limbs, and then we can figure out your routine and duties around here."

Leon's head whirred around to look directly at Sam, his mute face almost menacing. He blinked again. "Of course," he modulated through his vocabulator.

Sam smiled. "It'll be great having you around."

"I'm sure the pleasure will be all mine," Leon said.

Chuckling, Sam ran his hands through his scruff of wavy hair. "Well, I need to get to bed. Three comes awful fast."

"Awful fast indeed," Leon said, staring at his tightening fist rather than Sam himself.

Lying in bed, head against the pillow, Sam couldn't help but think now that Leon had all his limbs, there was something off with him. Soon enough, though, he surrendered to sleep and dreamed of better times.

The alarm sounded, and Sam's routine remained the same. On the way out the door, the pastry he held still hot from the toaster, Sam waved goodbye to Leon. "See you later, buddy!"

"Indeed."

Sam spent the next two days driving his route with the

same usual care, but found himself distracted and nervous. He worried about the conversation he was going to have with Leon, which was absurd; Leon was an android. He was built to be a tool for helping humans. He wasn't built to have a life of his own; indeed, he couldn't have a life of his own. Computers couldn't do that sort of thing. They could only imitate the things humans thought of as life.

And that was what Sam was having such a hard time reconciling.

Even though Leon wasn't able to feel actual human emotions, he was programmed to imitate the appearance of them. And at the point where someone as sensitive as Sam perceived that, Sam felt all the things he was supposed to in response to those imitated feelings. That was how it was supposed to work. That was why robots had eyes. And mouths. And why they were bipedal and had hands. It wasn't because hands and feet were beneficial, or that two eyes at the front of the face were the most efficient. They were not, as they used to say, "intelligently designed"; they were designed to cause a reaction of emotion in human response, to put them at ease when dealing with artificial persons of artificial intelligence.

In a way, the form of a human body had become intelligent design, but only when humans themselves became gods designing creatures to interact with themselves. And the evolutions they went through were their own learning models, constantly updating their databases and programing.

That afternoon, Sam ate his peanut butter and jelly sandwich and munched on his carrots in silence. He would have waited until he was driving to snack on them in an effort to get home faster, but the dashboard camera would alert the company of his distracted driving, and they'd dock him points. Enough docked points and he'd lose his job. It's why he left the radio off, too. Too much singing could trigger the same response.

It wasn't fair, but it was what he signed up for.

Computers making everything more efficient.

Sam tried humming to himself, tunes he remembered from childhood. Favorites his father used to play for him, or that his mother used to sing. At least that way, his mouth wasn't moving, and he might not get docked.

It helped keep his mind off what he increasingly felt would be a difficult conversation with Leon.

After a thousand houses and a thousand bundles of other people's waste, Leon took his evening walk from the street car stop to his home, bracing himself.

He wondered if this was what parents felt like, asking their children to do chores or to pay rent. He felt like Leon may have already had a hard life and maybe it wasn't fair to ask him to do too much. But then he had to tell himself again that it was just the way he was programmed as a human and the way Leon was designed as a learning, thinking android. There was nothing to be afraid of. Still, Sam found himself twisting his hands together, wondering why Leon had been discarded from his former employ. Aside from the missing limbs that were easy enough to replace, there was nothing really wrong with him.

Sam had searched and searched through the neighborhood looking for the arms and legs but couldn't find them. Had someone tried to prevent this by scattering the body parts elsewhere?

Paranoia. That's all it was.

Sam entered his small home to find the lights off. Not unusual.

"Hello!" he called out. "I'm home."

But there was no response.

Sam navigated to the living room and drew the curtains

on the side wall to let in the last bits of sunlight. He always preferred the sunlight when he could get it. It was cheaper than running the lights, and the beams of the evening sun in spring cut radiant beams across his grandmother's paintings.

He turned to see the couch empty, and the familiar sight of Leon on the coffee table was absent.

Moving through the kitchen, he still saw nothing of Leon. Then, into the bedroom…still no Leon. "Leon?"

No one answered.

Sam looked everywhere. The closet. Under the bed. The bathroom. The dusty little utility room with the furnace and the vacuum. Leon was nowhere to be found.

Finally, back in the living room, Sam scratched his head and turned about in the dwindling sun. He looked up to the wall, looking for a boost of serenity and strength in the final rays cast across his grandmother's paintings.

But they were gone.

"What?"

There were faded spots on the wall where they had hung, but the paintings themselves were gone.

Vanished.

Just like Leon.

Despondent, Sam circled the block on foot, looking for any sign of Leon or the paintings. He checked his own garbage bin. He checked every corner of the yard. He knocked on the doors of neighbors' houses. No one had seen anything. By the time night fell, he knew he had to get to sleep.

Three o'clock came early, and he couldn't lose his job.

After work the next day, he spent his time making signs to post around the neighborhood. He'd taken a few pictures of Leon. Lost robots weren't terribly common. Someone would see him and help him get back to where he was supposed to be. Maybe he just went outside and wandered off and got lost. Maybe Sam had done something wrong with the registration protocol and he was still tied to a previous owner. Anything could have been the issue. But the signs would help. Sam pasted them around the neighborhood, but he also posted them to all the major social media networks, especially those based in the city and the region. Someone would see them.

Then the grind repeated itself. He made his lunch. He went to bed. Three o'clock came. He got to work. He ate quietly in his truck. He came home. He kept looking for Leon and his grandmother's paintings.

Wash, rinse, repeat.

It all ended with an email.

It had a blocked return address, but Sam could only assume it came from Leon. It was a crudely generated version of one of his grandmother's paintings and a laughing emoji.

Sam was heartbroken.

The painting was close enough that he recognized it, but missing the heart and soul his grandmother had put into the original. The detail was missing. The colors were splotched in the wrong places.

None of it made sense.

Sam wanted to punch something.

He regretted ever rebuilding Leon in the first place.

There was something in him that told him the only way he'd get his grandmother's paintings back was either to trace the email back to Leon or to recreate the artwork himself, with his own two hands. He thought tracking Leon would be easier, so he set to work doing that.

After a week of trying, he received a second email with another twisted facsimile of another of his grandmother's paintings and a photograph of one of Leon's hands, crudely making a gesture with his middle finger.

Doubling his efforts to find the android, Sam still came up with nothing. The android was a ghost. A program. A system. Even if Leon still had the paintings, he'd taken their worth and twisted them into something else.

The only remaining choice was for Sam to recreate them until Leon decided to return the originals on his own. If Sam just ignored him, if he didn't give him the attention he wanted, perhaps he would just give them back of his own volition. Maybe it would work, maybe it wouldn't, but Sam would try.

After work the next day, he sat on the couch and pulled out the sketch pads and art supplies. The canvases and the palettes, the brushes and the paint cups, the watercolors and the acrylics.

He was going to find the soul of his grandmother.

The goddamned robot wasn't going to help.

He couldn't.

Sam was going to have to learn how to do it the hard way.

Mixing the paint with the brush, starting with the color of the cobalt sky, Sam started to feel like his grandmother might've felt, a connection to her he didn't know could exist. Then, putting brush to canvas, his soul met hers, and they danced together in color from beyond the grave.

Sam scoffed.

He'd like to see Leon do that.

Bryan Young (he/they) works across many different media. His work as a writer and producer has been called "filmmaking gold" by The New York Times. *He's also published comic books with Slave Labor Graphics and Image Comics. He's been a regular contributor for the* Huffington Post, *StarWars.com,* Star Wars Insider *magazine, SYFY, /Film, and was the founder and editor in chief of the geek news and review site* Big Shiny Robot! *In 2014, he wrote the critically acclaimed history book,* A Children's Illustrated History of Presidential Assassination. *He co-authored* Robotech: The Macross Saga RPG *and has written five books in the BattleTech Universe:* Honor's Gauntlet, A Question of Survival, Fox Tales, Without Question, *and the forthcoming* VoidBreaker. *His latest non-fiction tie-in book,* The Big Bang Theory Book of Lists *is a #1 Bestseller. His work has won two Diamond Quill awards, and in 2023 he was named Writer of the Year by the League of Utah Writers. He teaches writing for* Writer's Digest, Script Magazine, *and at the University of Utah. Follow him across social media @swankmotron or visit swankmotron.com*

LIBBY'S RED ROVER

MARY JO RABE

Libby ran her fingers through her short, light brown hair and hummed contentedly though, as always, off-key. She stretched her leggy frame out on the blue-cushioned recliner with its communicator hovering at eye level, waiting for her commands. The library and research center in the Robinson habitat was her workplace, yet her favorite place to relax. Here was where she flourished, searching for new data.

The air in the room with its faint scent of cinnamon was the cleanest on Mars, something Libby had insisted on when she was recruited as colony librarian. Her sensitive nose ached in the other rooms when she detected the annoying stench of peroxide from the caustic dust in the air.

It hadn't been cheap to put the library on the surface of Mars. The local plastics factory created special protective, slick, completely dustproof windows so that the library had a three hundred and sixty degree panoramic view that stretched to Pavonis Mons.

Her users felt like they were free, out on the surface instead of trapped in habitat containers. They appreciated the ambience as much as they profited from her competent help.

Librarians love nothing more than helping their users acquire the knowledge they need. Libby herself was an information junkie. She never had the feeling that she had enough data. She also liked to see this data put to good use. She updated the databases from Earth regularly, but occasionally the speed of transmission and position of the planets forced a temporary delay.

As much as Libby enjoyed finding information, helping the nice people in the colony was even more fulfilling, more or less frosting on the cake. Therefore, it was only logical for her to expand her searches, accessing all the information available in the colony as well as back on Earth. Technically, she had no right to most of the colony information, which was why she had invited Sheriff Long to the library that evening.

The doorbell played her favorite Sousa march, and she went to the door. "Come in, Sheriff," she said as she opened the door. Sheriff Curtis Long was a bear of a man, well over two meters tall and sturdily built, the only person in the colony who towered over Libby who herself boasted a proud one point eight meters, though on a thinner frame.

"Why, thank you, ma'am," Sheriff Long said, his remaining blond hair neatly combed over his balding head. He looked around expectantly. He wasn't what anyone would call an intellectual, but he was the most observant colonist Libby ever encountered.

Libby gestured to the larger recliner chair, the one she was sure could manage the mass of Sheriff Long. "I have you to thank for coming," she said. "I could use your advice."

Sheriff Long sank into the chair, looked over at her as she also sat down, and said, "Any time I can help. I always help good people, and you are one of the good people here."

"I don't know if that's completely true," Libby began, "but I also like to help the good people." She gazed briefly at her communicator.

"There aren't just good people here on Mars," Sheriff Long told her sternly. "Some people get mad when I say that, but it's true. Keeping the good people here safe is up to me and the judge. I try to catch the criminals and protect the innocent, but I don't always succeed. And sometimes the judge won't let me protect anyone because he says I don't have enough proof. That makes me mad."

Libby had of course already started gathering information about the colonists, though not exactly legally. She knew, for example, that Sheriff Long's expert instincts came from his working experience back on Earth. He had been a bodyguard and "enforcer" for a fairly notorious group of gangsters.

They had been good to him, had rescued him from a terrible family situation as a child, and he had been loyal to them, somehow defining them for himself as good people.

Out of gratitude, his associates had bought him his ticket to Mars when things got a little messy and the authorities were considering offering him immunity in exchange for information. The billionaire who was subsidizing the settlement on Mars recognized his talents and made him the law enforcer for the colony.

"You know, librarians are pretty good at searching for information," Libby began. "I think I could help the colonists better if I knew more about everyone, if I had an idea who the good people and who the bad people were. For example, if I could read all the sheriff's and judge's records."

"I can use all the help I can get," Sheriff Long said. "I won't stand in your way. I'll put you in the colony records as my deputy. Make use of any information you can get access to.

Like I said, you're one of the good people, and we good people have to stick together."

"Thank you," Libby said as she stood up. "I won't disappoint you. Let's go enjoy the view of the surface. Can I get you some refreshments?" And so, they moved to the south window where Libby encouraged Sheriff Long to tell her about his current cases, which criminals he wished he could catch, and which criminals he wished the judge had agreed were guilty.

The next day, Libby skimmed through the information Sheriff Long had given an override for her to access.

She decided to go shopping for a surface vehicle after her shift in the library ended. The bureaucrats had finally allowed independent and unsupervised travel on Mars some months ago. So, of course, the rent-a-rovers were immediately booked for weeks at a time.

Gerhard Michaels, an ambitious though otherwise less than commendable entrepreneur, had seen this development coming, or, more likely, had influenced it. The mayor of the Mars colony did decide to relax the rules at precisely the time Mr. Michaels had enough rovers ready for sale.

Libby called to ask about buying a rover both for business and private purposes, but before she got more than a few words out, an aggressive advertising pitch blasted through her communicator. Gerhard Michaels would be overjoyed to reserve a rover for her and give her a good deal on the price, or at least what he called a good deal. And, of course, she could have her dream rover right away.

Libby told him she would come late that afternoon.

Libby showed up at the tunnel entrance to the rover store shortly before closing time. Gerhard Michaels was one of the few businessmen who invested in a surface-level store with transparent brick walls on two sides. According to his colony-wide advertising, these transparent walls were necessary to showcase his products adequately. The customers should be able to imagine driving on the surface when they chose their rovers.

Libby opened the door, and Mr. Michaels, a thin, short, bald man, forced a brief smile across his thin lips and motioned for her to come in. As she walked into the showroom, she noticed oversized indicators on the walls that seemed to claim optimal radiation and air pressure levels. Libby made a note to herself to check her sources to see if this in fact was true. The stench of peroxide already gave her a headache.

"Here are a few of my rovers," Mr. Michaels said as he pointed his bony hand to the ten vehicles parked along the transparent walls. "I'm sure you will find one that fits your expectations."

The vehicles all looked like enclosed dune buggies with oversized wheels, air tanks along the sides, and solar panels and satellite dishes on the roofs. The rovers looked light and fragile, like most of the machinery on Mars. They were two-person vehicles, with front seats and the backs filled with useful tools, or so Mr. Michaels had advertised. Libby immediately felt drawn to the dark red one at the end of the row.

"I assume the vehicles all have the same specifications," she said.

"Absolutely," he replied. "They are more or less indestructible and can manage speeds of more than a hundred kilometers per hour."

"Isn't that much too fast for safe travel on the surface?" she asked.

"That depends on the skills of the driver," he said with a smirk. "Beginners should drive much more slowly."

"Tell me about this vehicle," Libby said, pointing to the dark red one. She looked down at Mr. Michaels to catch his eye, as he was significantly shorter than she was.

He walked around the rover proudly, boasting about its sturdiness, its speed, its ease of use. "Look at this," he said, opening the hatch to the back. "Chains, pulleys, heavy-duty plastic ropes, extra oxygen tanks, a generator, a second communicator, plus a dolly with indestructible, solid plastic wheels. You'll be able to rescue yourself no matter what kind of problem you might have while exploring the surface, even if rare circumstances prevent your calling for help. I'll of course download a current map into the navigator."

"Maps are something I can research for myself," Libby said smiling. "I'll take it," she said, pointing at the dark red vehicle. "Can we take care of the formalities right away? Give me the data, and I'll transfer the Martian credits to your store's account." She held up her communicator.

"Excellent," Mr. Michaels said, handing her a sheet of plastic paper, which she used to enter information into her communicator.

He peered at his smaller communicator, which he then handed to her. "And here you can see that I have registered ownership, insurance, parking space rental in the new private rover garage, and everything else. The information should appear in your records."

Libby smiled. "When would you be willing to take the rover out for a trial run with me? I need to know if there are any tricks to driving it before I make any mistakes." She tried to look needy and slightly helpless, despite the fact that this was usually an exercise in futility considering her height.

Mr. Michaels's face darkened for a nanosecond as he frowned. "That's really not necessary," he said. "Anyone can drive one of these rovers; they're like toys. No one has ever had trouble with them, and you have a personal hotline connection built in that will give you any advice you need. I include a one hundred percent guarantee on all repairs and returns for a Martian year."

"The hotline can't work if communication is down, like in a dust storm," Libby interrupted sweetly. "I'm sorry. If you can't accompany me on a test drive, I don't know if I should buy the rover. Maybe I should cancel my payments." Libby looked at her communicator.

At that point, Mr. Michaels managed to force a salesman's smile across his face. "I'm sure you'll have no trouble," he said. "In fact, I'm so sure that I promise I'll come and help you myself during the first year. Just call me."

Libby stared at her communicator and moved her fingers toward the keys. "No, you have to come with me on a test drive. If you refuse, I have to wonder if you are sufficiently reliable."

Mr. Michaels coughed and rolled his eyes. "Naturally, if you feel you need company on your first trip, I'd be happy to go with you," he said sullenly. "Ordinarily, I would send one of my associates, but they have all left for the day. I was getting ready to close up shop, but we can drive the rover first." He didn't look at all happy, but seemed grudgingly willing, perhaps because of the potential profit he would make from the sale. "I'll get my surface suit out of my office; you can use one of the customer suits in the lockers."

That was what Libby had counted on with her precise scheduling. For one brief second she wondered if she should forget the whole rover business. If she kept the rover afterwards, she would have to explain why she wanted one in the first place. Nevertheless, that would be simpler than the alternative. After all, she could always develop a sudden yearning for solitary exploration of the planet's surface. She could say that she wanted the possibilities this rover had to offer, or that she wanted to roam freely without having to wait for a rent-a-rover to be available.

"Wonderful," she said. "Where are the lockers? I'm ready to go."

Customer surface suits were in lockers next to the exit gate. All the surface suits were state-of-the-art, people-sized habitats with redundant supplies of oxygen, excellent self-sealing mechanisms, and powerful communicators built into the helmets.

The communications satellites somewhere above the dusty Martian sky were supposed to ensure that no one was ever incommunicado. They did a good job, except of course during dust storms. However, people protected by the newest surface suits could really survive any accident in one of them. Libby had done her research. Nothing should go wrong.

She maneuvered herself into the largest surface suit, adapted it to her needs, tried stretching and running, and then carried the helmet over to her new rover. It wasn't locked, and she was able to prepare for the drive.

When Mr. Michaels returned, they both climbed into the rover and put on their helmets, a safety requirement for any exit onto the Martian surface. After Mr. Michaels pointed toward the gate, Libby drove carefully into the exit container, Mr. Michaels pressed his remote control which sealed the inside door and opened the outside one, and Libby drove out onto the surface.

Driving on the surface of Mars at night was magnificent. The sky was black and deep. Phobos and Deimos seemed to buzz by overhead. Libby could see the tiny blue dot of Earth and had the feeling that she was seeing the present and the future quite clearly.

They drove for at least an hour, taking a route Libby had researched. Along the way, she experimented with all kinds of speeds and risky maneuvers, none of which seemed to bother Mr. Michaels noticeably. The rover had no trouble remaining upright and mobile, no matter what she did. She discovered that she loved driving. She couldn't tell what Mr.

Michaels thought; he was silent, and she couldn't see his face that well through the two helmets.

Finally, Libby drove the rover to the deep crevice that she discovered while researching her test drive route. "Can we test the integrity of the vehicle?" she asked. "If my suit malfunctions, I have to know that I'll be safe in my rover."

Mr. Michaels shook his head impatiently and took off his helmet, "Take off your helmet," he said. "You can see for yourself that the interior of this rover maintains perfect survival conditions. Then maybe we can drive back. You really didn't need any help with this magnificent vehicle."

Libby took off her helmet and pressed the button on the remote in her pocket that controlled contact with the communications satellite. "Yes," she said, "the rover is perfect. All it needs is a competent driver. Too bad you weren't able to drive yours without killing that little boy."

"Didn't happen," Mr. Michaels said coldly. "The hysterical parents and the corrupt sheriff tried to pin that on me. Fortunately, the judge agreed that there wasn't enough proof."

"Because you dumped the rover and the child into a crevice far from the habitat," Libby said.

"I don't have time for this," Mr. Michaels said. "Drive back." He pulled out his personal communicator, and Libby shot it in its center and Mr. Michaels in his head, in that order. Pistols were illegal on Mars, of course, but with a little research she had been able to purchase a tiny one from a source on Mars that Sheriff Long pointed her to. The pistol, smaller than her hand, fit well in one of the surface suit pockets.

There was quite a bit of work to do. She put her helmet back on and pulled the cards and keys out of his pockets. Next, she pulled the surface suit off the deceased Mr. Michaels so that she could return it to the rover shop. Fortunately, neither it nor the helmet had acquired any messy blood or body tissue. The equipment in the back of the rover proved excellent for lifting and rolling the body into the crevice, where he was unlikely to be found.

The drive back was even more pleasant than the drive to the crevice. She would leave it to the sheriff to decide if and when to inform the parents that justice had been served, late but better than not at all.

She returned to the rover shop, brought Mr. Michaels's surface suit into his office, returned her suit to the customer locker, locked up the shop, and left with the keys and cards. She could always throw them into another crevice on her next drive around the planet.

Naturally, she wasn't an expert assassin and probably only did an amateur job of cleaning up the evidence. Sheriff Long had assured her that he would register Gerhard Michaels as yet another missing person if she was successful in her endeavors. There would be plenty of volunteers eager to take over the rover store.

Libby doubted that anyone would ever look for that bastard anyway. The dust storm forecast for later that evening would cover much of the evidence nicely. She drove her rover back to the garage, used the rover-wash facilities to remove all impurities, and patted it contentedly as she left.

It was time to return to the obligations of her day job. There would probably be multiple research requests waiting in her library inbox. It was important to maintain a balance: first the library work, and afterwards, when she had time, the moonlighting activity.

Dr. (Dirty) Gertie Grob, who was head of personnel for the colony, for example, was responsible for numerous people returning to Earth because they couldn't stand her tirades. Others suffered clinical depression due to how the witch treated them. Many engineers and researchers expressed their desperation because of her meddling and micro-managing. Unfortunately, she had her political protectors back on Earth. The judge said there was no regulation against unkind behavior in the colony's constitution.

Interestingly enough, Dirty Gertie regularly strolled around the outside of the habitat buildings to find aesthetic untidiness that displeased her, which she could then insist someone repair immediately. It would be unfortunate if the breathing and communicating mechanisms in her surface suit were compromised while she was on one of those hikes.

Then there was the despicable duo Bud and Beavis who had bullied that child with Down syndrome and tricked him into exiting the habitat without a surface suit. The judge said the evidence was insufficient. Sheriff Long found it overwhelming. Libby would have to come up with a more creative solution for those teenage criminals. Perhaps she would invite them to race her rover over a stretch of her choice.

So much to do, but now she had a rover to help her with necessary transports. This could definitely be the beginning of a beautiful friendship between a woman's research skills and her trusty red rover.

MARY JO RABE grew up on a farm in eastern Iowa, got degrees from Michigan State University in German and math and the University of Wisconsin-Milwaukee in library science. She worked in the library of the chancery office of the Archdiocese of Freiburg, Germany, for forty-one years and lives with her husband in Titisee-Neustadt, Germany.

She electronically published "Blue Sunset," inspired by Spoon River Anthology *and* The Martian Chronicles *and has had stories published in* Fiction River, Pulphouse, Penumbric Speculative Fiction, Alien Dimensions, 4 Star Stories, Fabula

Argentea, Crunchy with Chocolate, The Lorelei Signal, The Lost Librarian's Grave, Whispers from the Universe, Draw Down the Moon, Mysterious Christmas, Particular Passages, Mystery Tribune, The Dark City Crime & Mystery Magazine, Dark Horses, Black Sheep, Möbius Blvd, Wyldblood Magazine, Luna Station Quarterly, Amazing Stories, ResAliens, Dark Dead Things, Epic Echoes, A Flight of Dragons, One-Way-Ticket to Epsilon Eridani *(Starry Eyed Press)*, Cutter's Final Cut Book 3 – Explorers, Boundary Shock Quarterly Book 19 – Sea Stories, Boundary Shock Quarterly Book 28 – SF Horror, The Pink Hydra, Blaze Ward Presents Book 6 – Small Gods, Blaze Ward Presents Book 5 – Crime and…, Blaze Ward Presents Issue 4 – Cloak and Dagger, Space Opera Mashup, Rocketpack Adventures, Future Earth Tech Earth Colonies, A Stitch in Spacetime, Short Story Town, Alternate Hilarities, *and other magazines and anthologies.*

For occasional musings about her short stories, including where they can be found, check out her blog at

https://maryjorabe.wordpress.com/ She indulges in sporadic activity on Facebook; you can find her at facebook.com/rabemj

MADAM ZOMALSKI AND THE MANTIS CLAW

H.K. SLADE

Discreetly as possible, I parted the many bangles and beaded bracelets on my forearm to steal a glance at my com rig. Mrs. Fonda's payment went through. I contained my smile and lay a comforting hand on the old lady's hunched shoulder.

"You've done a good thing tonight, my child," I said, bestowing the affirmation with the solemnity of a benediction. "Jerry's spirit is at peace now."

The old woman nodded, barely keeping the tears in her eyes. "Thank you, Madam Zomalski. Thank you." Briskly but not brusquely, I guided Mrs. Fonda to and through the front door before she could master her emotions enough to respond further.

What I do isn't grifting, not in any sense. I help people find what they need. It takes work and skill, and to my way of thinking, the payment is fair compensation for the comfort or entertainment I provide. Ultimately, Mrs. Fonda had received all that was possible for a medium like Madam Zomalski to provide. Prolonging the session wouldn't do anyone any good.

I stood in the doorway watching the old woman cross the street and disappear into the flow of foot traffic. Early August nights in Savannah aren't the ordeals the days are, but the steaming blanket of humidity still hit me like a physical wave. As soon as the old woman was clear, I retreated into the sanctuary of my tiny storefront waiting room and sealed the door against the heat and stink and the myriad of buzzing, biting insects.

The heat was nothing new to me, not in this life or my last. Once upon a time I was plain-old Brittany Siegel of Jacksonville, Florida, a name no one in the state of Georgia had ever heard of. But after three years in the lovely Gadsden Correctional Institution, I emerged a different woman: wiser, subtler, more spiritual. My time inside taught me that scamming the big boys was a sucker's game. By the 2080s, it wasn't the governments—and certainly not the little people— who controlled all the resources. It was the corporations, and they were vengeful on a biblical level. It's almost as if the powerful were waiting for someone to make a play for their money just so they could burn them to the ground.

Which was exactly what happened to me. But from Brittany Siegel's ashes rose Madam Zomalski, a kindly clairvoyant who invariably gave hopeful predictions to the tourists who wandered into her shop and closure to those who sought her out to contact their belated relatives. All for a modest price.

Tapping my com rig, the time appeared in the corner of my vision. I had grown tired earlier than usual. At 9:18 p.m. I went to the window to switch off the sign, a pink and blue neon emulator programmed to display a stylistic eye. It was an expensive unit. It even hummed slightly, just the way real neon did.

I heard the door open, and a wave of damp heat washed

over the room. I looked over my shoulder, already prepping a polite excuse, but then I caught sight of him.

The man was easily six feet tall. His suit said money, and his shoes and watch repeated it with emphasis. He had the square bone structure of one of the new-wave Okinawan holostars, the ones who seemed intent on bringing back "refined masculinity." The look was only slightly spoiled by some very faint scarring around his left eye. The repair work had been expensive. Back in Gadsden, I had seen enough scars that I could spot the difference.

My hand hovered over the sign's switch, but my decision was already made.

"Why have the spirits brought you to this place, my child?" I asked, facing the newcomer and resettling my shawl over my shoulders. "How may Madam Zomalski assist you on your journey?"

The programs I keep running on my com rig began to churn through oceans of public data. Facial recognition software is theoretically still illegal, but in the three years I'd been in Savannah and the four before that in Shreveport, I'd never had a problem.

"It's my father," the man said. His voice was completely clean, not a drip nor a drop of an accent. "He passed away fourteen years ago. We parted on bad terms. I need to speak to him. I've been told by friends that you can help."

"Your friends are wise. Yes, Madam Zomalski may be able to help. I am familiar with the veil between this life and the next. There are no guarantees, mind you. There are too many variables. Capricious spirits, clouded emotions...but if there is a way, I can help you find it."

"Excellent," he said. "Now is good."

My com rig alerted me that the search was complete, and the results appeared at the lower left corner of my vision. *Nothing.* I'd never seen that happen before. Everyone had a digital footprint, even me, and I'd paid good money to obscure my tracks. A voice in the back of my head told me to send the man away. I trust that voice. It's kept me alive, and the last time I ignored it had been the day they'd busted me for insurance fraud.

I forced a polite smile. "Preparation is the key to success in these matters. We will need a focus to have the best chance to contact this spirit, something unique and personal to the departed, such as a piece of jewelry or a family heirloom. With such an exceptionally long time removed from this plane, it's even more essential. Perhaps you could return tomorrow or next week with something?"

The man drew a thick fold of money from his breast pocket. Actual paper money.

I hadn't seen a government bill in twenty years. No one carried cash, not even the hyper-rich, but there it was. The bills were pinned together by a gold money clip set with a heavy turquoise nugget. The man kept the cash and handed the clip to me. The thing must have weighed half a pound and was probably worth more than old Mrs. Fonda's entire bank account. The voice in my head continued to object, but it seemed to be coming from farther and farther away. Without the dossier I was used to working from, I'd have to cold read the man, but that was still in my wheelhouse.

"Very well, my child," I said with the exaggerated pronunciation I affect when I need to sell the part. "What is your name?"

"Jason Sato," he said. "My father was Abe Sato."

"Jason, it is important that we are not interrupted and that our sanctum remains unspoiled. There is a restroom to your right. Please tend to any needs you have and make sure to wash your hands and face thoroughly. When you are ready and your mind and body are without distraction, you may enter."

Without waiting for a reply, I flowed through the beaded curtain with practiced grace. I had a minute, maybe two, to try and cobble together a story. Within seconds, my com rig began feeding me obituaries from the relevant timeframe. I struck paydirt with the second return: *Abraham Allen Sato of Seattle, Washington. Born July 23rd, 2008. Died November 16th, 2074 from liver cancer.*

That was interesting. The liver was the easiest thing to clone, so for him to die like that at sixty-six meant he was either poor, an alcoholic, or stubborn enough to refuse modern medicine. I ran a picture search and arrayed the images across the breadth of my vision, oldest to newest. Almost immediately, I had my answer.

Younger Abraham Sato had been every bit as handsome as his son. In fact, they were so similar in appearance that I might not have been able to tell them apart if not for the scars. All that changed as I worked my way from left to right and the pictures became more and more recent. By the late 2060s, things were obvious. The bloodshot eyes, the drooping lip, the bulbus nose shot through with spider veins…the drink had done it for the elder Sato.

I relaxed. I'd done more of these then I can remember. There is always bad blood when someone drinks themself to death, and the survivors usually only need to convey an apology for losing their temper or not being there at the end. I placed the money clip in the center of the table beneath the room's only lamp and flicked through the family records. I dug up something on an uncle, but nothing for Jason or his mother. Before I could drill down any further, I heard the latch on the front door cycle shut with a sharp snap. There was no buzzing from the sign, either. Someone had switched it off.

Jason Sato swept the beaded curtain to one side and filled the threshold as if he owned the place.

"My child," I said, only keeping the unease out of my voice by dint of my many years of practice. "Madam Zomalski prefers to leave the building open. It invites the spirits in and encourages their communication."

The man let the beads drop, and the curtain swung closed with an incongruous tinkle. "I understood you to say that we shouldn't be interrupted."

The hairs stood up on the back of my neck and the voice in my head, so faint only moments earlier, screamed for me to get away from this man. I told myself to stay calm. I'd had unstable clients before. I'd planned for this contingency and was paid up with the local syndicate.

Using the Tightwire function on my ocular implants, I sent a prepared message to Davante, my contact with the Gwinnett Street Posse. It bounced back, un-transmitted. Heartbeat pounding in my chest, I resent it.

Then my entire com rig system shut down.

I went for the stunner I kept beneath the table, but the man's hand shot out and caught mine, pinning it. His fingers were strong and cold, too cold to be alive—not human at all, but high quality synthskin. I looked up, having passed the point of trying to hide my worry.

With the lighting focused on the table, Jason Sato's features were mostly lost in shadows, but there was an iridescent emerald glow on the left side of his face. It took a few moments to work out, but I eventually realized that the man's damaged eye was a cybernetic replacement. The scars made sense. I tried to pull back, but his grip tightened until it verged on painful. We stayed like that, the two of us, staring silently at each other. Then the sleeve of his jacket peeled back like molting skin, and a spindly, spider-like appendage unfolded from his exposed forearm with a deliberate slowness that was far more terrifying than the lightning-quick move he'd made to snatch my hand.

"Do you know what this is?" he asked in his unnaturally neutral voice.

I did. I'd never seen one in real life, but that's because I didn't run in those circles even when I'd been a bona fide criminal. But on the shadow nets, I'd seen holos of mangled bodies, swollen and battered but surprisingly bloodless. Aware that he was waiting for an answer and understanding the consequences of offending such a man, I nodded rapidly.

He took a seat at the table but did not let me go. "I want to hear you say it. Aloud."

I swallowed, and my throat fought against me. "It's a mantis claw."

The folded appendage was light weight, a quality not particularly useful in a fight, but mass is only a part of the equation. When triggered, the small round hammer on the device would lash out with such velocity that it could break the sound barrier. Whatever the user held would be smashed to splinters. Fingers. Arms. Skulls. Spines.

It was the tool of choice for enforcers in the more elite criminal organizations. There were much, much more efficient ways to eliminate a problem, but a tool like that wasn't about efficiency. It was meant to send a message.

Jason Sato nodded slowly, apparently satisfied by my response.

"I need to speak to my father. Tonight. I've been told you're the best around at what you do, so you are going to help me have that conversation, and then you are going to forget everything. What I ask. What he answers. My face. Everything. If you fail in any way, I will stay here until the sun comes up, and I will spend that time hurting you. Are we clear?"

In spite of the countless times over the years that I'd talked my way out of a sticky situation, I couldn't keep my voice from quavering. "M-madam Zomalski does not control the spirits, my child. I-I'm a servant, and the most I can do is ask."

The man leaned in, the green in his artificial eye glittering in the table light. "Then ask well. Ask like your life depends on an answer."

I was in it now. No one was coming to save me. I drew a deep, stuttering breath, and on the exhale settled back into character. There was no way out except straight through.

"We shall form a circle. It would be better with others, but we will make do. Madam Zomalski has done this before."

I wanted nothing more than to pull my hand from Jason Sato's grip, yet I turned my palm over and took the cybernetic hand in mine. I rested the other hand lightly on the money clip that was still in the center of the table. The man looked at me, emotionless but clearly expecting instructions to be forthcoming.

"Complete the circle, my child," I said, my voice once again settled. He placed his free hand on the clip, fingertips brushing mine. There was enough warmth there that I knew that hand at least was real. He was meched out, but not a full borg.

Though I regularly employed all the modern tricks of my trade, my education in the craft had been heavy on the classics. I knew I'd have to do this one the old-fashioned way. Slipping off my shoes, I sought out the array of manual switches beneath the table. I used my toe to trigger the one that would lower the temperature in the room and almost imperceptibly dim the single lamp above us.

"Close your eyes, Jason Sato. Hold a specific memory of your father in your mind. I warn you, it must be powerful and clear to draw his spirit's attention from across the vastness of time."

The man nodded tersely, but didn't speak.

This won't do, I thought. "Do not be coy or shy. Do you have it? Is it clear in your mind?"

"I do," he said, his eyes still closed. "I am young, too young to speak. He's in a garden picking vegetables. The old man doesn't have a basket, so he pulls the hem of his T-shirt out and uses the fabric to hold the vegetables. The sun is behind him, and he looks like he has a halo. Everything smells of tomatoes and municipal water."

I raised my voice and dropped the pitch. "Abraham Sato, I call to thee. Your son calls to thee. We invite you into our sanctum."

I let that moment hang in the air. It's a rookie mistake to rush these things. If the answers come too easily, the client's doubts take longer to assuage. As much as I wanted to give the man exactly what he asked for and be done with him, I was walking a knife's edge. If I succeeded, he might kill me. If I failed, he definitely would. But if he even suspected I was scamming him, I knew I would spend the rest of my short life in excruciating pain.

"Abraham Sato," I called again, and this time, I put a little vibrato in my voice. "We beseech thee. Your progeny calls to you. Come to our sanctum that we may know your will."

Next came the dangerous part. It was a gamble, a high stakes one, but I had to go with my instincts, and my instincts were telling me I needed to draw him deeper into the process.

"My child," I said in a husky whisper, "your father is not responding. Is there another memory that you can summon? Something stronger?"

His grip tightened incrementally. I clamped my jaw but didn't try to pull my hand free. A hard frown creased his features and his eyebrows drew tightly together, but still he kept his eyes closed.

"We are at the pier," he began, and for the first time, there was emotion in his voice: pain or anger, something bitter. "It's night, and he's fishing and smoking, and I'm holding his beer. One of his biker buddies says something to him, a white guy with curly red hair and freckles. My father flicks the joint into the man's face. They're about to fight, but then the man backs down and leaves. My father laughs so hard he cries. It was the only time I ever saw tears in his eyes."

The memory was good, more data for the algorithm, but I was starting to question the wisdom of making this man relive such things. It simply *could not* put him in a forgiving mood, and that's where I needed him to be. Though I'd have liked to have gone at least one level deeper before the turn, I decided not to press my luck.

"Abraham Sato," I called for a third time. "We mean thee no harm. You will find no iron or salt here, but we demand your presence. For your family, for your memory, for the blood of your blood, you will reveal yourself. Madam Zomalski commands it!"

Just as my voice reached its crescendo, I pressed the switch to send the light flickering. Just as it had been programmed to, the ultra-tone resonance generator in the crawlspace began to vibrate the floorboards beneath us.

"He is here," I gasped. Across the table, Jason Sato's breathing sped, and his jaw tightened. I could see the hook was set, but I avoided congratulating myself; there were still so very many ways to fail.

"Is it my father? Are you sure?"

The next step was to personalize the experience. Scent was always a powerful tool. Though I could load targeted odors if I had prep time, I always left the system set up with a few boilerplate options: pine forests, city smog, popcorn, and cotton candy. Nothing seemed to fit the situation exactly. There was a sulfur stench that I could make work, but I was out of practice, and the trigger was too close to the amalgam of perfumes. I could play the array like organ pedals, but mistakes happened. I calculated the risk wasn't worth it and just raised the room's temperature and stopped the light from flickering.

"There is so much anger," I whispered, doing my very best to feign awe. "It is dangerous to host his spirit. We must remain calm and accept that the convergence will be brief."

"Is it my father?" Jason Sato repeated, and this time there was an edge in his voice.

"Spirit, we seek the shade of Abraham Sato. Are you with us?"

The tap of a switch produced a sharp rap in the ceiling directly above him, and then the creaking of a floorboard. Jason Sato stiffened in his seat, and his eyes slowly opened.

It was terrifying.

I felt a bead of sweat run down my scalp as the temperature in the room rose. I'd rushed things, damn it, and now all I could do was try and recover. Not daring to look down at the mantis claw, I lifted my eyes to the ceiling and called to the spirit world, "I am but a vessel through which you may once again connect with the corporeal plane. There is business unfinished, answers owed. Madam Zomalski will help you meet these obligations that you might journey on to your rest. Will you answer our questions, Abraham Sato?"

Another single knock, this time from the wall behind me, and an accompanying flicker of the light.

I dropped my voice even lower and met Jason Sato's eyes. It was like looking into a deep, empty pit. "Your father is with us," I told him, "but he is a shadow of who you once knew. Say your piece in a loud, clear voice. Ask what you need to know; yes or no questions are best. Be warned that more complex answers will require interpretation."

"He can see me?"

"Yes, though it is like looking through a thin curtain."

His gaze roamed the room. His lips drew tight. Finally, he found a point in a corner of the ceiling, and his eyes locked in like he was seeing a familiar face. I'd been meticulous in setting up the space and, with the light dimmed as it was, knew for a fact that someone sitting in that chair wouldn't be able to see anything but shadows outside the table. But his voice relaxed, and his gaze went soft, and he spoke as if talking to someone he knew. "I turned out alright, old man. I need you to know that I'm as tough as the bikers and bouncers you used to hang out with when you were my age. Tougher. Tough enough to admit my mistakes."

It was an odd opening statement, but not unprecedented. I knew enough to sit quietly. Jason Sato was working up to something, but he was having to take a running start at it.

"Remember that night in '63 when Jachai Brookstone got us into the Rip Tide with peeled IDs? I was porting with a college girl, and Jachai was taking hits of shine when you showed up at the bar, just walked right in and sat down with us. We both thought we were up to our necks in shit."

He paused, a ghost of a smile on his lips. He really was holostar handsome. While he was looking to the memory of his father, I stole a glance at the mantis claw that hovered over my arm like my own personal Sword of Damocles. It wouldn't do to forget how precarious my situation was.

"I wish I had that night to do over again," he continued. "If I was who I am now, I would have ordered you a beer and introduced you to the server, come up with some dumb joke you could have pretended to laugh at just to help you relax. I would have let you be one of the guys and not my old man, even if it was just for a few hours. But I didn't do any of that. I was too young and dumb and angry to see beyond my own nose. No, I wasn't mean, not like you and your buddies. I was worse. I just ignored you until you left."

He shook his head slowly. "I wish I had that one to do over."

I shut down the heat and sent a creak through the floorboard, then I waited a few beats. When the room was entirely still, I triggered the concave acoustic panels hidden in the walls and ceiling. It cost a fortune to install, but it was the pièce de résistance. Anyone sitting in Jason Sato's seat would hear a voice that seemed to come from everywhere and nowhere. It was most effective when I had time to customize it, but even without my com rig to control it, the system would still play gibberish. I figured I could make it work.

"I sense regret," I said gently. "The spirit also wishes things were different. He…he asks…he asks about your anger. He is confused by it. He wishes to make things whole between you two."

Jason Sato's face hardened so quickly it was as if it had turned to stone. "Why was I so angry?" he growled, any hint of wistfulness or regret burned from his voice. "You can't be serious. You don't remember how all those nights you'd come home from work and start right in on the booze and cannie? You didn't know what an angry drunk you were?"

A frown broke the stern mask. "No," he said, "you always had mom to compare yourself to. You probably thought since you didn't pass out you were better than her. Let me refresh your memory, old man. Night after night, you'd stagger down the hall, stand in the door to my bedroom, and bang a fist on the wall so you could tell me what a disappointment I was. The first time each night wasn't bad. You'd run out of words and stumble off, remember? It was always the third and fourth beratings that were the real tests. I was only ten. I could smell the weed and the bourbon on your breath as you called me a worthless piece of shit."

His grip on my hand tightened, and something popped. I

bit my lip until I tasted tinny blood, but I didn't make a sound. I was in deep waters, and the storm was raging.

"What was it you used to tell me? 'Life's a cold iron bitch; get over it.' You had a choice, just like the rest of us. You could have sucked it up and done something with it. But you were too small and weak to hold in all that pain and frustration, so you poured it into your family. And you have the balls to ask why I am so angry? I'm angry because you installed that program in me. I didn't have the drink or the drugs, so it came out as rage."

A tear welled in Jason Sato's right eye until a blink sent it down his cheek. His Adam's apple bobbed up and down. The crushing pressure on my hand abated some, and he spoke again, his voice tight. "But that was the secret to my success. After that, what's some stranger going to say to get under my skin? There wasn't a prison guard or drill sergeant or pit boss out there that had a patch on you."

I decided it was time to wrap the session up. I was seeing, almost too late, that Jason Sato wasn't there for healing or closure; his catharsis was confrontation. I needed to redirect him, let him have a win, and end it on that.

"Time is fleeting," I said. "We will not get another connection like this. Ask what questions you have. Do it now before it is too late."

His head tilted as if the suggestion amused him. Fortunately, he kept his focus on the ceiling and not me. "A question? You want a question, old man? Okay, here you go. Are you ashamed? Or were you so delusional that you really believed what you told the cops? The psychtechs spent months trying to make me believe I did it, but I never forgot the night you broke your hand on her jaw. That cast was a mark of your shame, but you weren't even man enough to own it. Instead, you blamed it on your little juvenile delinquent son. Did the guilt eat at you all those months I was in juvie? Did you feel any responsibility for what I did in there? What I became afterwards?"

He was shaking, not with fear, but the way a dam might tremble before bursting. I'd made a mistake forcing the question, one of many that night. His anger was driving his decisions, and angry men do violent things. It was like swimming with a shark. I had to end it before the situation reached the point of no return.

I punched the switch to flicker the light and, in desperation, triggered a few more effects at random. Multiple knocks echoed around the room. The floor rumbled. The smell of pine battled with the stink of sulfur and lost. The magnet beneath the table powered up and jerked the money clip two inches to the left. Apparently, it wasn't real gold after all.

"The spirit is trying to leave," I said through gritted teeth. "I cannot hold it much longer!"

"You don't get to leave, not until you hear what I have to say."

"Be quick!" I hissed. "We are in great danger."

Jason Sato lifted his head, and in a clear, self-possessed voice said to the room, "I don't want anything from you. There is nothing in this world that you have the power to give or take from me. I've waited this long to talk to you so we were clear on that point. I have carried this hate and rage my entire life, and finally, I am ready to let it go. I'm here to forgive you, old man. I forgive you for your mistakes. If you have any guilt, any shame, or hatred of me, leave it here in this room next to my anger. We will walk out of here, both of us, and never look back."

There! I thought and smashed the switch to kill all of the effects. Instantly, the knocking and rattling stopped. Fresh air blew through the room, chasing away the rotten egg smell. The light above the table brightened and settled.

Sweat dripped from my forehead and splashed on the table cloth. The pressure on my hand disappeared, and the flow of blood returned with a vengeance. I opened my eyes, only then realizing that I'd squeezed them closed.

For a fleeting moment, Jason Sato looked human. The mantis claw had retracted into his forearm. He wiped his cheek. Then he stood up, and his face vanished behind the glare of the table lamp. Deftly, he closed the seam on his sleeve, and his right hand slid inside his jacket to where I was certain he wore a gun.

It was all over. Either I'd put on a good enough performance or I hadn't. It probably didn't matter anyway. There was no reason for a man like him to keep me alive after I'd heard what I'd heard. I'd been a dead woman since he walked through the front door.

Jason Sato reached down and picked up the money clip. "You are going to forget everything," he said. "What was asked. What was answered. My face. Everything."

"Of course, my child," I rushed to assure him. *A glimmer of hope.* "Madam Zomalski is nothing if not discreet. I hope I have been of service. I hope you have found some measure of peace here."

The green light in his eye flashed dangerously. "By five tomorrow, this building will be a pile of rubble. By next week, it will be a pit." He pulled the cash from his breast pocket and folded it into the money clip before tossing it on the table. The heavy metal landed with a thud. "Take that and be somewhere else, Brittany Seigel. Savannah's dead to you. I wouldn't go back to Shreveport or Jacksonville, either. Try somewhere up north."

I didn't move, didn't reach for the money or even open my mouth. My heart in my throat, I sat silently while the killer who knew me for the fraud that I am unlocked the door and disappeared into the steamy summer night.

. . .

H.K. Slade is a writer living in North Carolina who specializes in police procedurals with occasional forays into horror and science fiction. When not writing or playing with his two dogs, he spends time designing an elaborate custom game each year for Halloween. In 2022, his short story "Last Gasp" was selected for the honor roll in Otto Penzler's The Best Mystery Stories of the Year. *You can find more of his work in* Mystery Weekly, Black Cat Mystery Magazine, Black Cat Weekly, Dark Horses, Black Sheep, *and* Behind the Shadows II, *as well as his website, hkslade.com*

MERCY

SIENA BUCHANAN

"Sariel of the Ibis, High General of the Ibis armies, wife of Astrid, mother of Aileen, you stand trial today for the destruction of the Kennu spaceship known as the *Bright Fire,* and the murder of all 70,553 Kennu aboard. In addition to these crimes, you are also charged with reckless endangerment of the Li Li people on the planet Lilandra below."

Sariel stood before the podium in the Hall of Song, head bowed, staring at the marbled floor beneath her. The floor, with its marvel of colors, stood in symphony with the rest of the Hall filled with crystal pillars that held up the cavernous ceilings, brightly stained wood benches, and podiums that had witnessed the major trials and coronations of the Ibis species.

This trial would be one recorded in the history books, Sariel knew. Behind her, every bench was packed with Ibis, in all their chosen forms. Because Ibis had no consistent form, each adopted what suited them—from tiny mouselike creatures to those as large as horses. Many, including Sariel, took the form of humans. It was a tradition so ancient, even

Sariel didn't remember its origins. Queen Mariana herself took the appearance of a pale young woman with hair so blond it could have been white, a circlet of gold nestled among the tresses.

Sariel had attended the coronation of that queen—in this very room, in fact, years ago. Though...had it been her or her mother? The queens were starting to run together. There had been too many since Sariel had been born.

Even among her kindred, who could live for thousands of years, Sariel was *old.* Six thousand, one hundred and eighty-four years. The oldest one left. She hadn't considered that, but it was true. She was the oldest now. Now that—

Her mind screamed at that thought, rebelling at it, rebelling against that which was true but could not be true. A field of jagged glass that cut her no matter how carefully she tried to walk through it. A screaming void begging to be filled, an open wound that she couldn't heal.

Sariel couldn't finish that thought even in her mind.

Thankfully, she didn't have to, as Queen Mariana continued speaking. "Sariel stands trial for her crimes and is joined here with her daughter Aileen, who will argue her mother's side." Aileen had insisted on being there, despite all Sariel's attempts to convince her to stay away. She stood resolutely next to Sariel, to her left and a step behind.

Sariel couldn't look at her.

"I, Queen Mariana, stand as judge. My Clerk is Ibis Hyacinth, with our witnesses Saal, Captain in the Ibis army, and Calliope. All others in attendance not mentioned shall remain silent through the course of the proceedings. May the Goddess guide us in our judgment."

A pause, a terrifying moment meant for reflection, for serenity, for thoughts that Sariel didn't want to have. She looked up, meeting the queen's dark gray eyes. No sympathy lay there, no pity. Only cold and unyielding steel.

"Ibis Saal, step forward please."

The man began to speak, and Sariel lost herself in memory.

* * *

THE PLANET outside the spaceship window bloomed in deep blues and greens with swirls of white clouds. Most might have called it beautiful, and it was—but there was so much beauty in the universe that Sariel could not call any one thing more beautiful than another.

She had witnessed the births and deaths of stars. She had stood on the edges of black holes, observing how they pulled light in, the vibrant red of light on the edge of being devoured. She had traveled to every corner of this galaxy, leaving no stone unturned.

There were many things that could be called beautiful: the way the starry sky stretched above, the way falling leaves were picked up by the wind, even the swirling lines etched in the cold white interior of the Ibis battlecruiser the *Fragment* where Sariel stood. Yet, as one of the nearby doors hissed open, Sariel saw a beauty that exceeded any of those. Her wife, Astrid.

Sariel couldn't help but smile as she saw her, with her long black hair in a braid over her casual pink shirt and the dark jeans she had always preferred. Even the pair of wickedly sharp swords at Astrid's side didn't stop Sariel from hurrying over and swinging her arms around her in a hug. Sariel buried her head in Astrid's dark hair and inhaled the scent of Astrid's energy—like freshly opened apple blossoms, bright and sweet.

"It's been too long," Sariel whispered.

"Seven years. Yes, it's been too long." Astrid tucked one of

Sariel's curls behind her ear. "I heard you got a promotion, General."

"I'm finally the same rank as you, General."

"I still outrank you. For one thing, I've been at this level longer, and for another, I'm older than you, so..." Astrid smiled as she shrugged, the playful coyness audible in every syllable.

Sariel moved her hand down, touching the ring that Astrid wore tied around her neck. "It's only fair that you still get to outrank me in *public.*"

"That sounds like a little bit of a promise."

"A promise, or a *threat.*"

"Well, I for one can't wait to see what that threat ends up being."

"Oh, I know you can't," Sariel replied, leaning in and kissing Astrid, pulling her into an embrace. They stayed that way for a few long moments before they broke apart.

"Unfortunately, that threat will have to wait until *after* we deal with the current situation," Sariel said quietly, her eyes flicking back to the window and the blue-green planet below.

"How long before the Kennu arrive?" Astrid asked.

Sariel rattled off the time without needing to check her watch. "Thirty-six minutes and fifty-three seconds until they drop out of hyperspace."

"Briefing will be in a couple of minutes, then. We should head that way."

The two of them walked, hand in hand, toward the bridge of the ship.

* * *

"THE ARRIVAL of Astrid and the other Ibis coming in from Ihengar occurred about thirty minutes before the Kennu dropped out of hyperspace; that is correct, your Majesty."

"And the reason for their arrival, Saal?" Queen Mariana asked from where she sat behind her podium, the circlet of gold on her head catching occasional flickers of light from the glowing crystals above. "Were there concerns that the Ibis you employed would be incapable of managing the threat?"

"No," Saal stated, "simply that they had finished with their mission, and we were the closest major ship for them to link up with."

"So, you didn't expect any resistance from the Kennu?"

"There were no expectations of resistance; that is correct, your Majesty. Though there is a long history of conflict between—"

"Irrelevant to this case," Queen Mariana interjected.

Calliope piped up. "With all due respect, Queen, I would argue that the definition of the conflict is the *exact* purpose of this case, because whether actions were justifiable depends on whether military authority was justified here. Which depends on whether the Ibis and Kennu are, in fact, at war."

"The quandary between the Kennu and the Li Li was very specifically *not* against the Ibis personally," Queen Mariana replied. "There has never been war between the Ibis and Kennu."

"You could make an argument that their actions *constituted* a declaration of war," Calliope shot back.

Hyacinth looked up from where he sat to the side of the Queen, taking notes. "We are not here to debate whether we were at war with the Kennu. Even if we assume that we *were,* Sariel still committed a crime, by either four hundred and ninety, subsection twenty-three, if we were not at war, or nine hundred and twelve point three, if we *were.*"

The Queen interrupted him. "Thank you, Hyacinth. However, in this case, Calliope does make a good point that the *severity* of crime committed does depend on which of those subsections we should follow. That makes establishing the circumstances of the case important. Saal, please, continue with your account."

* * *

"The Kennu offered the Li Li an ultimatum. Submit to their rule peacefully, or be taken by force," Sariel said, her eyes flicking through the room at the Ibis gathered around the large metal table in the center of the bridge. There were thirty-two Ibis in total, so many marshaled in a single place—though compared to the armies that she had once been a part of, it was nothing.

Sariel's eyes returned to the timer in the center of the table, counting down. Twenty-nine minutes and eleven seconds until they had to be ready.

"Have we opened a line of communication with the Kennu? Do they know we are here?" That was Calliope—a sharp young Ibis who preferred the form of a short human with keen eyes that didn't quite match the rest of her soft exterior. She had potential to be a great fighter—*if* she ever managed to stop following every rule to the letter.

"We have requested to speak with the Kennu leadership multiple times, but they so far have denied our requests," Sariel said.

"And the Li Li?" Calliope asked.

"Lack a central government," Astrid said, stepping in smoothly before Sariel had a chance to form her own response. "The Kennu are working to take advantage of that. They would have a harder time with a singular authority. We have informed those we have been able to contact, but they are few and far between."

"So, we should expect no help from them," commented another Ibis from the back of the room in the form of a sallow, middle-aged man who looked like he could use more time in the sun. It took Sariel a moment to wrack her brain to find the right name—Captain Saal. He had interviewed her once while writing a history book.

"Correct," Sariel said, "and they have no defenses against the Kennu unless we interfere. Lilandra is on a crucial hyperspace route, which makes it likely the Kennu won't give up their crusade easily. They have repeatedly defied our requests to stay out of the way of less advanced civilizations. We will, of course, try to broker negotiations on the Li Li's behalf if given the chance, but—"

"That makes it sound like you are expecting a fight, General."

"Not anticipating a fight," Astrid said smoothly, "but *preparing* for one. The Kennu have a long history of defying Ibis rule. While they have never attempted to make weapons that could kill us, that doesn't mean they aren't dangerous. They have an advantage too, the possibility of using the planet below as a hostage. We can't let them do that. Our priority needs to be protecting the Li Li and their planet of Lilandra, with a secondary priority of trying to kill as few Kennu as possible to get our point across. Many of them are just following the orders of their leaders—and it is those leaders we have an issue with, not the rank-and-file infantry."

* * *

"THE MAKEUP of the Kennu aboard the *Bright Fire*, what was it?" Queen Mariana asked.

Hyacinth read from the projected holographic screen in front of him. “Around eighty-two percent general infantry troops and starfighter pilots, seventeen percent maintenance and crew, and one percent leadership.”

“Any civilians on board?”

“Depending on how you define civilians. According to the Kennu or Ibis definitions—”

“As this is an Ibis trial, the Ibis definition would be most useful.”

Hyacinth coughed. “Ah. Yes. Well. According to Ibis definition, there were non-combatants on board, but no civilians.”

“Though the question of whether they were innocent in what befell—” Calliope added quickly.

“Should be taken into account, but that is a question for later,” Queen Mariana finished with a long sigh. “Continue the testimony, please.”

* * *

“GENERALS, THERE IS A HYPERSPACE DISTURBANCE NEARBY.”

Sariel let out a low string of the most ungodly, heinous curses from fifteen different civilizations across the galaxy. She checked the clock ticking down in front of them. “I thought we had more time.”

“The estimate was based on our best knowledge of Kennu hyperspace technology to date. It seems they had a breakthrough while we weren’t looking.”

Sariel took a deep breath. Detection of a hyperspace disturbance still meant they had a good five or ten minutes until the Kennu arrived, barely enough time to put their plans into action—if they hurried.

“Captain Dorian, take your squad down to Lilandra. Put up shields and prepare for a potential orbital attack. Captain

Phoebe, ready interceptor ships. Captain Saal, you and your group stay here with me and keep lines of communication open between all groups. Captain Ezra, you have the most experienced group, and therefore the most important job. Find a way to get past the Kennu shields and onto their ship. Inform them that the Ibis will not tolerate the Kennu taking control of another planet. Reason with them before resorting to fighting."

Next to Sariel, Astrid spoke. "I'll join you, Ezra. There is little use in both Generals remaining on the same ship, and Sariel and I can communicate telepathically to keep in closer contact."

Sariel squeezed Astrid's hand. "Are you sure?"

"Yeah." She shrugged. "Besides, Ezra wouldn't be able to see a peace treaty if it was right in front of him on a giant neon sign, so…"

"Unfair," Ezra replied, though there was a slight smile on his face.

"You're one of our best warriors, but you aren't exactly prone to giving up easily," Astrid shot back.

Astrid leaned over and gave Sariel a quick kiss. "Keep the lines open."

Then she disappeared, following Ezra out of the room.

Without her, the bridge felt darker, and Sariel felt a flicker of fear. She pushed it aside and was quickly distracted by question after question.

Sariel was busy making a notation about orbital shielding mechanics when a dolorous chime rang through the battle-cruiser. Silence fell among the chattering Ibis as they each looked toward the nearest window. Outside, a massive spaceship blocked their view.

Massive was relative. Sariel had seen ships that were big enough to be mistaken for moons, and this was nowhere near that. Still, this was the ship of a full, spacefaring civilization. It was as large as a small city and held a comparable population.

There was a moment when the entirety of the Ibis ship's crew stood in tense silence before returning to their duties with an increased urgency.

Sariel herself took a deep breath and called the newcomer ship, switching from the soft musical tone of the Ibis language to the hard clicks and chirps of the Kennu language.

"This is Sariel, High General of the Ibis army and current commander of the *Fragment*. I am calling the Kennu ship that has recently arrived in this sector. You have repeatedly been warned to avoid engagement with the Li Li people. If you continue on this path, we will be forced to engage you directly."

There was silence on the radio for a moment, and then a reply.

"Greetings, Sariel. This is Weaver Nine, commander of the Kennu ship *Bright Fire*. We are requesting that you lay down your arms and surrender."

"Weaver Nine, are you aware that you are standing against a full contingent of Ibis? You are outmatched."

"I will give you one final warning, Sariel of the Ibis. Withdraw from this battle and let us take Lilandra, or face our wrath."

* * *

"SAAL, you remained in the bridge with Sariel, is that correct?"

"Yes, your Highness."

"Did you overhear her discussion with the commander of the Kennu ship?"

"I did."

"What did you think of it?"

Saal shrugged. "The Kennu should be aware of the Ibis's power in battle, your Majesty, but the fact that this Kennu was acting rashly did not seem to be out of the ordinary. They do tend to try to make enemies back off through bluffs."

"So, you did not believe their threats had any merit?"

"No, your Highness. I did not."

Queen Mariana turned to Sariel. "And you, I assume—"

"I had no reason to believe the legitimacy of their threats, no, Mariana," Sariel replied.

"It is worth noting, your Majesty, that in over twenty-five recorded encounters with the Kennu, there has never been a single incident when an Ibis was harmed," Hyacinth added. "They had not developed the necessary hyperspace technology required to kill an Ibis. That requires a lot of intense research and understanding of hyperspace mechanics. There is a reason only four civilizations have managed it."

"Until two weeks ago."

"Precisely, your Majesty. There is no reason to believe that General Sariel made an error in her estimates. To the best of her knowledge at the time, the Kennu threat was empty."

The mistake she had made in discounting the threat dug into Sariel's mind. The mistake and the results. The pain, the jagged open wound, that nobody in the courtroom felt but her.

* * *

"ANY FURTHER RESPONSE FROM THE KENNU?" Saal asked.

Sariel shook her head. "They are refusing my call. Any updates from Dorian or Ezra?" As she said it, the radio came crackling on.

"This is Phoebe; our ships are in the air and in position."

"Copy, Phoebe. For now, do not engage directly. Keep a safe distance from the *Bright Fire* and watch for Kennu starfighters. If you spot any, distract and try to keep them away from the planet."

"Heard and understood, General."

"Just got a message from Dorian," Saal said. "They have reached the surface and are spreading out along it."

"Reply to Dorian; make sure they establish a proper Zefsgaf shield—a full one, not partial," Sariel ordered quickly.

"Understood," Saal shot back.

"General?" came another voice.

"What is it?" Sariel asked, turning to see the small form of Calliope looking at a screen in front of her.

"General, there is a hyperspace disturbance in the middle of the Kennu ship."

Sariel turned, leaning over Calliope to examine the readings. Calliope was right. There was an upsurge of hyperspace energy in the lower decks. Unusual. Potentially dangerous. Hyperspace energy could be used for a lot of things—traveling quickly through space being the most obvious one—but it also interfered with Tidal energy, the type of power that Ibis used and were created from.

The most likely cause was some sort of leak—perhaps there was lingering hyperspace energy from the jump. A malfunction like that could be dangerous to the Ibis on the ship if it continued to escalate. They needed to know. As soon as possible.

"Saal, message Ezra. Tell them to investigate." Even as Sariel said those words, she was also reaching out to Astrid, their mental link snapping into existence.

Astrid. Where are you on the Kennu ship? There is a leak of hyperspace energy in one of the lower decks. I need you to send someone to make sure it doesn't cause issues.

Negotiations are going poorly. They are refusing to listen to us at all. I'd take any excuse to get out of here. Where did you say it was?

Sariel checked the readout Calliope had put in front of her. *Fourth deck, in one of the engineering bays. And hurry, it's getting stronger.*

I'm on my way, Astrid replied.

Sariel turned to Saal. "Who among your crew would be best in a crisis?"

"Uh..."

"Never mind, just find a few of them who would be willing and send them to meet with Ezra and the rest. They might need backup. It sounds like the negotiations are going badly, so we may have to scratch ending this peacefully."

"Our whole goal is to at least *try* to resolve it without fighting."

"Yet the ideal world and the reality are often incompatible," Sariel shot back.

Sariel? Astrid whispered.

Did you find it? Sariel asked.

Sariel, it isn't a hyperspace malfunction. It's a weapon. I don't know if it is a weapon capable of killing Ibis, but it's certainly dangerous, both to the ship itself and to the planet below.

Sariel shot up in her chair, her heart suddenly pounding in her chest. "What?" she said aloud before she remembered Astrid wouldn't be able to hear her. *Astrid. You need to get off that ship.*

Ezra is trying to disable it. Once he does that, we will have to make sure that—

The world around Sariel flashed white, in both actual vision and power. Hyperspace dampened Ibis abilities, and this was no exception.

Amid the brightness and the blindness, Sariel heard a

scream she knew echoing in her head, a voice as familiar to her as her own heartbeat.

The moment the light faded, Sariel stood, looking out at the ship beyond.

"General, it is advisable for you to stay—" Saal started.

Sariel ignored him. She gathered her energy, her power, and flung it outward, creating a portal connecting two points, a path that she stepped through and found herself in the Kennu ship.

Kennu lay all around, many dead or dying, their mandibles bloody, their six legs curled around themselves, their eyes glazed over.

In the middle of the engineering bay, next to a large device, knelt Astrid.

The moment Sariel's eyes saw her wife, she rushed over. "Astrid. Astrid! You're okay?"

Her relief was replaced with terror as she saw the extent of the wounds along Astrid's skin, rippled raised marks as though burned. "Astrid—"

"Sariel," Astrid whispered, "it detonated as soon as Ezra tried to disarm it. We should have been more careful, but we didn't even think they could have built something like that."

Sariel took in a sharp breath. "The others?"

"Dead," Astrid said. "Ezra shielded me from the worst of the blow in his final moments."

"I should have told you to come back. I shouldn't have let you go in. They even—they told me. They threatened me, and I didn't think anything of it. What kind of general am I, that I couldn't see what was right in front of me? I never should have kept you or any of them on this ship. It's my fault."

Astrid let out a weak breath and coughed. "And if you did call us back? If we hadn't detonated it early? Would it have destroyed the whole Ibis ship and you along with it?"

"There would have been a solution."

"I don't want to spend my final moments arguing with you about this."

Sariel shook her head. "You are going to be fine. You must be fine."

"Sariel—the love of my life. My wife. My everything. I—am—dying. Even shielded, the blast was fatal. My soul is unraveling. You can feel it."

Sariel's mind was screaming. This couldn't be happening. She and Astrid had survived so much—they had fought side by side in the War of Shadows. Together, they had toppled empires and ended wars. Undefeated in battle or strategy, and in power, they had had made discoveries of the depth of the Tide. Their daughter had grown to become more powerful and wonderful than anyone Sariel could ever imagine.

All of that couldn't end here. It couldn't be cut short as though by a ragged knife. It couldn't.

"There must be a way. Always a way. Always—"

"There isn't always a solution, Love," Astrid's voice trembled.

"There has to be." Sariel pled with her wife, with her power, with the universe itself as her energy flared around her, trying to find something to fix, something to heal, trying to let it take her instead, as punishment for her error in judgement.

Yet even her own traitorous power was telling her the same thing. Astrid was dying. It was Sariel's fault. She was the one who had told her to investigate the disturbance. It was her fault that her wife was dying.

"You can't leave me," Sariel whispered. Tears, hot and fast, sizzled as they fell onto Astrid's skin—though whether that was Astrid's power or her own, she didn't know or care.

"You're going to have to be very, very brave, my love. You

are going to have to be stronger than I ever could be." Astrid reached up and, with shaking hands, unknotted the cord around her neck and pressed the ring into Sariel's hands.

Sariel looked down at it, the ring she had given Astrid so long ago, thousands of years ago, the day they had promised themselves to each other.

"I can't," Sariel whispered.

"Please."

Sariel took the cord with her own shaking hands and tied it around her neck.

"Shhh," Astrid said, drawing a ragged breath as her eyes drifted closed. "Don't think of me like this. Don't let this be how you remember me. If you can, remember the Swan Nebula, the way the colors bled together in that glorious dance, the canopy of trees, the way you kissed me—and the day you gave me this." She reached out and tapped the ring now hanging on Sariel's neck. "And our daughter…our glorious daughter. Take care of her. And…" Astrid's voice grew softer, and Sariel leaned in to hear her words, a final sentence for her alone.

Astrid released a long slow breath, and her form flickered. The power that kept an Ibis together in a single shape waned and revealed Astrid's true essence, a wisp of pale pink mist that smelled like apple blossoms.

Then Sariel's love, her wife, her everything, was gone.

And Sariel shattered.

* * *

SARIEL REACHED up and touched the wedding ring she still wore around her neck.

"How did the Kennu even learn how to create a hyperspatial weapon?" Saal asked. "It doesn't make sense. We had no record of them even researching advanced hyperspace technology, much less figuring out that it was the secret to kill an Ibis."

"Advancements can be quick. It's happened before," Queen Mariana said. "Though believe me, we will be conducting a full investigation into how this was missed by those Ibis stationed on the Kennu home world. However, neither of those things are the purpose of this case. The creation of a weapon capable of killing Ibis is a true and heinous act. The priority upon finding such an object should be its destruction."

"Which Sariel did," Aileen said. It was the first time she had spoken throughout the proceedings.

"Destroy the weapon, yes. Destroy the entire ship—"

"Was excessive, I agree. But the Kennu killed her wife. My mothers have been together for over four *thousand* years. Grief is a powerful thing. When I heard the news, I could barely contain my own anger—and I wasn't even *there.* She should have shown more restraint, yes. But her actions are... understandable, considering the circumstances at play."

"So were the actions of Etharian going after the Sun Empire, and yet we locked him in the Sanctuary," Queen Mariana said.

Sariel tried to ignore the thread of anger in her chest and forced herself to take a deep breath. She had chosen to face her consequences, and she would go through with it.

Aileen shrugged. "If the purpose of this trial is to determine whether Sariel crashed the Kennu ship—that's not in question. If it is to determine if her actions were justifiable, that's different."

* * *

SARIEL SCREAMED, and her power roared in response. Like the wings of a phoenix, bright blue fire bloomed around her, and the room was filled with the electrical smell of ozone.

The device in the center of the room, the weapon that had killed her wife, shattered. She didn't care if it killed her. She had no cares left in the world.

Sariel still needed more.

She strode through the ship, a force of nature itself, a goddess upon the universe.

The Kennu died. They tried to fight her, but with their primary weapon destroyed, they had no recourse, no way of fighting back.

She dealt death with every blow. Death, fire, and destruction surrounded her as she strode through the ship, higher and higher until, amid the flames on the bridge of the *Bright Fire,* Sariel held a sword aloft, her power flickering through her form.

"Mercy," Weaver Nine begged, cowering behind the control panel, his four eyes darting around the room for an escape route he wouldn't find.

"This is mercy," Sariel whispered.

The ship rumbled around the two of them. The force of destruction Sariel had unleashed broke it apart and sent it crashing toward the planet below.

"What do you want? What can I give you? I could make you a queen of Kennu. You could live among us. You could be empress—I have the votes, I can—"

"There is only one thing I want you to give me," Sariel hissed, "but you can't give it to me. You took my wife from me. You took the one I loved the most. Now, you face the consequences."

Sariel's sword came down, and the ship around them shattered fully into flames and darkness.

* * *

"THAT'S the end of the information we have, your Highness. I could pull up some of the data we have from the *Bright Fire,* but most of it is corrupted beyond salvaging."

"No need, but thank you, Hyacinth. I have a few more questions for Sariel herself."

Sariel raised her head to stare directly into Queen Mariana's eyes, who didn't flinch.

"Do you feel remorse, High General Sariel, for your actions two weeks ago, when the *Bright Fire* came crashing down?"

Sariel opened her mouth to respond and then shut it. Her instinct was to say yes. It was to say of course she felt remorse for what she had done. Of course. Why else would she be here? Her sentence likely depended on her response. The obvious and simple answer would be that of course she felt guilty.

It would be the thing everyone expected her to say.

But was that the truth?

No.

Sariel took a deep breath. The honest, raw truth. "No. I do not regret my actions. The Kennu had created a weapon capable of killing Ibis. I did what had to be done."

Hyacinth opened his mouth to say something, but Queen Mariana held up a hand to silence him before she herself spoke. "Doing what had to be done would have been to destroy the weapon, not a ship full of those who had very little to do with said weapon. Do you feel that killing those who did not have to be killed was wrong?"

Sariel swallowed. "Perhaps, in time, I will feel the weight of what I have done. But not now. Not while I am under the shadow of my own grief."

Queen Mariana nodded and then took a few moments of silence, as though she were thinking.

"I have come to a judgment, Sariel of the Ibis. I find you guilty of second-degree massacre of the Kennu and first-degree endangerment of the Li Li."

Queen Mariana motioned for Sariel to kneel.

For the briefest moment, Sariel felt a flare of fury within her. Her wife had been killed, and they were charging *her.* Sariel wanted to scream, she wanted to fight back, and she wanted to *burn.* She had done what she had to do. How could they not understand that? But no. She would not do this. She would not become more of a villain than she already had.

Instead, she took a deep breath, and she knelt on the cold stone floor.

A murmur rose around the Hall of Song. Queen Mariana raised a hand to silence them. "For the crime of first-degree endangerment, the defendant is hereby stripped of her rank and position in the Ibis military, with no chance of it being reinstated. For the crime of second-degree massacre, the defendant is hereby sentenced to exile from her kindred, away from other Ibis, and every day of her sentence shall mark one of those she killed, in the reckoning of the Ibis calendar. Hyacinth?"

"As far as we can ascertain, that will be a little over one hundred and ninety-two years, your Majesty," Hyacinth replied, with the faintest hint of a smug smile that made Sariel want to smack him.

The queen nodded. "One hundred and ninety-two years. Return to me then. And if, by then, you feel the guilt that you should—then, perhaps, we can talk about an end to your exile. In the meantime, you are forbidden from contacting your kin and forbidden from reaching out to any non-Ibis allies or friends."

Sariel swallowed. "I acknowledge and accept the sentences, Queen."

As far as a sentence went, it wasn't being locked up in the Sanctuary. It wasn't having her life reduced to imprisonment. It was temporary. One hundred and ninety-two years. A blink of an eye, and yet also an eternity in which the universe would move on without her. An eternity without her friends, her allies, her daughter.

She glanced toward her daughter, who was regarding Queen Mariana with a frown. "Your Highness, might I offer a suggestion?"

"Aileen. You may, though I cannot promise I will take it."

"I would ask that you not strip Sariel's rank entirely. She did something wrong, and I don't deny it, but my mother is one of the most brilliant strategists among the Ibis. When it comes down to it, in a few hundred or a few thousand years, if war breaks out, you will need Sariel by your side. You will want her leading your army."

Queen Mariana seemed to consider this before her eyes flicked back to Sariel. "I appreciate your request and your willingness to speak your mind. However, Sariel's actions have shown that despite her skill in strategy, she is not to be trusted with command. Sariel's title will remain stripped, *permanently*."

Sariel felt a flicker of annoyance and frustration. To have her title removed, just like that, after she had worked so hard to get where she was—it stung.

Aileen swallowed and nodded. "I understand, your Highness. Please accept my apologies."

"As I said, I appreciate you stating your opinion, even if I disagree," Queen Mariana conceded. "Now, Sariel of the Ibis, Former high General of the Ibis armies, widow of Astrid, mother of Aileen, your first day begins. Leave this place with no intention to return until your time has passed."

Sariel turned away from the stand, her eyes meeting the pale blue-gray eyes of her daughter, who nodded and gave the smallest smile before she turned.

Sariel took one step forward, and then another, and another.

One by one, following Aileen's lead, the Ibis in the courtroom turned to face away from Sariel as she walked down the long hallway to begin her first of 70,553 days of isolation.

SIENA BUCHANAN STUDIES biology in the Pacific Northwest. She writes primarily queer science fiction and fantasy, and she had her first anthology acceptance the day before she turned eighteen. Besides writing and schoolwork, she enjoys going for long walks, swimming, baking, watercolor painting, and reading very thick novels. She is an avid Brandon Sanderson fan and a proud member of the 17th Shard.

THE NAME GAME

KEVIN A DAVIS

I stared at the smooth fingers wrapped around the handle of the coffee mug in front of me. They weren't mine.

The girl sitting across the table was maybe eleven with mousy brown hair curled below her shoulders. There was a quieter boy with short hair beside her. They, too, were not mine.

We were eating outside on a patio of a restaurant in Midtown Manhattan. The sound of traffic dominated every direction. How did I know *where* I was if I didn't know *who* I was?

"Dad, are you listening?"

I nearly jumped out of my seat, and I did spill my coffee.

"Dad, you spilled your coffee." The girl, someone's daughter, plucked extra napkins from the dispenser.

"I did." What was I supposed to say; who are you? My hands, someone's hands, were manicured and young. A fat wedding ring was on the appropriate finger — for whoever this was. I wasn't married.

How did I know that?

I smiled at the girl and took the metal napkin dispenser under the guise of getting more. The reflection was hazy, but a goatee grew on a thin face with a long nose. A blue polo shirt hung over a trim body that needed some actual muscle. None of it was mine, but I couldn't remember what I should look like.

"Dad, are you okay?" Her voice rose high enough that an older woman nearby checked, as did the younger boy at our table.

Not at all, kid. "I'm fine." I patted my pockets. A key fob, change, and a wallet in the front pockets of navy blue slacks. I opened the wallet under the table out of sight.

Darren Peterson. Who the hell was that? He liked plenty of cash and credit cards. He had AAA and insurance, so he drove.

The waiter noticed both the spilt coffee and the wallet in my lap, so he exited the restaurant to head for us. I shoved the wallet back into my pocket and swallowed the last gulp from the mug.

The girl watched as I gagged on the bitter black coffee. Worse, it tasted like decaf. The boy put down his burger and turned up from his lap to study me. The nosy old lady snuck glances from the table behind the kids. I smiled at the nonplussed waiter as he arrived.

"Everything okay?" Young with a pinched smile and dead eyes, the man wanted no trouble from me.

"Fine. Maybe some regular coffee?" I handed him the cup.

"Dad!" The girl was mortified.

I ignored her and gazed at the waiter. Despite being completely wrong, the situation barely disturbed me. That, in itself, was disturbing. Did I expect to be in someone else's body with their kids, drinking their coffee, and trying to figure out who the hell I was? Most people would be shouting and running away; I was digging through his wallet for clues and ordering proper coffee. "Thank you." I checked to make sure there was sugar at the table.

There was a list in my head: Darren Peterson, father of two; Midtown Manhattan; prefers sugar in coffee. I was not young, smooth, and didn't have a goatee.

"Mom says you can't have caffeine." The girl brandished a ketchup-dipped French fry and pointed it at me.

Married. I glanced at my own plate. Sweet potato fries? And no ketchup. What was wrong with this Darren?

"This once." My voice sounded distracted. A movement across the road caught my attention. Just a city worker with a truck, blocking a lane. He climbed out of a manhole wearing a bright orange safety vest. His eyes were sad and fierce at the same time.

Danger.

Where the hell had that come from? I knew it as clearly as I knew this was Manhattan. I almost stood. To do what, tackle some poor worker?

The waiter startled me, fresh coffee in hand. "Do you have a pen?" I asked him. The urgency in my voice surprised us both.

The two kids had stopped eating. I smiled, took the pen, and figured I'd learn their names. "Name game?" I asked them. Using Darren, the only name on hand, I ran through the lyrics of the song with a goofy smile on my face.

On the napkin, I wrote "Darren Peterson." It was very familiar now.

The song almost brought a smile from the kids at "Marren," but they were still suspicious. I added Manhattan to my list and ran the song with "Dad."

"30th" appeared on my list, and I found a street sign behind me at the corner. I obviously knew where I was; or Darren did.

"You try it." I added sugar to my coffee and really tried for a fatherly smile. The old lady at the table behind us wasn't buying it.

I didn't care. Something terrible was going to happen. I wrote a "T" on my list of things I knew. As Darren's daughter started, I sang "Becky" before she did. I knew at least one of the names. She smiled as we stumbled through her lyrics twice.

I'd finished the "T" word: "Transcedence Zetta." I even understood what it meant. The forced transfer of a consciousness from one individual into another. Me into Darren. Great. Now what the hell was I supposed to do inside this poor schmuck?

Billy, the son, annoyed me and everyone on the patio with his attempt and his sister's assistance. Billy and Becky. Darren and his wife didn't reach too hard for those names.

The street worker leaned into his work truck, manhole still open. The sense of danger focused me there. Was I supposed to stop something? What was I? A super-agent who popped into people's bodies and stopped terrorism? That seemed rude.

I studied the street. Wouldn't they just send SWAT?

Down that hole were three converging gas and fuel lines. They led to the water by the United Nations building. I almost wrote that on the napkin. "Gas, Fuel, Un…"

How. The. Hell. Did I know that?

What if I were the terrorist? That would make more sense. An operative trained in taking over dads' bodies and then blowing them up in a suicide attack — with their kids.

Either the transfer had gone bad, been interrupted, or this was a lousy way to do whatever I was supposed to do. As it was, I wasn't blowing up Becky and Billy.

Knowing what I was meant to do should be at the top of the list for potential success.

"Sugar? Dad?"

The coffee had still been bitter. My spoon rattled absently in my partially filled cup. "In a mood today, Becky." That sounded awkward. Sweet potato, decaf, sugarless, Darren was having a dreadful day.

I assumed, knew, transcedence could be reversed. Was Darren's consciousness in my body in a tank somewhere freaking out? I believed so.

Darren Peterson

Manhattan

30th

Transcedence Zetta

Danger

Gas, Fuel, U~~n~~N

2:10 p.m.

The time just skidded onto the paper, but I knew it was important. How long did I have?

My chest tightened in panic, and my hand went to my side where my cell was supposed to be. Becky, chewing on her burger, tilted her head to let me know she still thought I was acting weird. "Where's my phone?" I asked her.

Billy lifted it slowly from his lap; a game bounced on the screen. From his expression, I couldn't tell if he'd always considered Darren a little dim, or just me at the moment. I still didn't want to see him die in a raging gas main explosion that would topple buildings. Maybe just singe the single eyebrow he raised at me.

"What time is it?"

Both eyebrows went up and he tapped his wrist.

Darren wore a watch. Of course. Rolex knockoff, I guessed. It was 1:54 p.m., if the time was correct. Sixteen minutes to do what? If I were the criminal, this would be easy. I just wouldn't do what I was supposed to do. What if Darren were the criminal, or worse, a terrorist, and had already done something?

"Crap." I searched around my feet for a briefcase, duffel of HMX, or even a suspicious paper bag.

"Language, Dad." Becky spoke with her mouth partially full and eyed Billy knowingly.

"Options:," I scribbled on my napkin. She tried to peek, and I tucked it under the edge of my plate, hiding it behind the burger bun. I used "T" as a code for terrorist in case she saw. I wasn't at my cleverest.

1. I'm Big T — do nothing and everybody lives.

2. Darren was Big T — already did something — hope I remember and stop it.

3. I'm Agent — attack random city worker and *hope* he's the Big T.

4. I'm Agent — forgot what to do. All die."

Becky nearly stood on her chair to get a look, and I covered my list with my hand. "Eat your burger."

"You eat yours."

I folded my napkin and tried to tuck it into my vest pocket. No can do, just a polo. Thanks, Darren. Not trusting the girl not to snag it, I stuffed it in my pants pocket and grabbed my burger with a smile.

I needed a minute to think and had about fourteen before something horrendous happened, or didn't. Chipotle sauce on a really mushy burger. Wait. Darren was a vegetarian?

Chewing slowly, I studied my best options.

The city worker still leaned into the open back of his little vehicle. Caution markers blocked the area around the manhole. One lane of traffic squeezed by him heading toward the water two blocks down. I knew too much about what was underground to be here for anything else.

I stood, veggie burger in hand as if that made me less conspicuous. Hopefully, more data would filter through this failed Transcedence, and I wouldn't end up with "Darren et al." etched on a memorial somewhere.

"Stay here," I told Darren's kids. As I passed the nosy old lady, I leaned down with chipotle breath. "Watch the kids."

Some part of me logged every pedestrian, the truck driver and loaded dolly, the sedans and vans turning onto my street, and the vague shape of a shopper through the tinted market windows across from the restaurant. The city worker was the danger. Darren's burger raised as if I might take a bite, I strode quietly and quickly to the manhole and peered down.

A canister, three feet by a foot, had been wedged at the edge of the pipes with a very ominous cap on the top. Wires ran down the side. A shape-charged bomb had a wireless detonator, based on the dual antennas. It wouldn't need a timer if the relay had one. They had built this for suicidal deployment with nothing complicated or tricky. Easy.

It only bothered me slightly how much I knew about the bomb. I assumed it was my knowledge, not Darren's memory.

I stepped forward, ready to drop in and yank out three wires, which would defuse it. My eye twitched as I considered a fourth optional wire. Someone had screwed up the transcedence something god-awful. There were maybe eleven minutes left, *if* Darren's watch was correct.

"Shit." The city worker spun when he realized that Darren, in his polo shirt and slacks, was prepared to snack on a vege-burger beside his manhole. "Back up."

The man hadn't shaved. Sweat drenched his work shirt. I could smell sewage, but not the chemicals of an explosive. His eyes flicked from surprised, to sad and resigned, then fierce. In his right hand was a clipboard, a prop for any safety vest. His left hand was in his lower pocket at an awkward angle.

"Burger?" I asked as I took a step forward, nearly straddling the opening.

My terrorist was not dissuaded or fooled. From his eyes

that were locked on mine and his slow moves, he did want a special moment, though, even if it was just with me. Darren's stomach churned, and my focus tunneled onto the terrorist's movements.

If I failed, Darren and his kids would die quickly, but I still hated the thought. The city would be split down the street where hundreds, if not thousands, would die. The targeted people at the UN would be among them. I couldn't let it happen.

The terrorist could have released the dead man's trigger in his pocket, but he wanted to witness my expression, knowing I was going to die, before he let go. For his joy in causing fear, I despised the man.

Darren's body was not made for combat. My mind could move the limbs about with some martial experience, but there were limitations to not having toned muscle. The burger fell apart as it dropped into the manhole. Best place for it.

The three fingers of Darren's left hand hurt, even jammed a little, when I shoved them stiff and tip-first into the terrorist's windpipe to crush it. The punch had been a blur.

Even the terrorist's eyes didn't react as I whipped my stolen body through the motions. Darren's right hand was strong enough to overlap the man's thumb holding down the bomb's plunger.

My victim's pupils dilated as I forced Darren's whining body to twist his wrist until the terrorist's bones shifted and cracked. I disengaged with the plunger freely in my control.

He would suffocate in a couple minutes, but fanatics could be resourceful and resilient. Instinctively, I tilted to kick the man away from me and the manhole. I needed to be free to descend and defuse the main weapon. This all felt comfortably according to plan.

A bullet tore through Darren's triceps brachii on the back

of his left arm. The impact spun me in time for the second shot to miss me as the city buildings echoed the gunfire.

The street had that moment of silence, that intake of a breath, before the people around us reacted. Left arm flapping and right hand clenched, I crouched to scan the area.

My pinched-faced waiter pointed a small Glock 42 and tried to aim better as I dodged to the asphalt.

The nosy lady stared wide-eyed at me. Darren's kids were gawking at our waiter.

The terrorist in the safety vest toppled to the road beside me. His clipboard rattled as he pointlessly clutched his throat.

Like a crashing wave breaking the unnatural silence, the screaming and uproar of the crowd deafened the New York street. In that brief moment, a driver found a car to crash into.

There was no noise when the side of the waiter's head sprayed onto the sidewalk. I didn't glance up and to the right where the shot had come from. Maybe it wasn't a SWAT team, but I obviously had friends nearby. The Glock 42 dropped from listless fingers.

Darren's body wasn't doing well with the shock of the gunshot wound. The scent of sewage hung heavy at the edge of the manhole. I rolled his legs into the opening and shoved into the sewer with his right hand clenched on the trigger and the left fairly useless when it came to climbing.

I was halfway down the ladder when a police officer, or someone dressed like one, strode in front of slow traffic to blast rounds into the asphalt next to me. At ten yards away, he was a bad shot, and from his deadly grimace, not a friend. I dropped the last six feet, nearly onto the bomb.

Rolling with the jarring impact to Darren's legs, I managed not to break anything. Whoever I was, I did well with the agent stuff, survival, and all that.

The name game sang in my head. Joanna. Great. That finally worked.

Another car crashed above. Someone fired a weapon. Thumb and pinkie pinning the plunger, I dug a middle finger into the casing of the detonator and popped it off. Definitely four wires. I, Joanna, was sure.

The terminals were clipped on, but I managed to pluck the first one from the outer edge easily. My ticking clock was no longer Darren's watch. Anyone with the frequency could set it off. They had a cop and a waiter ready for suicide along with the city worker.

Maybe the others hadn't known the whole plan. Only the man with the dead man's switch might know this was suicide.

Second wire. Darren was exposed. Fish in a barrel — Darren in a sewer. I didn't turn from my work, but part of my mind watched every shift in shadows. His body was pouring blood from the gunshot. I'd need to patch him up, if he survived.

Third wire. Darren's watch could be ten minutes slow for all I knew. For Becky and Billy's sake, I hoped he was a type-A, sugarless, caffeine-free, vegetarian who set his watch every morning.

The fourth wire dropped free. However, I just couldn't bring myself to let go of the plunger even though the Joanna-me knew I'd defused it. I'd studied bombs like this all my life. I was pretty sure of that. Mostly.

Darren-me had two terrified kids who would need therapy for the next ten years. Plunger gripped and left arm swinging, I climbed the sewer ladder. Darren's wife was going to give him hell. Caffeination was the least of his problems.

Helicopters echoed above. That would be my people.

I poked Darren's head out of the manhole. More police

aimed weapons at me, unsure as they argued over their radios. One uniformed body sprawled on the ground. The scent of spent gunpowder was a welcome distraction to whatever was on Darren's shoes.

Wedging my shoulders against the opening with my feet on the rungs, I lifted the switch out of the sewer.

"Both arms up!"

I sighed and hoped I wouldn't pass out. I managed to flop Darren's left arm onto the asphalt. None of the officers moved. They were waiting for someone above their pay grade to make a decision. Smiling, I hoped Darren didn't have a threatening face.

I could tell from their expressions when my people got through to the local authorities. One very confused officer holstered his weapon and crept reluctantly toward the guy halfway in the sewer with a detonator. He swallowed before he asked, "Joanna?"

Yeah, awkward. "Mostly, yes." Me and Darren, having a party in here.

"Sabin wants to know the status." He kept licking his lips.

"Defused." I let the switch roll out of my palm.

He closed his eyes, but we didn't blow up. "I'll let him know." Poor kid was trembling as he walked back to the growing barricade of officers.

I had to get Darren's arm wrapped before he bled to death. As I crawled onto the road, I could make out a terrified Becky wedged under the table with Billy at her back. Police were trying to evacuate the restaurant and stores — a good thing, in case some terrorist tried to run for the bomb.

I sat tying up Darren's arm with his belt while the police moved in to secure the manhole and evacuate me. "Darren's kids." I gestured to the beat cops clearing the patio.

They had no idea what to make of me, but one nodded and detached from the group to secure Becky and Billy.

They moved me ten feet to the side, as if it were a safe distance from the bomb. Through the other officers, I recognized Margo's face wearing an EMT uniform. She dropped her box beside me and flipped open the latches. "Rough one," she said.

I forced a smile. "You have no idea; he's vegetarian."

Kevin A Davis is an award-winning fantasy author with three published series: the episodic DRC files with Kristen, the Khimmer Chronicles featuring the lively assassin Ahnjii, and the AngelSong series centering around the indominable Haddie. A multitude of his short stories have been published in anthologies. His newest series, the DRC Files, features the curly and curvy Kristen, a witch with exceptional skill in magic, as the new agent on a secret team that tracks down the worst to seep through the realms.

Residing in north Florida, he attends conventions throughout the year either as staff, vendor, speaker, or fan. As a panelist at fandom conventions and as an attendee, he travels to many events in the Southeast United States with a wide interest in speculative fiction from epic fantasy to science fiction. Kevin A Davis has published a dozen anthologies through Inkd Publishing. He is Director of the Authors Workshop Track at JordanCon. For more information, please visit www.KevinArthurDavis.com, www.facebook.com/KevinArthurDavis, or twitter.com/KevinADavisUF

NO GOOD DEED

LEAH LORE

"Wasn't there a clinical trial on our SleepEZ baby formula?" I plopped a spreadsheet onto my supervisor's desk.

Larry continued composing his email like I wasn't even there. When I didn't take the hint, he sighed. "Obviously there was a clinical trial. What's your concern, Amelia?"

"Infant safety."

He swiveled to face me. "Are you insinuating this company is endangering kids?"

"Of course not, I just—"

"Did you ask Joel or Cody before bothering me? The guys have been working here a lot longer than you."

The guys treated me like a child. Just because I didn't have real world experience didn't mean I was stupid. I had a master's degree, for fuck's sake.

"No." I pointed to the spreadsheet. "Listen, I found a strange correlation between our SleepEZ baby formula and a slew of developmental disorders in young children. I wanted to dig into it, but I don't have access to R&D's files. I'm sure a look at the clinical trial will disprove my findings."

"I'll look into it." He slid my spreadsheet into his drawer and closed it with a snap.

I blinked. "Shouldn't I—"

"Don't you have work to do?" His dismissal was clear.

My feet felt heavier with every step back to my cubicle. I was out of my depth. College hadn't prepared me for industry. I knew statistics. I knew biology. I knew chemistry. I sure as hell didn't know office politics.

I collapsed into my chair and stared at my computer. Maybe I should have gone to *the guys* first, but I wanted to prove my worth. Instead, I just cemented my "silly girl" reputation with the boss.

Way to lower the glass ceiling, Amelia.

Ten minutes later I was still berating myself for my mistake. Larry wasn't concerned about the correlation, so it must not have been a real issue. I tried to focus on my work, but was distracted when Larry rose from his desk. He walked into the CEO's office with a spreadsheet in his hand.

My heart skipped a beat—*could it be mine?* I sat taller, staring over my cubicle wall. I could see the CEO through the closed glass door. He raised a thin eyebrow at Larry, then frowned at the spreadsheet in his hand. After a moment, a sneer pulled at his perfectly barbered goatee.

His gaze slid to mine.

Shit! I ducked behind the wall again. I shivered, even as my face heated. The CEO gave me the creeps. His clothes were always too crisp, his shoulders too straight, his jawline too perfect. I put my clammy hands on my keyboard and tried to calm my rapid heartbeat.

Just focus on your work. They aren't talking about you. You aren't import—

"Amelia?" Larry's rough voice made me jump. How did he get behind me so fast?

"Y-yes?"

He inspected me with narrowed eyes. "It seems I owe you an apology. We're going to look into that correlation you found. If you found that data, our competitors might too. The FDA might come asking, and we'll need to be able to explain it. Better safe than sorry, even though it's most likely a documentation error."

I blinked. "A documentation error?" That was one helluva documentation error.

"Boss wants to reward you for your diligence. There's a conference coming up in Vegas next week. Interested?"

"Vegas?" The excitement pushed everything else from my head. "Really? I'd love to!"

Larry chuckled. "Alright kid, I'll get you booked."

* * *

I STARED WIDE-EYED out the business class window as the plane descended. Mountains and desert turned to palm trees and city lights in a blink. I disembarked into a dim airport filled with slot machines and neon signs. A large arch boasted, "What Happens Here, Only Happens Here." It was right—I'd never been in an airport that smelled like a dive bar.

I followed the crowd to the exit, trying not to look like a tourist—and failing. There was too much to see. The company booked a driver for me, so I didn't have to rent a car. They were really going all out to thank me for finding that documentation error.

A man in a dark suit stood by the door holding a sign with my name on it. I hesitated, causing the couple behind me to curse. The man wasn't what I expected a driver to look like. His muscular arms made the paper sign displaying my name look tiny. Everyone gave the man a wide berth, so it was easy to approach.

"I'm Amelia Ray." God, could my voice sound any weaker?

He looked me over, raising an eyebrow at my hot pink carry-on. His expression didn't change as he reached out and took it from me. "This way."

I refused to wilt as I followed him into the parking lot. He loaded my bag into the trunk of a black sedan, then held the back door open for me. I slid in, putting my backpack on the seat beside me.

"This is weird," I said when he got in the driver's seat. "I've never had a driver before."

He didn't answer.

"What's your name?" I tried again.

He pulled out of the lot before speaking. "Smith."

"Okay, Mr. Smith. Do you know where we're going? My reservation's at the Bellagio." I pulled out my phone. I liked to follow the directions, even when I wasn't driving. "Google says to turn left up here."

He turned right.

"Um… You made a wrong turn."

No answer.

"Did you hear me?" I tried to keep my breathing even, but couldn't stop my voice from climbing several octaves.

Smith looked at me in the rearview mirror. His smile was out of place beneath his dead blue eyes. "I know where we're going, Ms. Ray."

Oh shit.

I tried the door, but it was locked.

"Let me out." My voice was somehow calm, detached from the panic in my brain.

Smith didn't answer. He didn't slow. He kept driving like I hadn't spoken.

Some of my panic escaped. "Stop the car! Let me out!"

Smith's smile widened.

Use your phone, dummy!

I dialed 9-1-1. A sharp tone screeched in my ear, followed by a mechanical voice. "Your call could not be completed as dialed. Please hang up and—"

Smith chuckled. "You think I'd let you keep a working phone? This isn't my first job."

Think, Amelia! You always have a plan B—what is it?

I smacked the window and screamed for help, using the distraction to covertly pull my belt from my jeans. I ran the leather through the buckle. Smith's chuckle cut off when I wrapped the belt around his neck and pulled the cinch tight.

He struggled against me, but I braced my legs against the driver's seat for leverage. After a few excruciating moments, Smith lost consciousness. I covered my head with my arms as the car veered toward a telephone pole.

The windows shattered on impact, slicing my exposed skin as glass rained around me. I scrambled out of the wrecked car, pulling my backpack behind me. I bolted down the first street I saw and ducked into an entryway to catch my breath.

Think, Amelia. You aren't safe yet. Where can you run?

The desert? It was close. I could run there. Hide and... then what? Die of thirst. I had no food or water.

What's plan B?

The crowd. I had to get back to civilization.

Still gasping, I dug through my backpack for my sweatshirt. I pulled it on, wincing as it rubbed over my skinned arms. The evening was too warm for the heavy sweatshirt, but my blood would draw unwanted attention. I pulled out my phone. It hadn't worked in the car, but maybe—nope. The screen was shattered, and it refused to turn on, no matter how much I pleaded with it. That car crash must have caused more damage than I realized.

The sound of footsteps drawing near had me cowering deeper into the dark alcove for cover. A man ran past my hiding spot. He was limping and looking around manically. I held my breath, expecting to be discovered any second. I wasn't, though. The man continued down the street. Once he was out of sight, I stepped from my hiding place and made my way toward the Strip, using the Strat Tower to navigate.

The sun was setting when music hit my ears, followed by the raucous chattering of people. I turned a corner and was immediately swallowed by the large crowd milling along the Strip. I trudged down the crowded boulevard, dodging the street performers and club promoters vying for my attention. From one step to the next, the scent of pastries was replaced by grilled meat. My stomach rumbled, and I contemplated stopping for a quick meal. After all, no one would attack me around all these people.

No. Get somewhere safe first.

I pulled my arms closer to prevent them being bumped—my cuts burned where they rubbed against my sleeves. I winced with every step, but gritted my teeth against the pain. I needed to clean myself up. The sweatshirt was the right call. Bloody arms would have stood out on the surprisingly clean street.

Pain shot down my arm when someone grabbed my shoulder.

I bolted, shaking off the grip and darting into the most populated area I could find—the Shops at Caesars. I sprinted down the escalators and darted past the Roman statues. My constant checking over my shoulder drew stares from the shoppers I passed. When I made it to an exit, I forced myself to match the crowd's pace.

Haunting cello music drifted from the walking bridge above me. I skirted the acrobats doing flips on the sidewalk. I barely noticed the Eiffel Tower or the Bellagio Fountains as I hurried to the safety of my hotel.

Once I was through the double doors to reception, I

could finally breathe. The decorative glass on the Bellagio's ceiling held my attention for only a second before my exhaustion set in. I wanted a bed, and I wanted it now. The front desk staff sniffed at me when I asked for my room key, but didn't comment on my bedraggled appearance. They offered to help me with my backpack, but I declined. I'd already lost most of my belongings; I wasn't going to risk anything else.

When I got to my room, I let my backpack slide from my shoulders and land with a thud on the floor. I dug my phone charger out of the front pocket and plugged in my broken phone in the hopes the battery was just dead. When the shattered screen lit up, tears sprang to my eyes, and I collapsed onto the bed. After running for my life across Las Vegas, I wanted to sleep for a week. I needed to shower, to at least clean the cuts on my arms, but I'd have to move. The last of my adrenaline was abandoning me, and everything hurt.

I'd heard of girls getting kidnapped in big cities, but I thought I'd be safe with a driver. Didn't the company run background checks? Once my phone charged, I was going to give Larry a piece of my mind. I could have been killed!

Unless…that was the plan?

No. I couldn't think like that. Why would they buy me a business class plane ticket, then try to kill me? I helped them find that documentation error…

Unless it wasn't an error.

I sat up on the bed. If it wasn't an error… If the SleepEZ formula really *was* causing developmental disorders in children, the company was trying to cover it up. If the correlation was real, then I knew too much.

If I knew too much…

I remembered the CEO's sneer right before he met my eyes. The look gave me chills. Even now, I felt goosebumps at the memory.

Shit, they're trying to kill me!

I grabbed my phone. I had to get help. I had to tell someone. I had to blow the whistle on this whole operation before anyone else got hurt. I searched the number for the FDA and dialed, praying they would have someone on the phones at this hour.

It rang once, then a familiar gruff voice answered. "Hey, kid."

I blinked. "Larry?"

"Did you really think we wouldn't intercept your phone calls? We've got agents everywhere, kid."

"W-what's going on, Larry?"

"You threatened to cut us off from our food source. We couldn't allow that to happen."

"Food source? What are you talking about?"

"For a smart girl, you really are obtuse. Dreams, kid. Your species' offspring give off the most delicious creativity in their sleep."

My species? I was too dumbfounded to form words.

"Its unfortunate creativity is a finite resource," Larry continued, "hence the developmental disorders you discovered. Otherwise, we could have fed from you indefinitely."

"Who are you?"

The line crackled with static as Larry chuckled. "You won't have to worry about that for long."

I hung up. Nausea turned my stomach as my mind raced. I was in the hotel room they booked for me. They knew where I was. Should I run? Could I hide anywhere? They could track me.

I raised my hand to smash my phone against the wall, but hesitated.

Guess it's a plan B kind of day.

I logged into Instagram and started a live post.

"Hey all, Amelia here." I slid to the floor and leaned

against the bed. "I made it to Vegas in one piece, but since arriving, I've realized some things about my company. About the higher-ups, anyway. I don't know how deep the conspiracy goes. They've blocked my calls, but hopefully they can't block me from posting. I probably don't have much time. Someone's chasing me... I'm just too tired to run anymore." Concerned comments started rolling in from my friends and family. I sobbed.

Thank God people were watching.

"I know it sounds crazy, but they're doing something to the children. The formula they manufacture is helping the babies sleep, sure, but it's also causing developmental disorders. I found the correlation, but there's so much more I don't understand. Please... Someone needs to look into this. I don't—" I sniffled. "I don't think I'll have the time."

The door flew open with a crash. I flinched, almost dropping my phone.

"Here he is now." I pointed the camera directly at Smith. "The man trying to kill me. Smile, Mr. Smith, you're streaming live on the internet. Get a good look, people! Take screenshots!"

The deranged man hesitated, then gritted his teeth and pulled a gun from his waistband. I turned the camera back toward me.

"I guess Smith doesn't have a plan B." Tears streamed from my eyes. "You don't have to watch this part. I love you all."

I slid the phone under the bed, letting the stream continue. I closed my eyes.

A gunshot thundered through the Bellagio.

Leah Lore is a fantasy and science fiction author from southwest Ohio. An avid reader from a young age, she was constantly daydreaming stories to escape reality. When not writing, Leah can be found at the stable with her unicorns or hiking in the woods with her partner and their rescue dog. Leah was a finalist in the 2024 NYCMidnight Short Story Challenge, and her debut novel will hit the shelves in 2025. Her stories are character-driven adventures with an emphasis on mental health and self-worth. Leah has an MS in biology. Her education and love of nature have been pivotal elements for creating beautiful yet realistic worlds brimming with magic. If you enjoyed this story, you can follow Leah's progress on her website and social media at https://linktr.ee/leahlore

PARSEC

TIM LEWIS

Cargonauts

"Engines are stable, sir. We have gone to plaid."

"Tucker, no one gets that reference," said the captain as he focused on the display.

"You do, sir, and that's all that matters," obliged Tucker.

A heavy slurping noise like a person biting on the butt of a ripe Georgia peach came from Tucker's right.

"Shut it, Anderson," said Tucker.

"Captain," said Anderson in a mocking tone, "I *too* like pre-century vids and would *love* if you and I could—"

"Stow it, both of you," the captain barked. Then, chuckling under his breath, added, "I'm surrounded by Assholes."

Metal whined from far reaches of the ship like a behemoth's roar, a common sound when a vessel faces intense structural loads at a molecular level, like those of a 150-ton vehicle crossing the envelope of space and time to travel faster than light.

The captain pressed a few highlighted pips on his screen, and a trajectory view showed a blip for his *Osprey*, a modified

FTL Orion Class personnel transport ship built in the Philadelphia Yard in 2132. "Wiley, give me our closure rate adjustment."

"We just left our solar system. We shaved nine weeks off our transit, sir, *relativity* speaking, of course."

"Math, someone," sighed the captain.

Tucker sat up straighter in his chair, reciting in a single breath, "With velocity increased to 3.65 times the speed of light, our 9.84 week relativistic reduction will translate to an observed time dilation of 11.3 weeks for the outpost on Proxima b — sir."

Another elongated slurp came from Tucker's side, this time with the added effect of a moan.

Tucker's hand swung out and barely caught Anderson's left shoulder as she instinctively dodged from the playful slap.

"Sir, I have been assaulted," said Anderson in a mock formal tone. "Under United Transport Regulation 32.73 subclause 5b, I request judicial—"

"If you two don't stifle your banter, I will pull this ship over," said the captain, straining to look over his shoulder, "and you will be strapped together and tossed overboard in an endless frozen embrace for a millennium until solar radiation breaks you into your useless atoms. Bright-line?"

"Bright-line, sir," came dejected voices in unison.

The captain went back to his display and cycled through several more screens. He enjoyed that they had grown into a family, which made the long journeys tolerable, but sometimes he preferred it when their military training kicked in and they did what they were told.

Wiley, the *Osprey*'s navigator, would occasionally recite measurements to the captain without a speck of emotion. The two monitored the *Osprey*'s primary FTL reactor as they validated the drive enhancements they made at the Eagle base in the Sea of Tranquility. The silent look between them told of their anxiety and hope that their adjustments would get them to Proxima b before everything went to shit.

Tucker and Anderson went about their work scanning the path ahead for celestial debris. Tucker, the flight engineer, was a recent graduate of the Academy. After serving four years enlisted to pay off part of his student loans, he opted to go the officer route. Anderson was career enlisted, and she was the youngest systems engineer promoted to chief. The two tweaked the instrument array to adjust for gravitational parallax to the navigational system to avoid "intersection."

A reassuring ping came from Wiley's console. "BIT parity is good. All calculations confirmed. The *Osprey* is a solid ship, sir. You did a fine job with the enhancements," said Wiley in rote fashion, never taking a glance from his display.

"We. Yes, we did," he said appreciatively as he patted his hand over a familiar panel on the bulkhead.

The spot had a slight sheen from being polished by the captain's hand over the years: sometimes a rub for luck, sometimes a pat for a job well done, and sometimes he just rested his hand there to be connected to the girl.

"I knew when they said 3.3c was the max speed of light she was capable of more, just by looking at her."

"Well, this is great, Captain," said Anderson. "So that just means we get there a little quicker? So what, we can turn around and come home that much sooner, so we can spend a year in dry dock going broke while they figure out how to clean excess antimatter from my engine's coils because we ran her so hot?"

The captain ignored Anderson as a general rule. "I got a request from high up before we started the trip. The shipment we carry is not only essential to Proxima b, but critical for their survival. About six months ago they ruptured their atmosphere accumulator at site Hawking and have been operating solely from site Milner."

"Um, site Milner can't support the population, Captain," said Tucker. "The consumption specification for a population size of—"

"I am aware of this, Mr. Tucker," the captain said with practiced patience. "They have rationed, and they're cycling half the team off planet in the *Largo*'s cryo chambers to extend the system, but even that could only buy them a year and half."

"Sir, didn't fleet report the *Largo* started its return four months ago?" asked Tucker.

"Do the math, Genius," said Anderson. "Brass is distorting reality again to cover up the issue."

"But that would mean—" started Tucker.

"You two done?" came the captain's voice. "We were going to barely make it under normal power, then Command asked us to take the initiative, so now with our adjustment, the people are going to have a better chance to survive this snafu."

"That's great, if we don't burn up from dark matter exposure," said Anderson.

"That's not a thing," said Tucker.

"Shut it," snarked Anderson.

The captain ignored them and moved on. "Command recognized the risk we're taking, and as such, have authorized an additional commission of, well, let's just say that the *Osprey* can be in dry dock for three years before you cargonauts need to worry about funds to buy your next shot. Sometimes it's a good thing the military went corporate."

Last Trip

"I TOLD YOU, I adjusted the overflow to account for the particle inversion."

"But did you—"

"Yes, sir! I also vented the hydrogen increase, and I set it to cycle for a pressure of 683kpa."

"Then tell me, Lt. Wiley," said the captain, "why did I wake up only halfway through our trip to find us rotating dead-stick at a paltry speed of 1.6c?" The captain cycled the control column haphazardly for emphasis that they lost all flight control. "We've completed a parsec, but we still have 0.94 light years to go, give or take a billion miles. At this rate we won't arrive for twenty… uh, twenty…"

"31.9 weeks relativistic." Tucker hesitated and took a deep breath. "40.9 weeks observed by time dilation on Proxima b."

"Yes, a long damn time. And that's if our trajectory holds. One bump by solar wind or an errant micrometeoroid greater than a gram, and we could end up in the next quadrant," the captain barked, as he spun and knocked his tablet off the console.

Tucker watched the tablet soar and oddly hover through the cabin before it bounced off a panel then smoothly slid across the floor in the four-fifths artificial gravity.

The cabin went silent. By the time they reached Proxima b, the terraformers would have been dead for four months, and without planetary maintenance, not a usable resource would survive on the planet to support their return trip.

The ship sat in a dead zone with minimal communication ability to either base. If the *Osprey* managed a return vector to the moon, it would be 106 weeks at their current speed. With their current stores, Command could collect their bodies that would have suffocated 47 weeks prior.

Even traveling faster than the speed of light by

momentum alone, they were still essentially adrift like a raft on an ocean of black.

The captain could see despair eating away at his crew one inexorable bite at a time. "Hey! Work the problem."

"The problem is pretty well worked; the solution is the challenge now." Anderson slammed her hand against an overhead panel.

"Anderson, are you offering to step outside and buy the rest of us a few weeks of rations?" asked the captain.

"No, sir," said Anderson.

"Then I suggest you focus on a solution. Work—the—problem." Each word was staccato and calm as he directed their actions.

Wiley ignored them both, his forehead pressed to the cold borosilicate of Port 7. No one on the ship knew, but "last trip" was the promise he'd made. As the ship slowly rotated along an oblique axis, he watched the brilliant glow of the Milky Way pass as if they floated into oblivion on its waters. This last trip was supposed to be less than six months and would get him enough experience for a promotion, then he'd ride a desk in the applied physics department until retirement.

Chemistry 201

THE HISS of atmosphere filled the cabin as the pressure equalized from the hatch to the maintenance corridor. Wiley and Anderson crawled through, and the captain could see their look was grimmer than the day before.

The captain braced himself with a hand on his bulkhead spot, as much to comfort her as himself. "What's the story?"

"The engines are mucked, sir. Antimatter built up in the injection chamber quicker than the calculations forecasted. I think the heavy water we loaded at Eagle Base was not fully recycled. Would have been fine for a normal burn, but we lost about seven percent cooling efficiency."

"Fu—bureaucratic—corporate—pencil pushing—"

"Captain?" Tucker's face was ashen as his mentor broke character.

"It's fine. It's fine," said the captain. He reached over and tried to give Tucker a reassuring pat on the back. "She's a solid ship, and now we know the issue. We just have to work the problem."

The crew stood silent, a rare occurrence, as the captain slowly calmed his breathing. He performed several paces in the cramped cabin, his mind focused on the problem.

Finally the captain turned back to the crew. "Okay, we got this. It's a simple matter of chemistry that we all had in the Academy. Wiley, pull up specs for the CO_2 scrubbers. Tucker, get me a count of all salt packs from the MREs. And Anderson..." he hesitated, a grin stretching across his lips.

"Sir?"

"Build me a phased ionizer from the secondary OME. We're going to filter some agua."

Beep

"WELL, maybe if we had five more kilos of salt and a year to distill the deuterium," said Tucker, "then we could get enough heavy water to purge the system and bring the reactor back online without melting a hole in the hull."

"Use the water we have in stores to make more," said Anderson. "Then you can all start peeing in the reservoir if that will help with the salt issue."

"Not the same," said Wiley with a chuckle, but frustration started to settle on his face.

"Heavy water has a different chemical structure to handle the heat. Regular H_2O uses the protium isotope of hydrogen, which would vaporize, whereas the hydrogen isotope deuterium makes up D_2O, heavy water, which can handle the cooling needs of a reactor." Tucker took a deep breath to continue, "It's because the neutron—"

"Thank you for the science lesson, Mr. Tucker," said Wiley. "And everyone, please don't urinate in the engines."

"I told you, Wiley, use the salt as a catalyst, not the reactant, and then use the Orbital Maneuvering Engine as an ionizing reagent on the hydrogen in the secondary tank to create the deuterium. Then it's another simple controlled burn of the OME to create our heavy water," said the captain.

"You're starting to sound like Tucker. This concerns me," said Wiley, his dry tone carrying all the requisite levels of snark.

"Lt. Wiley," warned the captain, turning on him with a placid look that told everyone the discussion was over.

"Bright-line, sir. You're right, the science is spot on. It works. But with the equipment we have on board... Sir, I'm making it a beaker at a time, when we need kiloliters."

Beep.

"Then plus up the production. Get the spare carbon-spun tanks in storage and build in the gym," said the captain.

Beep.

"Sir, excuse me," said Tucker.

"I can try, and considered that, but we just have the one tank, and with that size, it will still be months," said Wiley.

Beep.

"Sir!"

"Then carve out the ensign's empty head and use it as a vessel to produce more." Nearly enraged, he turned. "What is it, Mr. Tucker?"

"Sir. Long range proximity alarms show an object approaching."

"Well then, Ensign, get out and push us so we don't run into it," said the captain with little concern, since it would be days before the object would pose any threat.

"That's it, sir, it's already adjusted *its* course."

"What's adjusted its course?"

Tucker keyed in a few commands trying to attenuate the Comm array. "Anderson, the signal is weak; can you increase the gain on array two by twelve hertz?" He adjusted more controls with practiced fingers honed at the Academy.

"Today, Ensign," said the captain.

"Um, it's the *Largo,* sir," said Tucker.

"You're mistaken," said the captain, turning his view to the front as if to look at the ship that sat millions of miles in front of them. "That's impossible."

Rendezvous

"ALRIGHT *LARGO*, so that's the situation. If you could spare a cup of water, we would be much appreciative," said the captain, working well to exude calm.

There was a crackle over the intercom. "Glad we caught your distress beacon. I think we can oblige," said Lt. Malvolia of the *Largo,* the crew transport ship stationed at Proxima b.

"Thank you. We got our maneuvering engines working to get us to a stop. See you in about two days, *Largo,*" said the captain.

"*Largo* out, *Osprey*."

The captain flipped the switch for the Quantum Entanglement Communications Array, and the hum dwindled as the system powered down.

"So do you think..." began Wiley.

"Yep," said the captain.

"And they'll probably..."

"Yep."

"Um, could you two translate for those of us who don't speak Sexagenarian?" asked Anderson. Tucker's face fell. "Pick your jaw up. It means 'old person.' Get your head out of the gutter."

"The *Largo* was locked in orbit at Proxima b to provide their cryo chambers as a method to reduce the terraformers' use of limited planetary resources," said the captain.

"Well, they probably got new directions to take their complement back home. No sense sticking around to be a popsicle," said Anderson.

"They didn't mention those directives," said Wiley, as if that answered the concern.

"Um, who really recites their orders to every passerby?" asked Anderson.

"Ohhh," came the realization from Tucker. "They think we're a normal supply run, not a rescue. So, they didn't talk to Command. So, their return trip is not an order, which means they stole the ship." He paused and took on a somber tone. "They're deserters."

"If I didn't think it'd go to your head, Mr. Tucker, I'd give you a gold star and cookie," said the captain.

Tucker smacked Anderson on the arm before she could eat another peach.

She smiled and rubbed her arm. "Captain, they have to know, right? Kidding aside, they have to know they'll get imprisoned when they return to Earth," said Anderson, "or even executed."

"Not if they didn't know Command sent a rescue, and they're playing this as the regular return trip of the *Largo*. That explains why the lieutenant, not the captain, is piloting. Also why they're willing to stop, so they don't draw attention as the ship that ignored a call for aid."

"Let's just Comm back to base or Proxima b and let them know," said Anderson.

"We're still in the dead zone. We don't have the signal strength in our Quantum Array to reach either location. We barely could reach the *Largo*," said Tucker.

"What's the play, Captain?" asked Wiley.

"If we avoid them, we drift in space unable to get anywhere." The captain sighed. "If we stop, they try to kill us so we don't get anywhere. It's a Kobayashi Maru."

The others looked at him questioningly until Tucker's recognition set in, "Hey, I got that!"

"Do you want another cookie?" asked the captain.

Tucker smiled, then his face took on a look of despair as the gravity of their rendezvous and getting out of a no-win situation took hold. "I guess we'll see in a few days who finds out if the other is going to cheat."

Status Quo

"Closure is a half a meter per second and three degrees low off your starboard, *Osprey*," came a male's voice over the intercom.

"Roger, *Largo*. Adjusting." The captain entered subtle commands to the control column, and the staccato roar of the OMEs adjusted the *Osprey*'s orientation.

From the side port, they watched as the *Largo* imperceptibly came to a stop. She was four times longer than the *Osprey* and twice as tall. Vessels like the *Largo* were slow, but perfect for the terraformers that had to move large industrial equipment.

The intercom crackled again with the male's voice on the *Largo*. "Alignment is good. Capture in 3… 2…"

A muffled clang reverberated through the hull as the *Largo*'s gangway connected with the *Osprey*. The hiss of pressure equalization quickly followed, confirming a soft seal between the two craft was complete.

"Play dumb. Get the agua. Get back on course." The captain clipped out clear instructions.

"They know," said Wiley ominously.

"They might suspect something, but they don't know. Besides, if there are any issues, we have Tucker," said Anderson, giving him a nod.

"Um, thank you." Tucker's cheeks flushed.

"He's a natural when it comes to playing dumb. It's like he doesn't even have to try," said Anderson.

The captain couldn't hide his grin. "Let's go meet our guests. Wiley, you have the bridge."

The three made their way through various connecting halls and past rows of improvised cargo containers before arriving midship. Anderson spun the lock before swinging the half-ton door easily on its hydraulic actuators.

Before them stood a group of three in ill-fitting flight suits, the woman in front clearly in charge. She was tall, even by Proxima b standards, where humans only a generation out from Earth grew unfettered by the reduced gravity of the planet. She had raven hair, with eyes to match, and a perpetual lift on the left side of her lips that seemed to dismiss her lessers.

"Ahoy, Captain," came a raspy voice. "I am Lt. Malvolia. This is my First Engineer, Danmere, and my Load Master, Toddes."

Toddes gleefully looked to each person and the ship behind the crew, whereas Danmere held his gaze impassive.

"Thank you for stopping, Lieutenant." He gave a nod over his shoulder. "This is Chief Anderson and Ensign Tucker."

The lieutenant gave a nod to each. "So, time is money for us long haulers. What's the story?"

"We got some bad water on Eagle, and it fouled our engine," started the captain.

"The quality of the deuterium caused errant chrysalis in the conversion chamber that obstructed the flow regulation, creating a cascade shutdown of the secondary manifold," added Tucker with his usual, oblivious charm.

"Corporate." Malvolia said the word as a sneer and gave a slight smile that evened out the twitch in her face. "Well, that does put a damper on things."

"Uh, yes, the chief can reset the manifold, but we need clean water; otherwise, we wouldn't get a million miles before it mucked up again," said the captain. "If you can spare ten kiloliters, we should be back on our supply run at a decent speed."

"Supply run? I thought Orion class were high speed people movers, not like my tug?"

"It was a special request from Command. Some politician's supply of vichyssoise was probably running low. I don't ask. They pay; I go." He played off being jovial, but followed Malvolia's glance to Tucker's blank, dumb stare. *The boy followed orders too damn well sometimes.*

"Right. Command always caters to the elite, leaving the rest of us hanging." She gave a nod to Toddes. "Billy will help you bring the lines over so we can top you off."

"Sounds good. We'll get our umbilical and meet you in the middle."

The two groups separated to their duties.

Tucker's head lurched forward with a smack on the back of the head from Anderson. "He said play dumb, not Ruprecht the idiot savant."

"It's fine, Anderson," said the captain. "The moment was bound to be tense."

"Vichyssoise?" asked Anderson, perplexed.

"It's some kind of fancy soup I guess politicians would eat, and not something a group of colonists would care about."

"What colonists?" Tucker rubbed the back of head, with a tussle to his hair, making him look more confused.

"Not a one of them has ever seen a day in the military," said Anderson.

"How could you tell?" Tucker swung his head to each of them.

"Tucker, you are dumb. The flight suits worn out of regulation fit tells you they're borrowed." Anderson shook her head. "But tell me this, what's my first name?"

Tucker stammered as he never really considered that Anderson even had a first name. Sure, he had probably seen it on formal documents here and there, but he had never said it out loud, as everyone referred to each other by last name or title in traditional military style. "Heather?" Then it looked like he paused to ensure he could recall his own first name.

"Enough. Get the lines ready. Let's get this done quickly without escalation." The captain turned, and they each split off to their assigned tasks.

* * *

THE *LARGO*'S crew took a little longer than the *Osprey*'s crew, but twenty minutes later the teams reconvened in the middle of the gangway. The connection of the two umbilicals was a little awkward in partial weightlessness, where the ships' gravity generators didn't quite reach the full length of the gangway.

"We're connected. Cycle the pumps," called Malvolia to an unseen Toddes at the *Largo*'s portal. A few seconds later there was vibration, and the slosh of almost iridescent water ran through the semitransparent umbilical connector.

"Flow looks good," said Malvolia.

"We have positive pressure," called an unseen Anderson, manning the pump panel at the *Osprey*'s portal.

"Yep, should have a full transfer in about twenty minutes," said the captain.

The crews stood watching the water slosh through the coupling like it was about to do a trick. The captain and lieutenant shared idle chitchat about travels, while Danmere stood rooted with his head down at the coupling, but his eyes watched the captain and Tucker.

About halfway through, Toddes came down the gangway to check the progress. "Wow, cool! Why does it glow?" he asked.

Tucker unconsciously jumped in with rote fashion. "Large volumes moving through limited gravity in the vacuum of space without a significant ground generate low level static electricity, and the molecular weight of the deuterium amplifies the reaction, which gives the faint lapis lazuli glow."

"Cool, never seen that."

Tucker looked up, confused, as intrusive thoughts took over. "You see this anywhere large pipes run through a manifold on a ship. I thought any crew member knew this?"

Toddes looked to Malvolia for help to answer the question, but her eyes were locked on the captain. A moment passed, then Malvolia's eyes narrowed as realization of unspoken knowledge on both sides passed between them.

"Ensign Tucker," said the captain, without taking his eyes off Malvolia. "Please check with Anderson that everything is still going smoothly on our end."

"Actually, Mr. Tucker, would you mind coming to our ship and helping *Mr.* Toddes? Your experience would be a great help."

Tucker hesitated. The captain only used their rank for direct orders to be followed without question, so he looked for his captain's confirmation before taking a request from another superior officer.

The captain made the mistake of looking at Tucker to give him a head jerk to move up to the *Osprey*. When he looked back, Danmere was already in motion with something metallic in his hand.

The captain put up his arm, but the force was enough to connect with his head. Blood flowed freely and hovered in the partial weightlessness.

A blur of white filled the captain's view just as a foot connected to Danmere's chin. There was a grunt, then the umbilical wrench floated freely in the air as Danmere glided to the ceiling of the gangway, hit his head, then bounced back down.

Tucker gave a side kick this time, bracing himself against the bulwark. The kick sent Danmere two meters backward toward the *Largo*'s portal before gravity took over and dropped him to the gantry in a slump.

After the first kick, Malvolia reacted and reached into her flight suit to pull out a pneumatic rivet gun. By the time the second kick was delivered, she had the gun pointed directly at Tucker's chest. The captain could see the orange safety catch removed, so the piston would be a lethal projectile.

"When did you know?" asked Malvolia.

"The moment we picked you up on our scan."

"I thought it was the first name." She gave a glance to Danmere, still in a slump.

"They said no ship could make it in time." Malvolia was defensive. "We were supposed to wait to die?"

"Timeline was tight, and they needed you worried so you would conserve provisions. Not all details of Command are shared with civilians. But it's done now. They'll know what happened when you arrive at Eagle base." The captain was stalling, and Malvolia knew it.

"Actually, they'll know when *you* arrive at Proxima b. But if you don't show up, then my arrival to Eagle is exactly what I tell them. We drop speed and ride this out for a few extra months, so the timeline matches, and tell them you never showed." She raised her voice an octave and made an innocent plea. "There was nothing we could do when relief didn't arrive. We made a run with what little reserves we had left, and survived by grace alone." Her self-satisfied smile was repugnant.

"That's why you didn't say anything to us," she continued. "You have to get there for them to know we already left. What was once our condemnation is now our salvation...all because of some bad water."

"And you're thinking you condemned a few thousand people, what's three more cargonauts alone on a vessel," said the captain, disgusted.

"Good point. Let's get the chief down here where I can see everyone." Malvolia leveled the riveter on Tucker's head and yelled up the gangway, "Anderson, we have an issue, can you check this out?"

The captain and Malvolia locked eyes in silence as the sound of boot stomps came down the walk.

"Hey Captain, we're about halfway and the flow still looks the same, so what's the iss—" She stopped short when she got far enough down to see Malvolia holding a device on Tucker. "What the hell did Tucker do?" she accused.

"This plays out two ways," Malvolia said to the captain, ignoring Anderson. "We take our water back and you live as long as your supplies last before becoming a derelict ship of ghost stories, or you do something stupid and become a ghost ship today." Malvolia glanced over her shoulder, "Danmere, you up?" There was a groan as Danmere moved slowly to his feet. "Change of plans. Mr. Toddes, head back to the top and reverse the flow."

Toddes stood slack-jawed, trying to put the pieces together.

"So we're going to wait right here until this is done, and then you'll—"

There was a sound of gurgling water and the glow from the connector reduced as the water slowed, drawing everyone's eyes but the captain's.

As Malvolia turned back, the captain lurched forward, pushing aside her weapon arm just as it went off. A muffled *thwump* sounded as the piston pushed the rivet bolt out of the cylinder and right over Tucker's shoulder — and through the Mylar gantry.

"Breach! Breach! Breach!" yelled the captain, a second before atmospheric sensors sounded the klaxon.

Anderson and Tucker spun on their heels as the captain gave them both a shove from behind, sending them half floating, half running up the ramp.

He looked over his shoulder as Malvolia pulled on a stunned Toddes. "Billy, move!"

The captain and crew stumbled until full gravity took over, giving them traction to sprint the remaining distance. He called, "Wiley! Disengage the—" at the same moment the end of the umbilical came flying through the portal.

"Move!" yelled Wiley, poised on the side of the portal. His hair flew across his face as the atmosphere was sucked from the *Osprey*.

The three leaped through the opening, sprawling on the deck as they heard the satisfying *thhppt* of the large door closing and sealing the vessel.

Wiley slid down the side of the door as the others rolled over. He gave the captain a nod. "So, Captain, did you play *too* dumb to maintain the status quo?"

"My charming demeanor isn't what it used to be," said the captain as he pulled himself up to a squat. "Nice work shutting down the pump as a distraction."

The captain slowly got to his feet and pulled a rag from his pocket that he pressed to his cut. "Okay, cargonauts, let's work the problems. Ensign Tucker, calculate our engine efficiency based on the water we took onboard. Chief Anderson, eject the gangway before they drag us across the stars. Lt. Wiley, put some distance between us and the *Largo*."

"And..." hinted Wiley.

"*Aaand,* thank you for leaving the Comms open and catching that I said *three,* so you knew to come rescue our asses."

"Sir, don't we need to do anything?" asked Tucker.

"I just gave you an order, Mr. Tucker."

"No sir, I mean about the *Largo*."

"The *Largo*'s future is written. They can either drift until their stores run dry or go home and take their lumps. We'll call it in when we get to Proxima b, so Command will know long before they can ever arrive."

"Aye, sir."

"Okay, now let's get about the task of writing *our* future."

Lorentz Factor

"So, Tucker saved us?" Anderson gave an incredulous stare.

"Yep. He went all Krav Maga on the oaf and took him out of the equation, like a good mathematician," said the captain.

"It's really nothing; the Academy teaches zero-G hand-to-hand—" started Tucker.

"And then he let their boss pull a gun on him that nearly got us all killed?" asked Anderson, scrunching her face at Tucker.

"Well, I forced her to react and fire," said the captain.

"Because Tucker was too dumb to react, and you had to save his worthless butt. Well, at least you were there to prevent him from doing anything dumber," said Anderson before turning back to her console.

Tucker stared as the captain gave him a shrug, and his moment of glory visibly dissipated.

"Back to business. Did you finish the calculations?" asked the captain.

"Sir," said Tucker, still sounding a little dejected, "we were able to get six kiloliters, which will allow us to get up to 2.1c. That puts us a half a week behind our original schedule."

"Dammit. It's going to be tight. We need more time." The captain did a few paces and put a hand on his spot.

"Sir, isn't that only four days?" asked Anderson.

"No, because of math." He stared out the front of the ship, looking for alternatives in the inky black.

"But in that old *Star Trek* show—" started Anderson trying to lighten the mood, when the captain turned on her with fire in his eyes.

"Finish—that—sentence, Flotsam. Give me dominion."

"Sorry, sir." Anderson straightened. "I just don't think a couple extra days late is that big of a deal."

"We've increased our relative time on the ship to a half a week due to the reduced speed, yes, but we still have time dilation, so that puts us at two weeks as observed by the people on Proxima b. We were barely going to make it at our original speed, but now we may not be there in time at all." The captain went head down into his console, searching for a solution.

"I always hate this stuff. Just give me a date of arrival,"

Anderson sighed, turning to Tucker. "We get it. Because we're going even slower, slower than normal relativistic speed, our observed time to get there increases exponentially more."

"Obviously. This is just simple modified Special Relativity." Tucker looked from face to face, and Anderson mistakenly made eye contact with Tucker. The captain could see out of the corner of his eye that Anderson looked like she was going to hear a ghost story as Tucker launched like an excited puppy. "Time dilation increases to its maximum point right before the speed of light. A year for us near light speed would be like 70,000 years for an observer; that's why most ships travel less than 0.5c. At light speed, you would feel like you're getting there quicker on the ship, but it would actually take longer for the observers." Tucker was in his element and relished a moment to go full geek. "But once you cross the Lorentz Barrier, then time dilation decreases with increased velocity, *of course,* so the faster we go, the less the time dilation. That's why we have to accelerate through the band of 0.5lc to 1.5lc, so it's not observed as taking longer." Tucker turned over his vid tablet to show the modified Lorentz Factor calculation, like that would explain everything.

$$\Delta T = \Delta To / \sqrt{(|1 - v^2/c^2|)}$$

"*Mmm hmm,* got it," said Anderson, looking for support from the captain and Wiley, who still refused to make eye contact.

Thinking she didn't, and excited to talk to someone about his passion, he went on with more zeal. "See, it's now the absolute value of β. It's like the sound barrier. Very bumpy ride up to the barrier, but once you exceed the speed of sound, then the shock waves smooth the air currents. In this case, it's like a *timewave* smoothing our dilation."

"Said I got it," Anderson quipped. She pressed on her

entry board with more fervency, trying to disengage from Tucker's blather.

The verbal sluice was open, however, and Tucker's flood waters continued unchecked. "So while normal speed of light is a constant, once you cross over to faster than light, the calculation for time dispersion essentially inverts the tangent of the asymptote and the Lorentz Factor becomes a reciprocal, or rather the absolute value of one minus Beta. Your velocity between inertial reference frames becomes constant and the speed of light becomes the variable, or in this case the relativistic time dispersion compresses in conjunction with the modified Lorentz Factor—"

Anderson broke off in a sing-song tone, "Maath, math, math-math, maaath... Would someone give the ensign a cookie so he shuts up?"

Tucker lowered his tone. "Would it be easier if I draw you a diagram?"

"I'll draw a chalk line around your corpse," threatened Anderson, getting up from her seat.

"This is like the guylines holding the launch stand during high winds," said Wiley, without lifting his head from his console.

Hearing a full sentence from a man who usually only responded to direct questions from the captain brought Tucker and Anderson up short. "The *what?*" they asked in unison.

"The immense strain on the wires holding the launch platform at Tokyo Bay," said Wiley, still keying in commands without a break in tempo. "You can hear them hum while you're waiting to launch, almost like a tune." He input a few more commands, letting the pause hang in the air. "It's very similar to the level of intense sexual tension humming between you two."

Anderson drew herself up, "You can take that tune and go—"

"Enough!" The captain punctuated his order with a thump to his spot on the bulkhead.

Anderson mumbled something incoherent as she went back to her seat, and Tucker returned to his tablet. The captain was already back on his screens and cycled through several schematics of the *Osprey*.

"There. We can get more speed there." He zoomed into a section and then pressed a key that replicated his view on Anderson's console.

"Oh, hell no," came her reply.

"It has to be done Chief, and you're the only one who knows the subsystems well enough to make the repair to the inverter so we can increase the efficiency output of the main drive."

"I hate crawling into the ass of the *Osprey* when she's in dry dock, and you want me to go back there with engines running while we're hurtling through space?"

"If you have an alternative, I will consider it. But from my seat, that's our only option."

Anderson reviewed the data and reached the same conclusion. She buried her face in her hands and let out a few expletives before responding. "I better get a bonus for this."

"I'll transfer some of my own credits for you and Mr. Tucker to have a proper dinner and a movie next time we're at port," quipped the captain.

Anderson stared at the back of the captain's chair, which probably saved his life because she could not see his Cheshire grin.

Tucker added, "Should be a quicker trip because we're ten meters shorter now."

"Huh?" said Anderson, regretting it immediately.

"The Lorentz Contraction," said Tucker matter-of-factly. "At this speed with our current time dilation, our fifty-meter craft is reduced to only thirty-nine meters. Well, actually the front of the ship is contracted by less because it's going faster than the rear, which is essentially motionless because of the inertial frame of reference..."

Anderson spun around. "Captain, United Transport Regulation 32.73 subclause—"

"I concur," said the captain. "Mr. Tucker, if you don't stop warping our brains with your techno-babble verbal diarrhea, I'm going to bring you up on assault charges myself."

"No sir, assault charges against me," said Anderson, "because I am going to toss that breathing Wikimedia out an air lock!" She grabbed a weathered olive drab tool bag from under her seat and made her way along the relativistic thirty-nine meters to the rear of the *Osprey*.

BOHICA

"I'M TELLING you it's wedged," said Anderson over the intercom.

"You've got that fancy bag of tools; can't you just pry it loose?" asked the captain.

"I am elbow deep in the manifold, and it's not budging. The crystallization is worse than we expected."

"I can send Tucker down..."

"No!" came a quick reply. "I need leverage, not a science lesson. You send him down, and I'll go elbow deep—"

"I'll go," interrupted Wiley.

* * *

TWENTY MINUTES LATER, Wiley's voice came over the intercom, "Captain, we tried breaking it free and had a little movement, but it's being stubborn. Anderson is now wedged by a chunk of the crystallization. I'm going to try cycling the—"

A scream echoed through the maintenance hall and into the bridge.

"Captain, she's pinned! I can't hold it!"

The captain saw Tucker dart out of his chair and down the access ladder before he could give the order. They both hurtled down the maintenance tunnel, ducking beneath piping and leaping over conduit. As they reached the ass of the *Osprey,* they found Wiley standing upright with his arms braced against the centrifugal injector. Anderson was on the ground, her face sheet white with one hand pressed against the housing and her entire right arm out of sight in the innards of the converter. A small pool of blood was already wicking up the shoulder of her uniform.

"Tucker! Help me hold this, or it will sever her arm!" ordered Wiley.

He froze, staring at the two.

"Tucker, you idiot, help him hold it!" screamed Anderson.

Tucker ducked behind a unit out of sight.

"Tucker, what are you doing?" yelled the captain, as he ran next to Wiley to help him hold the injector.

"The charge is building in the magneto; we can't hold it," grunted Wiley.

"Screw it, Captain," grunted Anderson. Her face was ashen as she clenched her jaw. "Get the med kit off the wall back in ops. You can foam the…the stump, until you can get me to medical."

The three momentarily disappeared in a haze of pale yellow fog that filled the compartment. They all spasmodically coughed, and the cloud dissipated as quickly as it appeared. The captain looked down to see Anderson gagging with both of her hands on her face. He let go, and the inertia overpowered Wiley as the injector spun in normal operation.

The captain lifted Anderson to her feet and inspected the cut on her upper arm. "It's deep, but a few elastic stitches and you'll be fine, with a nice scar to enhance the story." He turned to Tucker who came out onto the walk. "What the hell happened?"

"BOHICA," said Wiley softly to Anderson.

She nodded.

"Captain, the injector's centripetal force was achieving critical mass regardless of external influence, so I extrapolated an alternative. The makeup of the deuterated crystals locking Anderson are formed by the recycled deuterium in a hexagonal lattice structure that—"

"English," said the captain.

"I expelled just a little fluorine gas from the reactor line, which was enough to force the hydrogen crystals to fissure so she could break free," he said with a satisfied smile and turned to Anderson. "I guess you needed a science lesson after all."

Anderson held back a swell of emotion, and simply said through gritted teeth, "Thanks."

"No big deal. Besides, a mechanic is not much good with only one arm," said Tucker.

She grabbed him by the front of the shirt with her good left arm and pulled him into a hug.

They both staggered back from the awkward exchange. Tucker, with cheeks beet red, stammered, "Although, you're not much better with two arms."

Anderson's face went red with her shoulders tightening like a bow getting ready to fire, and then a smirk slowly rose on her lips, "And you're only a little bit of an idiot."

Recovery

ONCE I HAD a star-eyed maid

Haul awa', haul awa'

I was content with her to lay

Haul awa', awa'...

Wiley sang the old sea shanty, keeping time with the clang of his boot against the metal console.

"Shut it, Wiley! It was just a moment of gratitude," yelled Anderson.

"What? I don't know what you're talking about. I like to sing while I compute trans-stellar equations against gravitational phenomenon."

In the comfort of her bed

Haul awa', haul awa'

Let me lay until I'm dead

Haul awa', awa'

Wiley continued, and there was a slight chuckle in his timbre.

"I liked it better when he was nearly a mute," mused Tucker.

"Mr. Wiley, give me an update based on the repairs," interrupted the captain.

"Sorry, sir. The blossoming romance in this ship makes this old heart sing again."

"Lt. Wiley." The captain's tone was level.

"Captain, we're not back to a peak efficiency, but the chief's work got us to 2.25c."

There was a long moment of silence while sideways looks from all three focused on Mr. Tucker.

"Oh, would you like me to do some *maaath*?" Tucker asked, feigning surprise.

"Ensign," warned the captain, drawing the word out like a knife.

"At 2.25c, our observed arrival time on Proxima b is now 23.35 weeks. Still four weeks shorter than our original arrival at normal speed."

"Hmm, your math was simple and relevant this time. Thank you, Mr. Tucker."

"Aye-aye, sir."

"Aye-aye, sir." Came Anderson's mocking tone in a hushed breath. "Wish he was *less* simple and *more* relevant."

Tucker just rolled his eyes and went back to his console. "Hmm, my mom was much older and drawn to my dad. I wonder if it will be genetic for me," he said absently.

"In your case, you really don't want to make any assumptions that will limit your prospects," Anderson shot back.

"Ensign Tucker," barked the captain.

"Sir?" Tucker snapped back to the moment.

"With our new velocity, what does that make our current ship length, by the Lorentz Factor?"

Excited for the question, Tucker hesitated, frantically doing some quick calculations in his head, "Um… 44.8 meters, sir."

"Hmm, still not far enough to *not* hear you two put this to rest if we throw you all the way in the back."

"Ew," said Anderson, giving an involuntary shudder as she turned back to her console. "Just *ew*."

Homeward

THE CARGONAUTS of ESS 73815 Orion Class transport ship, the *Osprey*, completed the preparations to engage FTL engines. Below, they could see the milky rust hue of Proxima b and the northern tectonic plate where they had just left Milner. The base would have enough supplies to maintain the pilgrims for another year while they got back to a self-sufficient state. More supply ships would come over the next few years to help rebuild Hawking base.

None of those would be the *Osprey*.

"The repairs look solid and will be enough to get us home in this lifetime." Wiley patted the captain on the back. "You did good, Virgil."

The captain gave a dagger stare. Very few knew his first name, and even fewer knew he was named after one of the original Mercury astronauts from the 1900s. His mother had high aspirations early on of him being an interstellar explorer rather than hauling cargo.

There were plenty of explorers, but Earth needed good crews to support forward bases. The captain never sought fame or recognition and preferred just being a footnote in history. He liked his job and the crew, but mostly his ship.

"Thanks, Wiley," said the captain. He glanced over at an agape Tucker, who quickly turned and managed to stare more intently at his screen.

The captain put a hand on his bulkhead spot and looked out into the calm and serenity of the black void. He could feel the warmth on his face from the red dwarf Proxima Centauri shining through the front portal. This was home, in these moments.

"Oh, and Mr. Wiley?" added the Captain, "if you ever call me Virgil again, I'm going to install a yardarm on this ship and hang you from it."

Tucker choked on his own spit and redoubled his focus on his console.

"Bright-line, Captain," said Wiley as he turned back to his own console with a grin, and reverently repeated, "bright-line."

"Course is plotted, Captain, all systems are nominal, 1.302 parsecs back to Earth," said Tucker. He sheepishly gave the captain a pleading look while Anderson just sighed and rolled her eyes.

The captain pointed two fingers forward toward the ship's prow. "Engage."

Tim Lewis manages rocket programs by day and collects hobbies by night. Writing has been his longest running hobby, going back to middle school and first place in a Halloween story contest. He took creative writing at Purdue, but his public works have all been scholastic and technical. Tim leans toward Sci Fi, Urban Fantasy, and Noir, where each contain an element of humor from a life spent as a smart ass. He published his first fiction work, "Switch," in 2019 and followed with short stories in notable anthologies as distractions from finishing his novel. For more about Tim, visit lewisventure.com

THE STAIN

MICHELE STUART

Keith Beaufort's death left a stain on the wall, right above the landing at the third-floor stairway. People had died in the house before. It was built during a time when illness or old age more typically resolved in the home than in a hospital and when many families endured painful childhood losses. But the stain left by Keith Beaufort's death was of a different nature. The wall was stamped not with his blood, but with his confusion and rage.

Not many knew about the stain. Some, like the man who rented the third-floor room for three years, are blessed with ignorance of such things. The woman who took the room after him though, fled after a single night, knowing only that those stairs terrified her.

Emily Carlisle felt the stain's presence the first time she mounted those stairs, in the summer of 2019. She brushed her fingers lightly against the wall, yanking them quickly back as if the paint had stung her hand.

"You okay, darling?" Amanda Wills asked from a few steps above.

Emily had known her new landlady for less than an hour,

not counting their email correspondence. She already thought of this short, stocky black woman not much older than Emily's parents as a woman of few words, and one of them was usually "darling." She insisted on "Amanda," not Ms. or Mrs. Wills, which would have been Emily's inclination.

Amanda thought this young white woman seemed nice enough. Probably a little sheltered. Polite. She marveled at how slight the girl was, like she might have to weight her pockets on a windy day.

"Just tired. It was a long, hot walk from the train station," Emily said. Her gift was the only thing Emily was adept at lying about, and that had taken years of practice.

Two doors opened off a small hallway at the top of the stairs. One led into the attic, the other to Emily's new bedroom. The antique bureau, the old-fashioned walk-in closet, and the colorful rug that covered much of the hardwood floor all delighted Emily. She appreciated the tiny refrigerator tucked into the corner of the closet, although she and the other tenants had kitchen privileges. She smiled at the sight of the patchwork quilt, folded across the foot of the double bed, ready to aid the thick, soft comforter against the chill Amanda had warned her about. Best of all were the two tall windows, showcasing chimneyed rooftops to the west and Salem Harbor to the north.

"I love it," Emily said.

* * *

HAD THUNDER WOKEN HER? Emily wondered, deep into her first night in her new room. Rain drummed against the roof. The streetlights made shadow puppets dance across the walls. But Emily had a memory of another sound, not thunder, but something like it. Something falling, maybe.

The puppets fled the light of the bedside lamp. Emily scanned the room. Everything in place. Maybe something in the attic. She shivered as she slipped out of bed and padded into the hallway. After contemplating the attic door for a moment, she descended the stairs instead. This seemed the right moment, in Emily's mind. Dark, wind-lashed nights are when stains like this are to meant be explored, she felt, without really understanding why.

Emily sat on the step above the landing and leaned forward, pressing her hand to the faded paint. Emotions buffeted her like the wave that had once tossed her end over end, until she'd surfaced, gasping, crying for her mother. As she had then, she retched.

This is death, Emily thought. *Someone died here.*

She washed her hands and rinsed her mouth in the shared bathroom on the second floor and found a sponge to clean the landing. Returning to her room, Emily found that sleep was not there for her, but the Internet was. Emily excelled at research. She loved it the way a kite loves a brisk breeze.

In another month, she'd enter Salem University's History program, where she hoped to focus on American Colonialism and the Witch Trials era. Her family teased her, affectionately, about being their black sheep, the sole humanities scholar of a very technical clan. *If they only knew,* Emily often thought. Not only a historian, but one with some kind of random, ineffable extra sense. Hers was a family of science and evidence. As a child, Emily hadn't had the language to describe the feelings that sometimes overcame her when touching certain objects. By the time she'd developed the language, she'd already deciphered her family's particular codes and mores. She opted to lie.

Emily did not yet understand that it isn't the nature of a gift like hers to be tested, verified, and documented. It's a fickle thing, like all such magic, which is not a word Emily ever applied to it. It does what it does, touches who it touches, and like the rest of reality, does not care if one believes in it.

Emily did not find a quick answer to the mystery of the dreadful spot. There was no police report, no news article, about a person dying at the address. Perhaps the event predated digitized records. She did learn that the house was owned by Keith and Constance Beaufort before Amanda bought it at auction. Constance had drowned in 2003, at the age of forty-one. It wasn't clear if she and Keith were divorced, or estranged, or if he had also passed away and Emily had simply found no record of it. She did not think they'd had children.

* * *

EMILY WOKE TO A BRIGHT, clear afternoon, her thoughts immediately drifting back to the previous night. She decided she would delve into the records that weren't online. Her family would get a kick out of that, she thought. Her second day in this historic, coastal city would be spent indoors, searching through old documents.

Emily heard no voices on her way down the stairs, so she was startled to find an older white man in the kitchen, sitting at the table drinking coffee and skimming a printed copy of the local newspaper while Amanda chopped parsley at the sideboard. The old, mechanical wristwatch he wore seemed to fit with the hard copy newspaper, in Emily's mind. She also thought that his blue eyes immediately scanned her for details and drew conclusions about them. This was true.

"Oh, hey, darling," Amanda said, breaking what Emily judged to have been a period of companionable silence. "Bobby, this is my new house guest, Emily. Emily, this is Detective Bobby O'Shea."

"Former," the man said. "Former detective. Retired. Bob or Bobby will be just fine."

"Bobby lives three doors up," Amanda said, nodding toward the back door. "Have some coffee. Just made a fresh pot."

Emily poured herself coffee, trying to think of something polite to say.

"Were you on the Salem police force?"

"Yes, ma'am," he said. "Lived here all my life, a lot of it in the same house."

"Oh, did you know the people who used to live here?" Emily asked. Her sudden excitement drained away as she felt all levity and good cheer flee the room.

Amanda sighed.

Bobby frowned. Something about the girl put him off, though Amanda had described her as charming. The girl seemed nervous, for no apparent reason. Could be she was just awkward or shy, he told himself, in which case meeting new people—especially ex-PD—probably did make her nervous. But why start asking about history that didn't concern her, again for no obvious reason? Maybe she was just making conversation. She couldn't possibly know how any mention of Keith or Connie threatened to swamp the defenses he'd built up over the years against the constant pounding of grief and guilt and loneliness. How could she know what he'd endured for all those years, without his closest friends, until he'd gotten to know Amanda and been reminded that there are still people worth putting on a clean shirt for?

"I did," he said. "Keith and Connie and I were good friends since high school. What makes you ask?"

"It's kind of my thing," Emily said. "History. Research. I always wonder what stories these old houses could tell."

"Well, you have come to the right city for that, darling,"

Amanda said, calling Emily's attention away from the former detective's unnerving gaze to her landlady's more comforting presence.

"I know," Emily said. She washed her mug and hung it back on its hook. "I guess I'll go out and see some of it. Nice to meet you, Detective. Bobby."

"You too, young lady."

Emily walked downtown, threading her way between throngs of tourists. She stopped to eat and used her phone to look up the buildings she wanted to see, deciding on Deeds and Probate first, library last.

Libraries were risky for Emily. She loved them, but she always feared choosing the favored volume of a beloved mother, donated by her grieving children, or the book used to strike an abused child across the face, becoming the focus of the child's rage and pain. Fortunately, such incidents were rare, and the risk worth taking.

This library delighted her with a robust selection of local history books dating back to the Trials and earlier, as well as collections of public records. The phone books were fascinating in their own right, especially the old yellow pages ads. Microfilms of old *Salem News* issues revealed two domestic disturbance calls to the Beaufort house in the eighties, as well as a couple of DUI stops for Constance, years later. *A troubled marriage,* Emily thought. She had found no divorce record for the Beauforts and no death record for Keith, but it seemed like he wasn't around when Constance died, and the city eventually auctioned the house.

It took no more than this to spark the idea in Emily's mind that perhaps Keith had stopped leaving the footprints we all stamp into history because he'd died. Maybe that awful stain on the wall was the last mark he made on the world. But the lack of evidence disturbed her. It ran against her grain to draw conclusions based on emotion, especially emotions not even her own. How to proceed?

* * *

Days passed as Emily pondered. In that time, she also toured the House of Seven Gables, visited her brother at MIT, and bombarded her family with pictures of her new city, but the troubling stain was never far from her mind, reasserting its pull on her each time she passed it. She sometimes imagined the house itself was urging her on. It certainly did its share of settling, as old houses do. Talking, Amanda called it. She said the old houses groaned about the cold settling deeper into their joints every year, just like people. But it was summer, and the third floor remained unseasonably chilly. Amanda said she'd had the heating and cooling system checked multiple times, and advised Emily to shut the AC vents off and open the windows to let the summer heat in.

Sometimes the house's complaints took on the sound of a footfall in the attic or the hallway. Emily dreamed, sometimes, that a man sat at the top of the steps, as if too polite to intrude into her room. She would wake up surprised, thinking a dream like that should have been a nightmare, but she never felt fear, no sense of threat. Only sadness. More than once, she woke in tears but could not remember which dream event had caused them. Those were hard mornings. She would go outside and walk until the sun's heat baked the sorrow away.

One night, after falling asleep with search results for "Keith Beaufort" filling her laptop screen, Emily woke in darkness, with the absolute conviction that somebody was sitting on the bed next to her.

"Keith?" she whispered, then woke again. It had been a

dream, one of those false awakenings that lull rational minds into believing in messages from beyond. Not that such things aren't possible.

"I'm sorry," she whispered into the darkness, unsure who she was apologizing to. To the person whose truth had yet to be uncovered? To the house? Did it want to be free of that stain?

She considered touching the spot again. Maybe she could glean more information. But the thought turned her stomach. Instead, the next morning, she decided to explore the attic. The door wasn't locked, just held closed by a small sliding latch. None of the doors in the old house hung quite true anymore, a quality that both charmed and annoyed Emily.

The attic was cavernous. Light filtered through small windows, littering the wooden floor with sunspots. This place demanded to be whispered in, even in the late-morning light. Old furniture stood here and there, waiting to be called to service again. Several piles of boxes marked "Christmas" took up one corner. Insulation filled the spaces between the exposed wall and ceiling beams. To the left of the door, a ladder of four wide, dust-covered steps led to a low loft.

Clearly nobody had traversed those steps for a long time, before Emily climbed them. The loft held only a few boxes and an old trunk. Hesitant at first, Emily quickly lost herself to the allure of the treasures she found. She examined an antique rag doll with a painted porcelain face dressed in a baby's nightgown. She braced herself before touching a World War II victory medal, but it held no impression at all.

The sun rose to its noon height and slid past it before she moved on to the trunk. She withdrew a 1979 Salem High School yearbook. Well wishes addressed "To Connie" lined the inside covers. Flipping through the pages, she found a picture of Constance Miller. She was a pretty white girl, her brown hair, like many other girls, cut in a feathered style that had been popular then. It reminded Emily of some of her mother's old photos. She also found Keith Beaufort. He was a little too blue-eyed and square-jawed for Emily's taste, but she could imagine many girls finding him handsome.

The trunk also held a couple of dog-eared novels and a shoe box. As soon as she touched the box, emotions swept over her. Love. Regret. A sorrow too raw, too painful, to call bittersweet. A pain that wondered if the love had been worth it after all.

She wasn't sure how long she sat in the box's grip. Tears blurred the already dust-fuzzed edges of the attic's contents and softened the sunbeams even more. Lifting the cover from the box, she found it full of old photographs. But something else caught her attention. Her shadow stretched across the attic floor, and another stretched alongside it, as if someone sat next to her. Some distant part of her wondered if she should be frightened, but another said no. No, there was nothing to fear here. There was only sadness now. A cloud moved across the sun, blotting out the shadows. She got up and brushed dust off her jeans, then heard the screen door swing shut, three floors below. Taking the shoe box, she trotted down the stairs to help Amanda with the groceries.

* * *

AMANDA DEVELOPED A FONDNESS FOR EMILY. She appreciated the way, if Emily were home, she'd come downstairs to help carry groceries. Emily always asked if Amanda needed anything before she went out, and she didn't seem bothered by whatever was wrong with the third floor. Amanda did feel a little guilty, not being more open about that, but she needed the extra income, and she was confident there was no danger. There had never been any furniture flying or phantoms dragging people into the shadows or other foolishness you saw on TV. It was more just a perpetual feeling of sorrow, as if the house itself suffered from a lingering grief centered on that floor. It seemed to her that most people didn't even notice, except for that one poor woman.

She was especially glad for Emily's company these recent weeks, since Bobby had drifted off into a funk. It happened, from time to time, often when he was reminded of his two old friends, Keith and Connie. Emily had meant no harm by asking about them; how could she know?

But Bobby could still be counted on for Tuesday nights, and she looked forward to seeing him. She'd put some dinner on later, then they'd go to the reading group she had talked him into joining with her.

Emily started a pot of coffee while Amanda put groceries away.

"Amanda," Emily said, "I have a confession to make."

"Oh?"

"I snooped around in the attic."

Amanda snorted and sat at the kitchen table. Emily put a cup of coffee in front of her, then poured one for herself.

"Find any lottery tickets or diamond rings I missed?" Amanda asked.

Emily's lingering nervousness melted away. "No. But I did find something." She set the shoebox on the table and sat down next to Amanda.

"Well, will you look at that," Amanda said, picking up a photo with no hesitation at all. Emily felt a fleeting pang of envy.

"Look, that's Bobby," Amanda said.

"It is?" Emily leaned over. "Which one?"

Amanda pointed him out, then started spreading the pictures across the table. There were many candid shots of Keith Beaufort as well as a few of Bobby.

"I suppose Connie took these," Amanda said. There were pictures of the friends at the beach, at a park, at parties. Bobby often seemed to be with different girls. There were other people in some of the pictures, though there weren't as many shots of birthday or holiday gatherings as Emily thought her own parents had.

Amanda didn't know everyone in the pictures but started talking about the ones she did. Emily was astonished by the flood of words. She should have asked questions sooner. *Some historian you'll make,* she thought.

Amanda told Emily she'd graduated five years before Bobby and his friends but got a job in the high school's administrative office. She hadn't known any of them well, but she remembered hearing that Keith lost his parents not long after high school, then that he'd left Connie with this huge old house he'd inherited from them.

"Connie passed quite young as well. I just hope Keith is well, wherever he is."

"Do you think he's still alive?" Emily asked.

Amanda looked at her sidelong. "Why would I not?"

Emily looked down at the table and thought about all the things she could say. *It's what I do. I'm a history buff. I chase buried secrets like a cat chases a red dot.*

"I'm afraid you'll think I'm crazy," she said.

"Spit it out, darling. It's obviously making a bad taste in your mouth."

Emily wasn't sure she'd ever been more embarrassed. She could not meet Amanda's eyes.

"I have a bad feeling about the third-floor stairs. I think somebody died there, but I can't find any record of that happening."

Amanda was silent for so long that Emily finally did raise her eyes. But Amanda wasn't looking at Emily. She was looking out the kitchen window, watching a squirrel race up and down a tree, while she let the thoughts that Emily's revelation inspired unfurl in her mind. Maybe her house really was haunted. Maybe that small guilt she felt over renting the space without warning was warranted. But to acknowledge that something felt "weird" was a far cry from saying you believed in spirits.

As Emily had a moment before, Amanda debated various responses, some less charitable than others. *You're right, I think you're crazy*. But that would be both unfair and a lie. *Lots of people have probably died in this house.* But clearly the girl meant something more specific than that.

"And you think it was Keith?" Amanda asked.

"I'm not sure," Emily admitted. "I mostly got interested in old houses because I like to dig into the history of places, but what started me on that was a thing I can do."

Amanda just waited for the girl to say more, and eventually, she did.

"Sometimes, when I touch a thing, I get feelings from it. Emotions."

"Psychometry," Bobby O'Shea said from outside the screen door. Amanda and Emily jumped. Neither knew how long he'd been standing there.

"Yeah," Emily said. She'd looked it up years ago.

Amanda furrowed her brow at Bobby.

"How on earth would you know that? And why are you lurking out there? Come in, if you're coming."

"You'd be surprised the things you pick up in my line of work, in this city," he said, stepping into the kitchen.

The despair that hunted Bobby as relentlessly as he'd ever hunted any criminal caught up to him as he looked at the photos on the table. He remembered almost every moment pictured. Not every—memory is a funny thing, shifting and reshaping itself with time and distance—but most of them.

"Where did you find those?"

"Attic," Emily said.

Bobby poured himself coffee, refilled the women's mugs, and started a fresh pot.

"Connie loved taking pictures," he said. "She got better cameras, in later years. Started developing her own film. Wanted to be a professional."

"Wanted to be?" Emily said.

"Keith had other ideas. He wanted a family. Didn't think that would work out if she were traveling the world snapping pictures."

"They might have talked about what they wanted before marrying," Amanda said, with a dryness that Emily had never heard from her before.

"Young love," Bobby said, and Amanda sighed and nodded.

Bobby leaned against the counter, and Emily shifted her chair so she wouldn't have to look over her shoulder at him.

"Tell me about your psychometry," he said to Emily. Something in his tone reminded Emily that he'd been a police officer. He expected to be obeyed. She obeyed.

"Sometimes, I feel things," she said. "I get impressions from objects. Emotions."

"You don't see things? Have visions?"

Emily shook her head. "No. Just emotions. Don't even know whose they are."

Amanda looked at Bobby and wondered who this man standing in her kitchen was. She'd never seen him like this. The tone he had taken with Emily was disconcerting and, if she were honest, worrisome. There was no overt threat in either his voice or manner, but it put her on edge just the same. She felt a storm building, the air electric and hard to breathe.

"You believe in this sort of thing, Bobby?" Amanda asked.

Bobby shrugged again, without taking his attention from Emily.

His dismissal annoyed Amanda. She suddenly didn't care for the way he was leaning on her counter like it was his counter. She felt in danger, she realized, surprised. The smart thing to do would be to redirect, calm things down, or maybe get him and Emily to laugh the whole thing off, though Amanda still wasn't entirely sure what "the whole thing" was. But this was her house. A moment ago, she'd felt the need to lighten the mood. Now she felt like maybe a good storm might be just what was needed to clear the air.

"I asked you a question, Bobby," she said, with a sharpness that got his attention. "Do you believe in this sort of thing?"

"I suppose I do," he said, surprised. "I don't know how much I believe it. I don't know that I believe her." He nodded his head toward Emily. "But I guess there are things we can't explain, sure."

Emily blinked, as Amanda's question broke her from the sway the detective held over her. She glanced at the photos, then looked more closely. She was sure the watch Bobby wore, in several of the pictures, was the same one he was wearing now. It might mean a lot to him, if he'd kept it that long. On the other hand, it might be as dead as the medal in the attic.

Before she could talk herself out of it, Emily stood and stepped next to Bobby.

"Let me show you," she said, and clasped her hand over the watch on Bobby's wrist. He exclaimed something that wasn't quite a word and jerked his hand away from her. Emily was already turning and vomiting into the sink. It was worse than the stain on the wall. It was years of loneliness and sorrow and guilt. So much guilt. He had done something terrible.

Bobby grasped his wrist as if Emily had burned him,

furious at her, furious at himself for being caught off guard like that. Now she was throwing up in Amanda's kitchen sink. He didn't know what to make of that. Was she acting? Was this all some sort of scam? To what end? The girl choked on her sobs, trying to speak. He could barely make out her words.

"What did you do?" she was saying. "What did you do?"

Amanda sat rooted in her chair. She had not expected that from Emily, but she was sure it was no act. This girl had just experienced something that wasn't a good something. The pieces coming together in her mind formed an image she did not want to see. She looked at Bobby and saw again the man she'd grown so close to over the last decade. He'd never said, but she knew he loved her. She believed he was a decent man. He'd once told her he'd never had to shoot anybody in the line of duty. So, unless he'd lied about that, it was something else that Emily sensed. Some horrible thing.

"What did you do, Bobby?" Amanda asked, far more gently than Emily had. When he turned to her, she imagined she saw his heart break, and she thought her own might have cracked a bit. Her fondness for him ran deeper than she'd admitted to herself.

I can get through this, Bobby thought. He could walk out now. He could give Amanda some time to cool down, then come back and convince her that the girl was crazy, that there was nothing to this ability she claimed to have. But then their continued friendship, maybe something more than friendship, would be built on lies. *More lies,* he corrected himself, and he was so damned sick of feeling like a mule carrying too heavy a load. Maybe he should put it down. Maybe, if he just told some of it, she'd understand.

"Keith and Connie," he said, "had a hard time. I guess you've picked up on some of that. They made a go of it for nine years. Then she called it quits. Said she was leaving."

Emily rinsed her mouth and poured herself some water. Amanda waited for him to go on, so he did.

"She went up to the attic to get a suitcase. Keith followed her. They were fighting. She said she didn't mean to push him. She just wanted to get past him. But he fell."

He saw Amanda's expression soften. Her empathy might be the thing he most admired about her. But the damned girl just wouldn't let it go. She was like a dog with a bone.

"Why was there no police report? No obituary? You helped her cover it up?"

He nodded. "I did. She called me. It could have ruined her life. She might have been charged if they didn't believe her story."

His story didn't sit right with Emily. It didn't match what she'd felt from either the watch or the wall. Amanda looked about ready to take Bobby into her arms and comfort him, but Emily wasn't as convinced.

"So, he was dead when you got here," she said.

"I just said that, didn't I?"

"You didn't."

Bobby saw his chances of recovery slipping away. The girl wasn't sure, or she wouldn't be dancing around it, but she knew he was still holding back.

"He was almost gone. He'd landed badly..." He watched horror settle across Amanda's face.

"Oh, my Lord," Amanda breathed.

"You killed him," Emily said. It fit. Keith's rage and confusion. Bobby's guilt. It fit.

Bobby said nothing. He just watched Amanda's face, searching for any trace of the affection he believed she held for him. He wanted to snap the damned girl in two. He wanted to fall on his knees in front of Amanda and explain how it was. How Keith wouldn't have made it to the hospital. How Connie would likely have gone to jail.

But he could not. Should not. If he kept talking, he might say more things that should never be said. How Connie had started drinking and ranting while drunk, saying things people might listen to. No, he could not handle any more truth today. He set down his coffee mug and walked out of the house, for what he knew would be the last time.

Amanda waited until the sound of his steps had faded. "I don't suppose you recorded any of that?"

Emily blinked, surprised by the woman's calm. "That would have been a good idea," she managed to say, before she started trembling so hard her teeth chattered.

Amanda stood and pulled the girl into her arms.

"I am so sorry," Emily said, tears flooding her face again. "I'm so sorry. I never—never meant to cause—"

"Darling, none of this is your fault."

"He's going to get away with it," Emily sobbed against Amanda's shoulder.

Amanda felt tears stream down her own face and drop into Emily's hair. "Yes, he is," Amanda said as they finally parted, each wiping off her face and groping her way down her own path to coping with the enormity of what she'd learned. There was no way that any police force was going to bring one of their own up on charges for a murder that the women couldn't even prove had happened.

"Maybe," Amanda said, "just maybe it's enough that someone knows now."

Emily nodded. "Maybe we could do something for him," Emily said. "For Keith. Have a marker set up or something? Maybe include Connie?"

"We'll think about it. Maybe we could start with a private ceremony. A little remembrance for two imperfect people, from two imperfect people."

* * *

THEY HELD the funeral a few days later. There was no sudden sense of peace, no immediate rush of warmth, though Emily did think the chill abated. At Amanda's request, Emily hauled the boxes down from the loft so they could explore the house's history together. Eventually, the stain faded.

MICHELE STUART LIVES with her husband in the southeastern United States. Aside from the husband, she loves writing, reading, art, languages, theater, listening to podcasts, working out, and lying around. Find her on BlueSky @crystalbrier.bsky.social or at her website, https://michelestuart.me

A WIZARD, A WARRIOR, AND A KITE

A.R.R. ASH

Redheaded Valya and brunette Nerada held their hands over their noses and mouths to keep at bay the smell of the alley—a smell so pervasive and powerful that it coated the backs of their tongues and throats like a putrid patina and would require barrels of soap to wash the clinging stench from their hair.

"Ne'er did I experience such a stink," Nerada whispered through her covering hand. A white scar ran from her hairline, skipping over her right eye, down her cheek to the corner of her mouth. "I detect notes of overripe fish; stale, cheap ale; and, lest I forget, long-marinating urine."

"Shh," came Valya's harsh whisper. Then in a thoughtful tone and with a sideways glance, she added, "Forget not the reek of rotted meat."

Nerada opened her mouth in response, but the shriek of a black kite circling above ended the debate. The bird sported a forked tail of black feathers, black beak and claws, and black flight feathers, though the feathers of her body were a mottled brown.

As one, the two women rose from behind their concealment of moldering crates. Nerada, in her leather-wrapped chain, pulled her swords—named, appropriately, Long and Short—from their sheaths, their blades coated in black oil to absorb the moonlight and starlight. Valya, in her voluminous robe over form-fitting leather armor, pulled one of her dozen wands—this one, a sliver of redwood—affixed to a wide leather belt.

The two exited the main alleyway and moved to the entrance of a smaller side alley just as a cat burglar in all black touched the ground and two others followed down a rope grappled to a third-floor balcony.

The ground-level burglar, his head hidden within a balaclava, started at the sisters' appearance, then he whisper-shouted a single word: "Tumble!"

Nerada and Valya had been in the company of thieves enough to understand the cant—*Trouble*—a word starting with the same letter and which rhymes with the intended word.

The burglar pulled a dagger, blackened like Nerada's own, while the other two hastened down the rope. All three wore packs that bulged at the seams.

For their part, the ambushing sisters politely waited for the other two thieves to reach the ground.

"Be away with you while you can," the first thief said through clenched teeth. He angled his dagger toward them in a steady hand.

"The fullness of the situation seems to escape his perception," Valya said to Nerada while keeping her eyes on the thieves.

"By our count, the *fullness* of the situation is three to two." Though his mouth was covered, his sneer shone through.

"We'll be takin' your score," Valya continued. "You need not be harmed in the takin'."

"By the left hand of Laverna! Do you know who we work for?"

Nerada nodded. "We're counting on it."

Though only his amber eyes were visible, the sisters noted their slight widening and a stiffening of his stance. To their ears, the bravado in his tone was strained. "If you value your lives so little, we can divest you of them along with your valuables."

He took a menacing step forward. The circling kite dove and clawed the rearmost thief. His scream, pitched high like the raptor's shriek, distracted the other two. One took a bolt from Valya's wand for his distraction and found himself frozen in place.

Nerada crossed the few paces separating her from the nearest opponent and gave him a knock to the head with the flat of Long. He dropped his dagger as he instinctively reached for the site of the pain.

The kite shrieked again and surged upward, leaving the third curled like a babe upon the grimy cobbles.

"We'll be takin' your packs now," Valya reiterated.

"You'll regret this!" The first removed his pack, belying his bluster. He then moved to relieve his unmoving cohort of his pack.

The third, with shaking hands, slipped his off his shoulders.

Like a feathered lightning strike, the kite swooped down and snatched the pack's strap in her claws. She struggled with the weight but managed to fly down the alley, past Nerada and Valya.

Each sister retrieved a pack.

"Been a pleasure doin' business," Valya said with a smirk. "Tell your superiors to meet us this time tomorrow, near the statue of Marduk in the plaza, if they want their loot."

Nerada gave a wink and a flip of her dark hair, then took the pack from the kite.

Valya and Nerada retreated into the larger alley, then moved to the far end, where it joined a main thoroughfare. After traversing several side streets and doubling back to ensure the thieves did not follow—all the while, the kite watching for shadows from the sky—the sisters, wizard and warrior, retired to the room they rented at The Griffon and the Knight. They dropped the bags of stolen goods without a care for their monetary value, for their value to the sisters was far more than what could be accounted for by mere gold.

Nerada pulled off her black calf boots and, still in her armor, reclined upon the bed. Valya removed her belt of wands and doffed her steel gray robe, revealing the leather armor beneath, before settling heavily onto an unupholstered chair and releasing an "Ahh."

The cool breeze entering through the open third-floor window brought with it the kite, who alighted upon the back of another chair, her talons digging furrows into the wood.

Nerada, with a groan at the effort, raised her head and spoke to the bird, who busied herself preening her black tail-feathers, "Don't worry, Vicca. Soon we'll have the magician who did this to you, and, by all the cursed gods, he *will* return you to your form."

The declaration was met by a shriek that, to the sisters' ears, sounded hopeful.

* * *

VICCA THE KITE circled the Plaza of Marduk and, with the eyes of a bird of prey, spotted the ten thieves creeping among the shadows and down the five avenues toward the statue at the center. A pattern of shrieks and calls alerted Valya and Nerada to the treacherous rogues.

From the platform atop a high, rectangular, ziggurat-like structure overlooking the plaza, the two sisters watched as the thieves met at the statue of a bearded male holding a sword in one hand and a shepherd's crook in the other. The Temple of Marduk overlooked the eponymous statue.

"This is how you behave when we treat with you in good faith?" Valya called from the platform. Her voice echoed through the cool, clear night among the structures bordering the plaza.

The reverberating sound of her voice startled the thieves, who glanced quickly about. "Show yourselves!" one called.

At that time of night, the plaza was absent its normal denizens, save for the rats and mangy cats and dogs.

"Send your leader up, alone, or you'll never see your take," Valya called down.

Now the thieves focused their attention on the source of the voice. The ten rogues closed and conferred.

To punctuate their point, Nerada pulled a small golden figurine of a rampant dragon from a sack and tossed it to the ground, where it struck the cobbles with a metallic *thunk*.

The thieves ended their conference, and one separated to ascend the steps of the temple. After a brief wait, a head appeared above the landing of the stairs, though his footfalls had made not a sound upon the worn stone steps.

"You wanted to talk. Here I am." The thief's voice betrayed only the slightest hint of windedness. He wore soft black boots and a long, black, tight-fitting tunic, his face uncovered to reveal long, tightly curled black hair and a sneering visage.

Vicca the kite, continuing to circle the plaza, remained poised to offer a warning shriek should the thieves move upon the temple. Several of the rogues stood with arrows trained on the bird.

Valya held one of the doubly stolen bags. "You can have

this and the rest returned to you. We seek a mutually beneficial arrangement."

The thief took hesitant steps forward, his hand extended for the bag.

At the last moment, Valya pulled the bag away. "We relieved your thieves of the take with no trouble. You would benefit from this alliance."

"They will be punished for their sloppiness—as you should for your transgression against the guild."

Valya reached for a wand, one of ebony wood with an obsidian tip, but Nerada placed a gentle, restraining hand on her forearm. Though her body vibrated beneath Nerada's grip, Valya allowed herself to be placated.

The thief again extended his hand, and Valya slowly proffered the bag.

The thief took it, then he hesitated, eying the two women. "What do you propose?"

Nerada answered, "A break-in. The tower of the wizard Ushar."

The thief scoffed. "Madness!"

Nerada shook her head. "Our sister managed it."

"Impossible!"

"'Tis true," Valya responded, continuing to speak over the question she next anticipated from the thief. "She succeeded but suffered for it, and we seek remedy. We cannot gain entrance alone. You may keep any treasure of the tower. We desire only the wizard."

"Where is the rest of the take?"

"It is hidden. A note within that bag reveals the location," Nerada replied.

One with a hand upon Short, and one with a hand upon a wand of bleached bone at her waist, Nerada and Valya moved past the rogue.

The latter said, "Speak to your superior. If *she* agrees, leave a note at the location of the hidden loot."

The reference to the guildmaster's sex put the rogue back on his feet, and the sisters disappeared down the stairs.

* * *

TWO WEEKS LATER, the sisters and six thieves, their bargain struck, observed the tower of the Transmorpher Ushar from the loft of a high minaret. The night was cool and smelled cleaner so far above the city streets. A kite flew a wide circuit from the tower to the spire.

The thieves unfolded four frameworks of long, hollowed-out bones and thick canvas. Once opened, the contraptions appeared as long, triangular pairs of wings with leather harnesses on the underside.

The sisters warily eyed the contraptions.

"What are those?" Curiosity and skepticism married in Valya's incredulous tone.

"They are wings that will carry us to the wizard's tower." The thief Dagrim, leader of the roguish band—the same thief who met with the sisters atop the ziggurat—answered with the condescension of one who took pleasure in another's ignorance. Attired in the wonted color and garb of rogues, he sounded as a disembodied voice among the shadows of the loft. "The tower is protected from infiltration from below by all manner of trap and magical defense. As best as we can discern, the roof is warded against magical access, including magical flight, but not mundane."

"Enki's crooked staff, you are mad!" Narada's tone was as if the thief had suggested they coat themselves in dung to better conceal themselves among the shadows.

"You fear. I understand," Dagrim answered with a smirk.

"We have an artificer among the guild. He assures us these contraptions will function."

"As long as your artificer avers our safety—" Nerada rolled her eyes "—consider me assured."

Valya put a calming hand on her sister's shoulder. "You have naught to fear." She tapped a cedar wand, affixed with an eagle's feather, at her waist with her finger. "Should aught go amiss, I shall ensure we do not plummet to a rather abrupt death."

Dagrim gave an annoyed grunt. "The moon is new; clouds obscure the stars. This is the perfect night. Let us not waste it."

"The operation of such a contrivance is not known to us." Nerada spoke reasonably, calmly.

Dagrim grinned. "That is of no moment. We shall travel in pairs."

Valya scoffed.

Dagrim shrugged. "If you prefer to desist…"

Nerada and Valya looked at one another. Regardless of the danger, both understood the necessity. If Vicca were to be returned to her human form, no risk was too great. As one, they shifted their gazes to the thief and nodded.

"Then let us not tarry any longer." Dagrim gestured toward Nerada. "You can join me."

The warrioress inhaled deeply and nodded.

Valya paired with a short-statured thief who seemed none too pleased to partner with the irascible wizardess.

Each sister fastened an external harness about her torso and attached it to the harness of her partner with a thick metal clip.

In pairs, the last four thieves strapped themselves to the remaining two frameworks.

"Let us go!" Dagrim said with enthusiasm. He took several steps and leaped from the minaret.

Nerada summoned all her self-control to keep the scream lodged in her throat. The wind buffeted her face and made her eyes tear; her clothing snapped and rippled. The ground was so far below with nothing between her and a violent, splattering death but a metal carabiner and some bone and canvas. She cursed for not having relieved herself before embarking upon this madness. If she were to fall, she hoped Valya could offer some magical assistance. Her hands held the handles attached to the framework so tightly that she feared she would rip them from their fasteners.

They passed over the tower and alighted abruptly upon the roof. Nerada exhaled and gasped, having forgotten to breathe in her fright.

The other thieves and Valya settled shortly after, and all disengaged from the harnesses.

Vicca came to rest upon the low parapet.

Still breathless, Nerada said, "So that is what Vicca experiences. I've never known anything similar."

Valya shook her head. "Nor I."

Dagrim showed a smug countenance. "As I said." He glanced about the roof and indicated a trap door. "Wizard, can you remove the wards?"

"I believe so, *thief*." Valya selected a straight wand of iron, pointed it at the portal, and spoke a guttural word not of any mundane tongue. "It is done."

"That's it?" Dagrim's face scrunched in skepticism. "I saw nothing."

"Nor would you. You were correct about the contraptions, but this is my business."

After a moment's hesitation, he offered a grudging, "Very well," and beckoned the short-statured rogue.

The slim man moved to the door inset into the roof of the tower. Withdrawing the tools of his trade from a pouch, he went about opening the lock. After several moments, he smiled and pulled the door open.

"It seems our partnership is one of mutual benefit," Dagrim said. "Perhaps we ought to extend its duration."

In a dismissive tone, Valya replied, "Let us complete this mission before we plan another."

The six thieves descended the stairs from the trap door, and the sisters followed. Vicca swooped in behind them.

"Do you recall the way, Vicca?" Nerada asked in a hushed tone.

The kite dipped her right wing, a signal they had developed to indicate a positive response.

Valya retrieved a straight wand of sandalwood, a small crystal held by a golden claw at its tip. At a word, the crystal began to glow with an inner light. "Do as you wish. We have our own mission."

Without waiting for a response, Nerada and Valya moved down a corridor in pursuit of the sure-flying Vicca.

"How do you believe they will fare?" Nerada asked with a backward glance.

Valya shrugged. "They are upon their course, and we upon ours. We must take the Transmorpher unaware if we are to capture him."

The corridors of the tower were formed of smooth, mortared black marble and separated by a distance that was spacious for one but not quite wide enough for two. Valya walked a step in front, holding the light-giving wand; Nerada, behind, held Long and Short in hand.

Vicca flew ahead and would return to direct the sisters. In the utter quiet of the corridors, the only sounds were the flap of feathered wings, the slight rustle of cloak, and the creak of leather-wrapped mail. The two moved with slow, deliberate steps on soft-shod feet that left no more sound of their passing than the fluttering of a scarf.

An ambient scent of flowers and incense filled the halls, yet without an obvious source. Ensconced oil lamps lined the walls but remained unlit. The skulkers passed numerous doors, all marked by a single symbol that not even Valya recognized. The doors, banded with black iron, were hewn of a wood as dark as the stone of the walls, and the wizardess was certain each was protected by more than any simple mechanical lock.

As they came upon the entrance to a spiraling staircase, echoing footfalls reached the trio from within the stairwell. A glance between the sisters exchanged their mutual understanding of the situation: the footfalls moved briskly but not in haste, and, even under duress, the rogues would not sound so carelessly. It was likely Ushar the Transmorpher.

"Go. Hide." Valya flicked her head down the corridor. "I shall greet him."

Nerada would have argued the point, but the steps grew close. She disappeared around a corner.

Valya extended her obsidian-tipped ebony wand. As a body emerged from the stairwell, she shouted, "Halt!"

He did. Yet it was not the wizard, and Valya shifted her weight to her back foot in surprise. Before her stood a man so thick with muscle that he nearly filled the width of the corridor. He held a sword that seemed too large to be practical, particularly within the confines of the tower. His tunic stretched over his torso like a second skin, and his short kaunakes of colorful, overlapping feathers showed that his lower extremities were as powerfully muscled as his upper body.

His countenance and black eyes were expressive, passing from the shock of encountering the unexpected to anger at the brandished wand to the surprise of recognition all within the span of several heartbeats.

"Who are you?" Valya asked.

Once the hulking man settled upon his final expression, he issued forth, "Helvar?"

"No. I'll ask you but once more." Her voice was firm despite the obvious threat the man could pose.

The bulk of the warrior seemed to deflate at that—almost as if he diminished to the size of an average man—and his features fell in disappointment, so much so that Valya nearly held sympathy for him.

Then he drew himself to his full height, projecting his chest outward. "I am Valrok."

He made the declaration with such pride that Valya suspected he believed the name should carry some weight. She had never heard it. "Why are you here?"

"I have given my n—"

Vicca flew into view, and the man dropped his sword with a too-loud clang. Valya flinched at the sound. Without pause, Valrok pulled a bow from across his shoulders and an arrow from the quiver at his back. He nocked the arrow and sighted upon Vicca.

"Loose that arrow and I will skewer your kidney." Nerada had stepped from her concealment at the sound of the dropped sword and pressed the tip of Short to his lower back.

Valrok growled but did not show any indication of fear. "That bird. It is the wizard's familiar."

Valya's offense on behalf of her transformed sister found outlet in her response. "Vicca is slave to no wizard. She escaped his control." In a quieter voice, she added, "She is our sister."

Valrok lowered his bow and released the tension on the string. His thick black brows descended toward the center of his face. "Your sister?"

At a glance from Valya, Nerada drew her blade away, yet kept it at the ready.

"'Tis why we are here," Valya explained. Once she began, the words continued unbidden. "Vicca thought to burgle this tower. In her misguided attempt to protect us, she undertook the job without us. She was caught, and the wizard, rather than kill her, gave her this form. Yet, she wrested her freedom, found us, and, over time, managed to convey her story. Though her form is of a raptor, her mind is Vicca."

As she spoke, Valrok replaced his arrow and bow and retrieved his sword. When she finished, he said, "My blood boils at the affrontery of the wizard. I, too, am on a quest to find my sister. I have not seen her since we were children. When I first happened upon you, I thought you to be she."

"You still have not answered my question, Valrok. Why are you *here*?"

"Another wizard promised me information about my sister if I were to steal an item from his rival. He helped me gain access to the tower." Valrok pulled a jagged black crystal from a pouch. "A dragon's kidney stone."

"We seek the master of the tower to force him to reverse the transformation upon Vicca," Valya offered, shuddering at the fist-sized crystalline stone.

"Then by Moloch's horns, why do we tarry? Your quest is just, and I offer my sword and arm in support!"

A quick glance exchanged between the sisters was all that was necessary to agree to accept the warrior's aid.

Valya nodded. "Then come. With our thanks."

The trio followed the kite to an ebony door carved with a squiggly sigil. Presently, Vicca flew tight circles before the door.

"You sure?" Nerada asked.

The kite's right wing dipped.

"That is our destination," Nerada told Valrok. "The wizard is within."

"Then surprise is our ally." Valrok scabbarded his enormous sword, lowered his shoulder, and barreled forward.

Valya shouted, "No! Wait!"

Valrok struck the door with the force of a catapult-hurled boulder. The wood shattered with a sharp crash, and he continued forward with barely a slowing of his momentum.

Valya and Nerada ducked away. Behind the warrior, vertical blades emerged from the stone above and below the door, both within and without the chamber, and horizontally from the frame. Had he hesitated but an instant, Valrok would have been impaled by those blades. As it was, he stood triumphantly within the chamber and pulled his blade.

Nerada chuckled, and Valya uttered, "Idiot."

The sisters contorted themselves to pass through the extended blades, though Vicca remained without.

The circular room appeared to be an audience chamber of sorts. A cushioned, gilded throne sat at the far end upon a low dais. Around the circumference were woven sitting pillows displaying motifs of palmettes, scrollwork, and geometric patterns, with a low table before each. Sconces, placed regularly upon the wall and in the form of various animals—an adder, a fox, a kingfisher, a falcon—held oil lamps and emitted the earthy and woody aroma of frankincense.

A man draped in a loose, midnight blue robe covered in silver runes—who could only be the Transmorpher Ushar—stood at the base of the dais amid five scurrying ferrets. Another man, whom the sisters recognized as Dagrim, kneeled at the center of the chamber, his wrists behind his back and tied to his ankles.

The bound thief started at the explosive entrance, yet the wizard showed hardly any reaction.

"Ah, there you are." His voice, while aged, still held

strength and surety. "I do appreciate your coming to me. These rogues showed far less consideration."

At the comment, Nerada and Valya tensed at the realization that the ferrets were the other thieves.

Their suspicion was confirmed when Ushar said, "I've given the rogues a form better suited to their pilfering personalities." He paused and narrowed his eyes of royal blue. "You all, I suspect, like your sister, offer more trouble than value." He glanced beyond the trio as if searching for someone. "Yes, I know who you are."

Valrok raised his enormous sword. Nerada brandished Long and Short before her. Valya drew two wands—the obsidian, ebony-tipped one and one carved of a thin bleached bone.

At some silent command from the Transmorpher, the ferrets scampered across the black stone floor toward the trio. Other critters—serpents, rats, cats, scorpions, lizards, an owl—animals that should have been mortal enemies—emerged from behind the sitting pillows and charged. The combined calls and sounds of the creatures evoked a primitive terror, one reminiscent of dark, hidden dangers in the sisters' minds.

"Do not kill them!" Nerada shouted as much in warning as to overcome and banish her own base fear. "They are transformed and enslaved as Vicca was."

A shudder, beginning in her lower back and rushing up her spine and extending into her neck and shoulders, shook Valya. "Even the scorpions?"

Valrok swung his sword in wide arcs while stomping his large, booted feet at whatever neared him.

A visceral, primal scream escaped Dagrim's throat as he fell over and his body began to reform. A bushy tail sprouted, his neck elongated, skull and features shifted, hands and feet thinned and sharpened into claws, and black and brown fur burgeoned all over his body—all accompanied by a grotesque cracking and squelching of reshaping bone.

His scream was echoed by Nerada and Valya as they fell to the floor, doubled over. Then Valrok followed.

Nerada managed a shout, a single word: *Villa!*

Vicca swept into the room and surged toward the wizard, who instinctively threw up his hands in defense.

Abruptly, the pain abated, and warrior, wizardess, and warrioress rose. As they moved toward Ushar, the owl broke off to intercept Vicca.

The Transmorpher turned his attention back to the sisters and Valrok. His eyes went suddenly wide, and he bowed his head to glance at the shortsword embedded in his sternum.

Nerada stood with Long in one hand, her other arm extended in the follow-through of her throw.

Valrok crossed the room in a moment, bringing his sword in a downward swing that cleaved the wizard from shoulder to midback, biting into his spine.

Valya loosed a strangled cry, this time not in pain or fear but in desperation for a lost opportunity. "No!" Wands raised, she whirled on Valrok.

The animals abandoned their attack, though they turned their attention to one another. The adder lunged at a rat, and the owl swooped to grip the serpent in its razor claws.

"You killed him!" Valya nearly foamed at the mouth; her chest rose and fell in unchecked fury.

Valrok showed no fear or offense at the outburst, standing unguarded before the wizardess's wrath.

Nerada placed a hand on her sister's shoulder; if Valya was angry at anyone, Nerada knew it should have been her. "He only finished what I started. Ushar's death was inevitable."

"He was our only chance!" Valya raised the bone wand

toward Valrok, who eyed the item warily but still made no move.

"He would have transformed us before we could capture him." Nerada's calming voice and restraining hand again precluded a violent outburst.

"The draconic kidney stone!" Valya shouted as her body straightened in revelation. "They are said to have powers to counteract magical effects when crushed and drunk. Valrok, was there another such stone?"

Valrok shook head his head, but he reached into his pouch and pulled forth the black stone. "How much do you need?"

"The whole stone is required."

The expressive face of the large warrior drooped in regret. "Your…sister." His countenance formed into a pensive mask before his jaw set in determination. "Take it. For your sister."

Valya, still too consumed by a red haze, could find no words, but Nerada managed, "But what of your sister? The wizard's aid?"

The warrior's jaw twitched before he spoke. "I will find another way. I have been searching for much of my life. You are so close."

He extended the black crystal, and Nerada accepted it, then handed it to Valya, who deposited it within one of her many pockets.

Nerada extended her arm, and Valrok gripped her forearm in a warrior's clasp. She then moved to retrieve Short from the Transmorpher's chest.

A mewling from the floor drew the attention of the three. A bizarre, grotesque form—patches of fur and skin; mangled, misshapen limbs; not human, not animal—writhed upon the floor. Dagrim's transformation had been interrupted mid-change.

Without a word, Valrok drew up his sword and brought it down in a merciful blow, severing the head of the man-thing. "Let us be gone from this cursed tower."

"We have means to depart upon the roof," Nerada offered.

Valrok nodded in thanks but said, "My wizard provided me with my own manner of egress. I need only reach the appointed location."

"When next we meet, I trust we will raise a tankard with you and your sister," Nerada said, her voice thick.

Valya gave a stiff nod. "Thank you, Warrior."

Valrok grunted and was gone.

The sisters, with Vicca, returned to the roof. Presently, they examined the winged contraptions.

Nerada shook her head. "No."

Valya wrapped an arm around her sister, and Nerada squeezed the wizardess in a tight embrace. Valya pulled forth her feather-affixed cedar wand, and the sisters stepped from the roof. They floated slowly to the ground, beyond the paved courtyard and high wall surrounding the tower, while Nerada kept her eyes so tightly shut that she began to see white bursts of light. Not until she felt the ground beneath her boots did she open them.

* * *

As soon as the sisters returned to The Griffon and the Knight, even as the calls and tintinnabulation for morning prayers pierced the air, Valya crushed the black draconic stone and mixed the granules with water.

The kite sipped the concoction. However, by the time dawn came in full, Vicca's form remained unchanged.

. . .

A.R.R. Ash is a lifelong fan of both science fiction and fantasy, though he typically focuses his talents on writing grimdark. His first independently published novel is The Moroi Hunters. *He has had short stories appear in several anthologies— including* Behind the Shadows*;* Behind the Shadows II*;* Detectives, Sleuths, and Nosy Neighbors*;* Dragon Mythicana*;* Hidden Villains*;* Hidden Villains: Arise*; and* Noncorporeal II *by Inkd Publishing, as well as* Socially Distant: The Quarantales *by Impulsive Walrus Books—and he has received a Silver Honorable Mention and six Honorable Mentions from the L. Ron Hubbard's Writers of the Future Contest.* Xy: Descent, *the first book of his The First Godling trilogy, as well as* The Tribe of Fangs, *the prequel to* The Moroi Hunters, *are undergoing editing. He is currently working on* Xy: Ascent, *the sequel to* Xy: Descent, *as well as other short stories that pique his interest.*

In other trivia, his favorite dishes are burgers and sushi (but not together), and his favorite series is Dune, *though* The Expanse *by James S. A. Corey is making a run for the title. His sense of humor is decidedly an acquired taste. You can contact A.R.R. Ash and watch his interview with Cursed Dragon Ship Publishing through LMPBooks.com*

ACKNOWLEDGMENTS

Hidden Villains: Criminals emerged from the suggested theme of Editor-in-Chief Robyn Huss. An editor with powerful developmental and grammatical skills, she retains the author's voice while polishing every story. Robyn works with authors on multiple passes to bring out the best in every story.

Thank you, Robyn.

With over 200 submissions, Inkd Publishing would like to thank Heather Lewis, Heather Norris, April Davis, Tony Cioffi, Kalyani Poluri, Kristi Barnes, and Kevin Davis for their relentless hours helping Robyn read through all those stories. Thank you for your tireless work.

* * *

Producing anthologies can run into the thousands of dollars between editing, covers, and payments to authors. We couldn't do it without the loving support of our Kickstarter supporters who help to defray some of those costs.

Please join us in thanking the following for helping to make this anthology and future anthologies possible.

Kickstarter Patrons:

Kathryn M., Amanda Eschmeyer, Colleen Feeney, Ruth Ann Orlansky, Jessica K. Meade, Tim Lewis, Zack Fissel, Jared Nelson, Mary Jo Rabe, Patricia Bailey, Mark Lindberg, Kristina Kugler, Joy Kristen Allen, Kalyani Poluri, Michael Barbour, Stew Buchanan, Suzanne M, Boris Veytsman,

Linnea Lindstrom, Kyle Wilson, Ted Herman, Rachel Rada, Catarina Snyder, Florian Ammann, Ronald Pyatt, Sergey Kochergan, k.r.wesel, brunella segura, Alexandra Corrsin, StoicMan, Robert D. Stewart, Jarno van Roosmalen, Kara Rogers, crystalbrier, Sara Jordan-Heintz, Lexie C., Meyari McFarland, Claincy, 'Will It Work' Dansicker, Lisa Martin, Tyler Hulsey, Molly Twizzler Martin, Holly Williams, Rosemary Williams, Billy Todd, Alexis Horizon, Ariadne Davion, Grace Hoffman,and Melissa Slager

Thank you! Thank you!

Please visit us at InkdPub.com

TUCKERIZATION

In his short story "Parsec," Tim Lewis happily Tuckerized backer Billy Todd as the antagonist's minion, "Billy Toddes."

Thank you to Billy and Tim for supporting the Kickstarter!

ALSO BY INKD PUB

Hidden Villains

Hidden Villains: Arise

Noncorporeal

Behind the Shadows

Hidden Villains: Betrayed

Detectives, Sleuths, & Nosy Neighbors

Noncorporeal II

Behind the Shadows II

Impulse

Yay! all queer

Dragon Mythicana

Please visit us at InkdPub.com, join our newsletter, and follow us on Facebook and Instagram.

www.ingramcontent.com/pod-product-compliance
Ingram Content Group UK Ltd.
Pitfield, Milton Keynes, MK11 3LW, UK
UKHW040654120325
456161UK00002B/128

* 9 7 9 8 2 3 0 7 7 5 5 4 6 *